"What Wicked Imp Prodded You into a Deed of Such Folly?" Blazed Evain.

"Have you so soon forgot the black toads who would see us captured or dead?"

Shoulder-deep in the spring, Anya froze. She looked toward the black-clad man standing nearly invisible amidst twilight shadows.

Despite the warnings his conscience screamed, Evain couldn't look away from the ethereal vision of loveliness rising from moon-silvered waters. She stole his breath.

Anya knew she ought turn away from the blue fires burning in the depths of his eyes. She ought yet could not deny the fiery attraction which had steadily built since the first kiss given her as a man to a woman. She began moving through the pool toward Evain. The undeniable hunger in his expression stole her shyness and left her certain that coming to him this way was the most natural action she'd ever taken.

Evain locked her against his powerful body. Once inside the circle of his arms, the feel of his broad, muscular body overwhelmed Anya with burning sensations and drove the last tendril of rational thought beyond her reach. Her fingers twined in his thick, dark hair.

"You're taking risks, child," he said.

"I'm not a child—you only wish that I were. You wish it, but I am willing to dare any risk." As if to prove it she gently arched her body in an untutored invitation while softly moaning, "Evain . . . kiss me again. . . ."

Books by Marylyle Rogers

The Dragon's Fire
Wary Hearts
Hidden Hearts
Proud Hearts
Chanting the Dawn
Dark Whispers
The Eagle's Song
The Keepsake
Chanting the Morning Star
Chanting the Storm

Published by POCKET BOOKS

For orders other than by individual consumers, Pocket Books grants a discount on the purchase of **10 or more** copies of single titles for special markets or premium use. For further details, please write to the Vice-President of Special Markets, Pocket Books, 1230 Avenue of the Americas, New York, NY 10020.

For information on how individual consumers can place orders, please write to Mail Order Department, Paramount Publishing, 200 Old Tappan Road, Old Tappan, NJ 07675.

MARYLYLE ROGERS

CHANTING THE STORM

POCKET BOOKS

New York   London   Toronto   Sydney   Tokyo   Singapore

An *Original* Publication of POCKET BOOKS

POCKET BOOKS, a division of Simon & Schuster Inc.
1230 Avenue of the Americas, New York, NY 10020

ISBN: 0-671-87185-4

First Pocket Books printing May 1994

10 9 8 7 6 5 4 3 2 1

POCKET and colophon are registered trademarks of Simon & Schuster Inc.

Cover art by Sharon Spiak

Printed in the U.S.A.

Author's Note

During the millennium between the Roman invasion in A.D. 43 and William of Normandy's conquest in 1066 the number and boundaries of Britain's kingdoms fluctuated constantly. Although these centuries are shadowy and near uncharted, we have been given a picture—often through the eyes and ears of those who were there—by a number of sources. First, the Roman historians; then the writings of Gildas, Nennius, and Bede; and last the *Anglo-Saxon Chronicles, The Welsh Annals,* and *The Chronicles of the Princes of Wales.* Mere glimpses at the start become much fuller descriptions, less open to conjecture by the end.

The Roman invaders came into contact with a fierce Celtic race who bowed to the absolute supremacy of Druid priests possessing the secrets of past, present, and future. The Druid religion was not confined to Britain but rather spread across Europe. However, it is believed that Britain was to international Druids what Rome was to early Christians and present-day Catholics: the center of knowledge and power.

Because Druids were forbidden from putting their beliefs into writing, we have little concrete knowledge of their ways, only the distant echoes of rituals distorted but still observed—dancing, hands clasped about the Maypole; setting bonfires the night of October 31 (Samhain, eve of the Celtic New Year); and crowning monarchs above the Stone of Destiny, which has resided beneath the British Coronation Chair since 1297 when Edward I took it from the Scots who had crowned kings over it from time out of mind.

We do know that becoming a Druid priest was the highest pinnacle to which a Celtic man could aspire and necessitated learning endless poetic chants in the form of riddles whose answers explain natural phenomena—such as eclipses, phases of the moon, movement of stars—and all things unknown to men untaught. These priests held a dominant power to which even kings bowed. We know also that they possessed amazing scientific knowledge, some of which modern science has only recently rediscovered, which gave them the ability to awe their contemporaries with such things as accurate predictions of astral events. Some wonder what primal knowledge they may have possessed which is now forever lost.

In the Romans' wake came Christianity. Its advance drove the Druids into their natural havens, the wilds of forest and mountain, and they were deemed extinct by Roman historians late in the first century A.D., although pockets survived for many generations.

In A.D. 410 Rome was overrun by pagan hordes and, in a last attempt to save itself, called its legions home.

Britain was left with empty stone palaces and crumbling roads its natives knew neither how to use nor maintain. The Romans departed but Christianity remained.

Another invasion, foolishly invited by one of Celtic Britain's own, began when Angles, Jutes, and Saxons—all pagans—crossed the British Channel and North Sea. They steadily drove the native Celts into Cornwall/Devon, Wales, Scotland, and Ireland. Note that the Celtic Druid's belief in the power residing in nature itself was far different than the pagan Anglo-Saxons' panorama of warrior gods.

Not until the close of the sixth century did Saint Augustine bring Christianity to these invaders and then it came unevenly and with periods of backsliding into old ways. Also, when the Celts earlier accepted Christianity, it began with the lowliest and worked its way up. But the Anglo-Saxons' conversion was accomplished by starting at the top with the king whose example led entire kingdoms (often en masse) into the new religion. And even after Christianity was accepted by either Celts or Anglo-Saxons, old superstitions remained century after century. It was often deemed easier by the Christian church to "whitewash" old ways with Christian meaning rather than attempting to exterminate them wholesale.

With regard to the historical characters who appear in this book:

Wilfrid, known as an aggressive, self-centered, difficult, and worldly bishop, was expelled from his see (seat of a bishop's authority) in 678 by King Ecgferth. Though originally sent to Rome, he returned to Britain and spent the years of this exile in other Saxon kingdoms, earning the patronage of their monarchs.

Indeed, after King Cadwalla of Wessex conquered the Isle of Wight, he granted Wilfrid a quarter of the island and the booty he'd acquired by that action.

Aldfrith received the kingdom of Northumbria after the death of his brother Ecgferth in 685. Apparently Aldfrith was originally intended for the church as the extent of his education was so exceptional that he is reputed to have been the most learned king to rule England before James I nearly ten centuries later. Though it is recorded that he continued his brother's quarrel with Bishop Wilfrid, in 686–87 he allowed the man to return as Bishop of York . . . but to a much diminished diocese. Within a few years Wilfrid again came into conflict with the king of Northumbria.

Cadwalla's reign over Wessex was brief, lasting only a violent three years. In 688 he resigned his kingdom and went on pilgrimage to Rome. There he was baptized, apparently not having bothered with the rite earlier, and ten days later died.

Definition of Terms

FROM WALES

Cymry—When the Romans invaded Britain in A.D. 43 they found a Celtic race they called Britons. When the Anglo-Saxons invaded centuries later they drove the Celtic Britons back into the island's extremities—Scotland, Cornwall/Devon, and Wales. The Britons in Wales were cut off from their kinsmen in other areas by the mid-600s and began to call themselves the Cymry (fellow countrymen) while the Saxons referred to them as the Welsh, which in Anglo-Saxon meant foreigner (roughly equivalent to modern-day Americans calling Native Americans foreigners).

Prince—The highest title a man could hold amongst the Welsh (Cymry). While outsiders referred to Welsh leaders as king, the Cymry themselves called them princes.

FROM SAXON ENGLAND

Atheling—Anglo-Saxon word meaning "prince of the (royal) blood."

Bretwalda—Excluding the Celtic "outlands" the island of Britain was split into several Anglo-Saxon kingdoms (the number varies but in the later and more stable centuries it was seven). Each was ruled by its own king. However, at different times one king would gain ascendancy over the others and would be hailed as the overking or *bretwalda*.

Ceorl—Yeoman farmer, a free and independent landholder, and part of the basis of the Saxon kingdoms.

Ealdorman—A member of the ruling nobility of Saxon England. The king's viceroy responsible for a shire's administration and justice and for calling out the reservist army or *fyrd*. The term was not replaced by *earl* until approximately 1010, and was then likely influenced by the Danish *jarl*.

Thegn—A member of a select body, usually young warriors, who attended the king and usually accompanied him everywhere, acting as bodyguard and lesser official. On rare occasions, for good service, a thegn could be elevated to ealdorman. Older thegns were among the king's advisers.

Thrall—Bondsman or slave.

CHANTING THE STORM

Prologue

Early March, A.D. 688

Low-rolling rain clouds further darkened a dense forest. The only sounds amidst its shadows were the monotonous squish of horse hooves plodding through mud and the patter of a seemingly endless drizzle. For the small mounted band retracing a barely discernible path between close-grown trees these noises were the sole product of a fruitless day's toil. That fact made dreary weather seem an appropriate background to five men whose quest had come to naught.

In an attempt to foil rivulets of rain running over strong cheeks and clenched jaw, Adam pulled the hood of his black cloak lower, casting a deeper gloom on his handsome face. He was cold and wet and irritated by this waste of a day, annoyed by foes who refused to honorably fight in the open. Only the night past his wretched opponents had slipped silently through the darkness to fall upon a small cottage

1

snugly cradled inside a woodland glade. All those sleeping within had been slain.

This forest marked the border between Northumbria and Mercia, and the attack had been yet another attempt to nibble away at the existing boundaries between the two kingdoms. Months earlier King Aldfrith had ordered Adam, as his liege man and the Ealdorman of Oaklea, to lead a band of men from his own shire in the kingdom's center to the southeastern border. There they now joined the local ealdorman in defending against such assaults. Thus it was that early this morn Adam had led four men in following the evildoers' trail, which had grown ever fainter until it faded into nothing. The culprits who laid it had simply disappeared—a fact which increased Adam's irritation until his teeth ground together and leather reins bit into the battle hardened palms of clenched hands.

A warrior of considerable experience, Adam was frustrated by this childish, nay, cowardly conflict of stealthy attacks made by Mercians who then melted into shadows rather than standing to fight man-to-man. Jaw anger-tight, Adam wordlessly cursed the storm responsible for the current failure.

Storm? Nay, this weather was unworthy of such a fierce title. Heavy gray clouds following drifts of fog and endless rain were nothing so dramatic as a mighty clash of the elements. Rather they were the sorry sham of a tempest and in comparison a dismal disappointment. Same as the disappointment of this day begun with hope for wreaking vengeance upon the enemy but ending in a lack of any worthy event. Worse still, Adam feared this day too likely a portent of those to come.

After King Ecgfrith's death three years past, his half brother, Aldfrith, had assumed the crown of Northumbria. A most learned man, trained to be a monk, Aldfrith sought always to live in peace. Nowise could the present state of conflict be laid at his door. Nay, it had been precipitated by Ethelred, King of Mercia. Ethelred was a man determined to expand his kingdom and toward this end had turned greedy eyes upon the lands of the new monarch he believed proven a weakling by his love of peace. As with the previous night's attack, bit by bit Ethelred's warriors had begun chipping away at the edges of Northumbria until now outright war hovered like a black storm cloud over the horizon. Adam and his men steadily traveled onward through the stillness while his thoughts grew ever bleaker.

Z-z-zwing! Thw-w-wap! In the space of a single breath the air filled with the hiss of flying arrows and solid thuds of points piercing flesh.

Sword singing in its unsheathing, Adam whirled his horse about to catch a glimpse of his four companions-in-arms falling from their mounts, riddled with arrows. The forest erupted with men, gruff voices barking out harsh battle cries.

Adam didn't see the sudden blow that smashed against the base of his neck and knocked him from the saddle—senseless.

The thundering sound of a hundred steeds hurtling their masters into battle seemed to pound in Adam's head. While conscious thought slowly returned, that thunder was all he could hear until, gradually, he became aware of the welcome warmth of the crackling fire nearby. However, his lashes remained too heavy

3

to lift and for that Adam was thankful when he heard a voice familiar and unwelcome.

"Take our *guest* to where I've arranged he be held." The carefully measured words were restrained but were clearly stretched over an underlayer of satisfaction with this capture and reduction of his noble prey to tight-bound prisoner.

"Why?" A querulous voice demanded. "Surely there is somewhere nearer where Lord Adam could be confined with less waste of time and toil." Having made the argument before—and failed—the speaker added a claim that revealed a sense of injustice over his ostensibly devout cohort's usurping of a duty he deemed rightly his own.

"You haven't the wits to understand the dangers surrounding him." Impatient with the Mercian thegn's repeated challenges, the first speaker snapped out the denigrating words.

"Oh, aye. You shake at the prospect of all that Druid nonsense which so easily reduces you to a puddle of baseless terror." The one plainly demeaned sneered his defense. "And I resent such a waste of effort when my warriors are equal to ensuring that Lord Adam remain in custody, proficient enough to prevent the interference of Druid magic that has no power save the ability to strip your strength with fear." The words fair dripped with sarcasm.

"In payment for my support, your king agreed to ensure that our captive would be taken to the destination I have arranged. Thus, no matter your *baseless* boasts, you have been commanded to see him confined within the walls of man-cut stone waiting to hide him away from those certain to come seeking."

Adam heard hatred for him in the bishop's voice, a

black emotion which clearly had sunk into venomous depths during the decade since last their paths had crossed in violent confrontation. Aye, the less than pious bishop was readily recognizable but less certain was the identity of the other who ridiculed powers well to be feared. In a desire to have his suspicion confirmed, Adam slowly forced heavy eyelids to open.

Squinting against bright firelight's painful assault on a pounding head, Adam took Bishop Wilfrid's measure. Years of exile had done nothing to reduce the sizeable belly over which Wilfrid habitually crossed his hands, but Adam's attention quickly shifted to the man glaring at the portly bishop. He was vaguely familiar. In an instant, Adam recognized him as Torvyn, thegn to Mercian King Ethelred.

Torvyn looked so gaunt as to be weak but Adam knew from the experience of meeting him in battle that it was a facade masking a wiry strength and cunning mind. Yet the mere fact of his presence was no surprise, particularly compared to the shock delivered by the fact that Torvyn's unkempt hair flowed like dirty thatch from beneath a beaten-bronze helm crested by the form of a wild boar. Moreover, the roughly hacked ends brushed against the matted fur of a cloak only partially covering a leather jerkin studded with interlaced circles of bronze.

Too fervent to be restrained, a growl of disgust erupted from Adam. Both the helm and the jerkin were his.

The other two men's attention instantly shifted to their captive, bound and helpless on the dirt floor. The bishop's lips spread with a smile of chilling contempt and unshielded exultation before, without a single word more, he turned and led his fellow conspirator from the humble dwelling. Adam was left alone with a dying fire and the disheartening certainty that the small hut was ringed with men who soon would carry him far, far from the reach of even his wife's mystical powers.

And yet why? Why had this enemy of old not simply rid himself of the earthly presence of the man who once had not merely defeated but exposed him to disgrace? What purpose lay behind the bishop's inexplicable action?

Chapter
1

Late May, A.D. 688

Spirits of meadows and woodland bowers, of eternal stone and fleeting flowers, of gentle dew and mighty sea, thrice of you I plea. Sitting on a stool drawn close to one of a pair of small windows whose shutters were thrown wide, Anya exercised her habit of solemn patience while continuing an unspoken chant. *Once to grant serenity, twice to fire my beloved's memories, and thrice to hasten him back to me.*

Anya had been waiting in near this same position since dawn, gazing at the path leading to the door of Throckenholt Keep. Now as she earnestly repeated her soundless litany the deepening pastels of a setting sun lent a bright aura to her slender body and glowed on the cloud of pale blond hair cloaking her shoulders. Even while chanting she prayed that what power silence robbed of her words might be compensated for by their fervor.

7

The daughter of a Saxon Christian and Druid sorceress, Anya saw no reason to hesitate in combining a Christian prayer with a Druid chant. She worried only that her triads failed to possess the ethereal beauty and effortless rhythm of either her mother or Llys's chants. 'Twas the best she could do without the formal training denied her by a father's insistence that his children be raised as Christians and by a mother's honest belief that her half-Saxon offspring were by their mixed blood blocked from attaining mastery of Druidic forces.

Guilt-struck with this suggestion of an undeserved criticism, Anya shifted position and her stool creaked. She hadn't meant to blame her father when, as Ealdorman of Throckenholt, a shire of Christian Northumbria, the renowned warrior, Wulfayne, could hardly do less. Asides, he loved her and his action was well intended.

Nor could Anya claim it a fault against her mother. Lady Brynna was sincere in her belief of the limitations imposed by her children's mixed heritage. In truth, Anya's three younger brothers showed neither interest nor aptitude in such matters. Anya grimaced and shifted again. It was unfair to assume as much of baby Cenwulf. Yet if Cenwulf took after ten-year-old Cub and six-year-old Edwyn then 'twould be so.

Aware of a sudden that her unusual restlessness had drawn the notice of both her mother and Llys, Anya realized she'd allowed her mind to wander. From so early a time she could not name the day, quiet as a mouse, she'd listened closely and long since learned enough to know that serenity and unwavering attention were the first steps in wielding Druidic power.

Were her chants to be of any use, she must focus on them alone.

"Spirits of meadows and woodland bowers, of eternal stone and fleeting flowers, of gentle dew and mighty sea, thrice of you I plea. . . ." Leaf green eyes closed tight, Anya concentrated on her goal—Evain's coming.

Even the fact that Evain was journeying here not to see her but rather in answer to his sister's desperate plea failed to lessen Anya's delight. Blocking all thought of the keep's hall, of thralls laboring at the central hearth over a belated evening meal, of her mother and Llys, she fervently repeated silent triads.

Brynna sat in her shadowed herb corner at a long table burdened with an array of vials, measuring bowls, and pottery jars. The methodical pounding of a small pestle to grind tiny seeds in a stone bowl was a task so oft repeated over many years that it permitted her to work without thought to the sleeping tisane in which they'd be steeped.

Instead a gray gaze darkened with anxiety lingered upon the daughter filled with palpable anticipation. Despite the lovely vision presented by her golden child bathed in daylight's final glory, to Brynna, Anya had as well have been shrouded in bleak mists and leaning out over an unseen precipice. Brynna near wished that Evain would not answer the call too likely to tempt Anya into a headlong fall.

Over the years Brynna and Wulf had watched in amusement while as toddler and then awkward child Anya idolized teenage Evain—a harmless youthful fancy. But now Anya was a maiden full-grown, and her unwavering affection had become a worrisome thing. The young boy to whom Brynna had stood as foster mother, of sorts, had matured into a devastatingly handsome man. The potency of Evain's natural attraction had been increased by experience gained in having been pursued by a great many females during the past decade. Then, too, he was the more dangerous for his mystical powers—particularly to Anya.

Evain was a Druid sorcerer whose heritage and destiny demanded the fulfillment of an all-important duty owed both to the past and the future—one in which a half-Saxon mate could have no part. Thus, nothing could come from the deepening of Anya's feelings for him. Nothing but pain for Anya. And of that Brynna wished to spare her daughter. Regretfully, there existed no mystical chant able to alter human emotion.

The overworked pestle had ground seeds into an unnecessarily fine powder before it was stilled by another's gentle fingers settling atop Brynna's hands. A dark head highlighted by strands of silver lifted to meet the solace of Llys's sapphire gaze.

"Trust Evain." Llys spoke so softly only Brynna would hear. As the mother of a healthy pair of twin boys and a toddling girl, Llys could easily comprehend her foster mother's concern but also knew her brother too well to doubt his honor. "He cares too much to hurt her."

Brynna's smile failed to reach her eyes. "I fear 'tis as inevitable as the thunder that follows a strike of lightning." Seeing the other woman's distress over the truth in her statement, Brynna felt guilty. First, for thwarting Llys's attempt to comfort. Second, for even momentarily regretting Evain's coming when it was so necessary to aid in Llys's desperate cause.

Unaware that the two older women were quietly discussing her, Anya maintained her concentration by summoning to mind the image of the darkly handsome sorcerer, her beloved Evain. The fervor of Anya's chanting intensified until some inexplicable inner voice urged her to look through the window.

Green eyes flew open to glimpse the answer to her pleas striding through twilight's purple mists. Anya leaped to her feet so quickly her stool crashed to the side. Paying it no heed, she rushed to throw wide the iron-bound planks of an oak door, dash down the front path, and hurtle herself against the longed for figure.

"You're here! Oh, Evain, I'm so glad you've come at last." The words were muffled against his broad chest but she soon leaned back and tilted her chin upward to ask, "Why have you stayed away so long?"

One strong arm wrapped tightly around the dainty figure while the other held a stave topped with a crystal clasped in a bronze eagle's claw. Evain gazed down into a piquant face radiating an unshielded emotion he dare not return. 'Twas the answer to her question yet one he would not state aloud for fear of opening a subject best buried in silence. In truth, he wouldn't have ventured coming to Throckenholt at all but for his sister's urgent request that he meet her here. Aye, only affection for his sister and awareness of the desperate purpose behind her summons had forced him to risk reentering a tempting web woven by sweet innocence and forbidden love.

And yet nothing could prevent him from drinking in the reality behind too many daydreams and night fantasies. Large silver-green eyes dominated an elfin face with high cheekbones and pointed chin while her petal pink lips, top bowed and bottom full, were far too enticing. And the more inviting now when they were so brief a distance below his own.

"Come in, Evain." Calling from the cottage's open doorway, Brynna's voice was sharp and sundered the dangerous enthrallment she saw too clearly. But her tone softened to add, "There's stew and fresh bread waiting to be eaten."

Evain glanced over the top of Anya's blond head, smiling an apology for the momentary lapse in his guard and gratitude for the interruption. Asides, he was both hungry and thirsty.

"I pray you can spare me a mug of ale as well." Evain's deep laughter rumbled. The beauty continued clinging to his side but it was with a restrained brotherly affection that he wrapped his arm about her and led the way into the abode where burned a fire whose warmth was welcome against the spring evening's chill.

Three women and one man took seats at the high table of a lord gone to join his king in defending a threatened realm. When Evain chose to sit between his sister and foster mother, Anya was painfully aware that he'd chosen that position to make it impossible for her to sit close beside him. In view of the serious reason for his return and despite an aching heart, she acknowledged the rightness of his choice.

Anya had already known that upon entering the keep she must retreat into her usual shell of silence. By doing so she would be allowed to remain and feast upon the sight of her reluctant beloved, to savor his nearness while watching and listening. Speaking would be to risk being exiled from the chamber like a child, same as her brothers and Llys's children, who

had already been sent to bed. That prospect reinforced an awareness that her shell was her armor as
well. Knowing that once inside she became near
invisible to others occupied with weighty matters
strengthened Anya's hope for learning what actions
the three Druids meant to take for righting wrongs
committed against their own.

Settling into her seat at the table, Anya composed
herself to wait, as she had all the day long, in patient
serenity.

Patience? Serenity? The thought of these emotions
were a gentle jest that curled her lips into a slight
smile. They were the elements of which her shell was
formed and had become a useful habit through which
she had heard and learned many things that elsewise
would've been denied her. And yet Anya feared a lack
of patience would be her downfall. In truth, it was
amazing that despite their mystical gifts none of her
three companions had ever recognized the simple
truth that behind her calm exterior lay a fiery spirit
too oft struggling against her shell's restraining bonds.

Anya wondered if her mother, Llys, or Evain had
ever felt such tests of the controlled tranquility all-
important to a Druid. She feared they never had,
feared it was this lack in her which would prevent her
from winning her goal of sharing their secret talents.
And one thing more important—as well as more
difficult to attain—Evain's love.

Once Evain had made a worthy dent in his platter
of bread drenched in savory stew and quaffed a
sizeable portion of the ale provided in an earthen
mug, he quietly listened while his sister spoke of the
matter which had drawn him here.

"As you know, Wulf met with the foes of Northumbria. And you know, too, that after he saw one of their leaders wearing Adam's helm and armor, we thought him dead." Despite now possessing worthy reason to question that assumption, Llys's voice ached from months of what she hoped was needless mourning.

"Less than a fortnight past, to Oaklea came a traveler. After wending a path through the kingdoms of Wessex and Mercia he found his way to our door. For the price of a meal and night's abode, he delivered this missive." Llys carefully laid a square of folded parchment on the tabletop and nudged it toward her brother.

Evain went still before returning a full spoon to the trencher, which he thence moved aside. Gingerly he slid the clearly precious parchment nearer. The ragged paper crackled in its cautious opening and, curiously, several pieces of candle tallow fell to the table's bare planks. They were initially ignored while he gave his attention to the message in his hands. It was with unconscious gratitude for the wisdom of their foster father, Wulfayne—who had insisted that in addition to Glyndor's Druidic training, he and his sister learn the rudiments of writing and reading—that he read the scribbled message: "Healthy but in stone."

The letters were roughly formed and smudged, leaving little doubt but that they'd been written with a bit of coal salvaged from a fire gone cold and crudely sharpened. Yet, though cryptic and unsigned, its meaning was as clear as the identity of its author.

"Realign the tallow pieces," Llys urged, heart in her throat. Although she'd been certain of the letter's source the moment it touched her outstretched hand, she was anxious for the reassurance that her brother was as convinced as she that this was not merely a cruel hoax.

After Evain nudged the three largest chunks of broken tallow together the identity of the message's source was confirmed. Pressed into their center was a stylized letter *A*. One such as those so oft used in illuminating the manuscripts copied by the scribes in monasteries.

None at the table could doubt but that the mark had been produced by the ring whose metal strands were twined into the first letter of Adam's name. The ring was a distinctive one given Adam by King Ecgferth in thanks for having saved his liege's life. Ever secreted upon his person, Adam had long used it to mark formal approval of documents and sign personal correspondence.

"When Wulf returned from the unsuccessful negotiation between our king and his opponents, he told me of the foe who proudly wore Adam's helm and armor . . ." Brynna broke a long silence. ". . . And he spoke of looking for but failing to see the ring upon him."

"Adam was wise not to sign his name." Evain nodded both acceptance of Brynna's statement and his certainty that the letter had truly been sent by a captive Adam. "I fear that had it been recovered by his captors, his life would've been . . ."

Llys shivered while through her mind ran visions of Adam being tossed into the sea or a bottomless peat bog—both furtive but known practices for arranging the permanent disappearance of a foe.

Sensing the distress caused by the implication, Evain regretted not having better guarded his tongue.

To direct his sister's thoughts away from bleak possibilities, he asked, "From whence did this message originate?"

"The one who delivered it claimed 'twas given him in Wessex by a man who had traveled south." Llys's answer was immediate. "Said the first man was unable to recall precisely where or who had given it to him."

That the source of Adam's letter could not be firmly stated was no surprise to the listeners. Unless a lord sent his own trusted messenger, most written communication passed through many hands before reaching its destination.

When the meal was done, thralls removed the trenchers and retired to the small hut provided by their master. The hut was a gift of uncommon consideration for slaves but one also able to provide Wulf and his family with an even rarer treasure—hours of privacy. Alone and free to openly discuss secret matters unknown and never to be revealed to those unworthy of being taught, Evain and the two sorceresses reached an agreement. They would take the scrap of parchment out into nature's haven. Once within arms whose embrace was ever open to those able to commune with its silent voices, they would chant the rising moon.

Anya quietly rose when, to intently discuss needful details, the tones of her mother and the two siblings instinctively sank into whispers. Slipping from the abode unnoticed, Anya hastened down two wooden steps, around the keep, and into a circle of oaks. In his bride's honor, near two decades past, her father had planted these trees, joining them to the mighty one long growing at this site.

While approaching that venerable oak Anya softly

sang the triads of respect and gentle pleas for permission to use its shield which she'd learned from a mother unaware of how attentively her child listened. Then in a darkness preceding the moon's appearance, she hiked her pale yellow skirts up to billow over a low-riding belt of plaited reeds, leaving the hem to brush her thighs.

Once done Anya began to steadily climb. The bark was rough on her hands and she feared that, even carefully folded over a belt, her linen skirts would have tears difficult to explain. Still, she had no regret for the deed. Anya had just settled herself into a crook between sturdy limb and trunk when the other three entered the oak grove below.

Evain placed the missive from Adam in its midst. Next atop the scrap of parchment, he, Llys, and Brynna laid their crystals. The three then moved together, not into a circle but a triangle. Eyes shut and arms extended with the closed fingers of one's hand touching at tips against another's while thumbs met below to also form triangles at each joining, they began chanting an eerily beautiful tune. The wild song's deep tones sank and gained strength as the trio slowly revolved around soon glowing white stones. When the notes soared higher, the three Druids moved ever faster and the crystals burned so brilliantly 'twas as if the rising moon itself had come to rest in the grove's heart.

In branches above, Anya was awed by the charm of what, by a tale told far and wide, she recognized as the eternal triad of balanced power. Aye, though these haunting verses had a different purpose, this must surely be the same powerful rite that the three had once performed to send a massive army fleeing.

As the final notes of the otherworldly entreaty dipped, swirled, and soared through the treetops like rising sparks, each chanter bent to lift their own crystal and reverently hold it in cupped hands. Staring into bright centers, one by one they spoke of the vision revealed within luminous depths.

"I see men dressed in the armor of the ancient invaders." Brynna recognized the garb by virtue of the costume passed from generation to generation through her family until Glyndor had seen Wulf so attired to aid in a rescue of her.

Fascination filled Llys's voice as she said, "I see the southern forest and crashing sea beyond."

Both the eerie glow and waiting silence lingered until at last Evain shared his vision. "I see a sprawling stone palace . . . surrounded by dense forests and shrouded in storm clouds." His companions gasped but he gave them a grim smile. "Leastways I know my destination and go warned, prepared for the difficult quest."

"You go?" Llys's brief question held both fear and hope.

Evain nodded and while the brightness of his crystal, too, faded, the light of a fully risen moon rippled over the thick black mane a watcher above intently studied. "Both you and Brynna have children to raise and shires for which to care." He sensibly answered his sister, strong chin lifting in demonstration of his determination. "Alone I am better able to thread my way through the forest of foes and pass unscathed through the storm."

Brynna remained silent. She saw too well the verity of Evain's claim. Loving him as a son, she feared for the man but could not honestly dispute his words.

Asides, he'd been both well-trained to military skills by a great warrior, her husband, and taught all manner of mystical powers by her grandfather, the famed Druid sorcerer Glyndor. With these comforting facts she soothed her apprehensions for his safety.

From the branches overhead, Anya listened to frightening words. Although not totally unexpected, she had refused to earlier consider the likelihood of Evain's clearly stated intent. She laid her soft cheek against the trunk's rough bark, an unthinking echo of the need to face harsh realities. 'Twas true that neither her mother nor Llys could desert those dependent upon them—both children and entire shires. Not when the only males remaining in either Throckenholt or Oaklea were either very young or old and infirm. Anya forced an unwilling spirit to accept the unalterable fact that Evain must take up the challenge of finding and freeing Adam.

While Brynna and Llys retreated to the keep, like a new fire gathering strength, an idea slowly took shape in Anya's thoughts. The older women had duties to bind them near their homes, but not she. Focusing on that glowing inspiration, Anya straightened—an action that nearly sent her plummeting to the ground. She tightly clutched both a limb overhead and the one below to steady her balance. Yet even this immediate proof of her vulnerability did nothing to lessen her belief in the merits of a fine plan able to provide aid for Evain . . . and also permit a measure of the time in his company she craved.

Anya assured herself that the ease with which she'd recovered her secure position foreshadowed an ability to safely pursue her goal. Surely nothing existed to prevent her from assisting the success of Evain's mission. A cold flash of reality shivered through Anya. Nothing, that was, except Evain himself. Still, Anya reassured herself, she was sharp-witted enough to find a way around that impediment as well.

Maintaining a tight hold on thick branches, for an unmarked length of time Anya sat motionless to ponder the matter. She devised and discarded a plethora of convoluted ploys until in the end she settled on the simplest. Filled with a sense of success in overcoming the first obstacle, she glanced down only to discover additional difficulties. Not only had a deal more time passed than she'd realized but below rested another problem unforeseen.

Evain, as had his mentor, Glyndor, disliked having the barriers of man-made walls between himself and the spirits of nature, the source of his powers. Thus, when visiting Throckenholt, never did he sleep within its walls. Anya hadn't known where he made his bed until now when it was clear his habit was to sleep in this grove. Stretched out on his back, head pillowed on his satchel and wrapped in a long black cape, Evain lay sleeping directly beneath her towering perch.

This was a problem indeed. Doubtless the ladies inside the keep had thought her safely abed before they set out to perform the rite she'd witnessed. And were she not in her small chamber when dawn came, there'd be questions she couldn't answer without jeopardizing her plans. There was no help for it. She must find her way down from this tree and into the keep unseen. Moreover, to wait longer here would be to tempt the night chill to rob her fingers of necessary dexterity and make matters worse.

With senses honed by training as a warrior and sharpened by the skills of a sorcerer, Evain had become aware of being watched. That the attention focused upon him lacked any threat of danger prevented him from immediate action. It was not until he heard soft sounds above that his eyes opened to a too enticing sight.

Moonlight picked out the light-hued skirts tucked up beneath a belt riding slender hips and glowed on the elegance of shapely legs. Only a bit above his standing height small bare feet descended the rough bark of the oak's trunk with care. In the instant during which he was torn between rebuke and unabashed admiration, the dainty maid's toes slipped.

Despite desperately grasping fingertips, Anya fell with a soft shriek. Her heart-stopping fall had an even more exciting ending—caught in Evain's arms and crushed tightly against his broad chest. Not wishing to lose the joys of this unexpected gift of fate, she instantly buried her face in the crook between his throat and shoulder thinking that if he meant to hold her until her heart resumed its normal pace she would be in his embrace forever. But it seemed her future afforded no such good fortune, leastways not without her help. A fact made plain when he lowered her feet to the ground and started to put her aside.

To defeat what Evain likely viewed as an honorable choice, Anya twisted about to wrap her arms around his neck and wantonly pressed herself full against him. She loved the feel of his warm strength, the powerful muscles tensing where her breasts flattened against him. Her heart ran wild as she rose on tiptoes to lift her lips toward his.

Evain was thoroughly aware of the many reasons this must not happen but for far too many months, nay, years he had dreamed of sharing just such a burning embrace with the elfin beauty. Those heated memories were responsible for leaving him utterly unprepared to withstand the trembling maiden's innocent onslaught.

Firm mouth brushing achingly across hers, Evain gently bit at her lips. He probed and tenderly coaxed until he had heated the kiss she'd initiated as an inexperienced child into a devastating merger of souls. Wild sensations swept over Anya, stealing her breath and turning her bones to water. She melted against him with a hungry moan, tangling shaking fingers into the cool black strands of his shoulder-length mane.

The sound of Anya's hunger sent Evain over some vague precipice of blind pleasure, and he lifted her delicate curves intimately tighter into the curve of his hard form. But even as she yielded without sane restraint, Evain became achingly aware of his wrong. Having sampled the berry nectar of her mouth—indescribably sweet and the more precious for its scarcity—his guilt intensified under the realization that it could never, must never be tasted again.

As Evain abruptly pulled his mouth from hers, Anya cried out against the loss and lifted heavy lashes to gaze with palpable longing into the mesmerizing lights glittering in the sapphire depths of his eyes.

Irritated with himself for his foolish actions of questionable honor and with her for so easily knocking him off kilter, Evain struggled to mentally restore an even footing.

"Go to bed, little poppet." Evain employed the teasing name he'd long used for the dainty elfling child she'd been and still was—almost.

"I've grown up." Aching with a never before experienced frustration, Anya instantly took exception to his implication of inexperienced youth, never mind that 'twas true.

"Have you?" The cynically smiling sorcerer's tone left no question but that he doubted the fact and for the first time Anya caught a glimpse of what danger this man could be to her. However, 'twas a danger more thrilling than perilous and one she refused to fear just as she refused to rise to the bait inciting an argument.

Seeing Anya's delicate features settle into the lines of patience which were their wont, Evain cupped slender shoulders in strong hands and turned her toward the keep's path with another caution. "This adventure is *over.*"

Although Anya walked away without verbal response, she concentrated on her carefully designed plan and wordlessly disputed his claim. *'Tis not over! It has only just begun.*

Chapter
2

Anya awoke with a start. In the darkness of a window-less room it was impossible to tell how far the morning had advanced. Praying her late retirement hadn't led her to oversleep, with unusual awkwardness Anya hastily took up a taper from the neat stack ever waiting beside her pallet. She applied its wick to the glowing coal inside one of the small iron pots nightly left at bedsides by house thralls. After the wick took fire she let dripping wax puddle on a smooth wood square then steadied the taper to stand upright atop it.

By the candle's feeble light Anya poured water from a waiting ewer into the shallow bowl and rushed through morning ablutions before pulling on a fine linen undergown. This first garment was pale green and close fitting. To it she added a kirtle of wool the hue of a shadowed forest. While rapidly dragging a

bone comb through her hair she worried that her
mother might question this choice of favorite garb for
a day midweek. Anya could only hope serious concerns would so occupy the thoughts of both her
mother and Llys that neither would spare it their
notice. Nowise would it be possible for her to explain
that her selections had been made with a view to what
she deemed best suited to blend with her surroundings on the adventure ahead.

Once done dividing her wealth of silver-blond hair
into two fat braids, she turned her attention to carefully folding both a deep red gown and long-sleeved gray
under camise. These she packed into an old, use-aged
leather satchel. Setting it to wait beside the door, she
was ready to set forth on this first day in a quest
promising to offer the greatest challenge of her life.

Upon entering the hall Anya was relieved to find
proof that she hadn't overslept. Open window shutters revealed a day too new to provide adequate
illumination. And as torches held in metal rings down
each wall were rarely lit during daylight hours, the
only worthy light came from the leaping flames of the
central hearth. Despite the spirals of smoke that
accompanied twisting gold and orange spears she
could see Cub and Edwyn, as well as Llys's twin sons,
seated at the high table. Two thralls bustled about
serving the rowdy boys bowls of oat porridge along
with mugs of foamy milk and chunks of dark rye
bread.

Turning left Anya found the two women she sought.
They were seated at a long table amidst shadows
which preserved the potency of the medicinal herbs
and potions to which the corner was dedicated.

"Evain left last eve," Anya announced, striving to

steady the betraying tremor in her voice. "He chose to
linger no longer for fear of what might be the cost of
lost time."

Anya did not share her suspicion that he would go
first to his cave-home in the mountains of Talacharn
and, struggling with guilt for hiding her own plans,
was thankful for a wailing Cenwulf's interruption. It
was her mother's practice, upon leaving the bedchamber each morn, to bring into the hall the woven-reed
basket in which her baby son slept, and Anya hastened
to her infant brother's side. His waking cry gave her
the opportunity to turn away before the other women
could query her on how it was that she'd come by this
information while they slept.

Brynna did question the source of Anya's knowledge . . . but silently, too certain of the single answer
for both that and the reason behind the strain in her
daughter's voice. Again grinding seeds with her pestle,
though this morn's seeds were larger and required
more vigorous actions, Brynna resigned herself to the
certainty that Anya had spent some measure of the
night with Evain.

Watching Anya lift her tiny brother from the basket,
Brynna remembered Llys's plea of the previous day.
Aye, she remembered the words urging her to trust
Evain. And trust Evain she did. Elsewise she'd have
been a deal more upset. She comforted herself that
Evain's hasty departure proved his private time with
Anya had come to naught. Asides, her foster son most
assuredly knew that a relationship between himself
and Anya was effectively blocked—first, by the all-
important purpose of a sorcerer's existence; second,
by Wulf's dreams for his sole daughter's happy future.

She was certain that any bond betwixt the pair could have no end but anguish.

Brynna suspected the haste with which her daughter had turned aside after giving Evain's news was motivated by dejection over his leave-taking. She chose not to deepen Anya's distress by forcing a painful admission. Yet, despite sympathy for her daughter, Brynna was relieved that the handsome sorcerer's further danger to tender emotions had been removed from Anya's realm.

"Cenwulf's hungry and only I can calm his cries." With a gently teasing smile and gray eyes gone soft with compassion, Brynna rose and stepped forward to take the babe from her daughter's arms.

Anya returned the smile. Though her guilt was increased by an awareness of her mother's misplaced sympathy, she was thankful for this indication that the woman harbored no suspicion of plans Anya meant soon to put into motion. Once mother and baby disappeared into the lord's chamber, Anya turned toward Llys with a smile she hoped concealed her nervous anticipation.

"The miller's wife is feeling poorly, and I promised I'd bring them food enough to keep him and his young son fed until my mother's potions see her health restored."

Llys absently nodded, too busy restraining a curious toddling determined to poke tiny fingers into jars and baskets to spare Anya's words more than scant attention.

Pleased by the ease with which these first steps had been navigated, Anya's spirits soared. She lost no moment in taking two sacks of rough homespun from a neat pile on one of the shelves built against a long wall. Next, from a mental list earlier devised, she rapidly filled each with foodstuffs of a sort unlikely to spoil—apples, cheese, and parched oats. She left the keep's severely limited store of salt meat untouched but included round loaves of unleavened bread meant to remain edible for some little time. One plump sack she truly would leave with the miller, but the other even fatter sack would journey with her.

In addition to these provisions, Anya peered into a pouch attached to her belt. She had restocked this small linen bag by firelight the past night and anxiously widened its twine-drawn top edge to assure herself that it did indeed contain items deemed necessary. First, the flint needful for striking fire. Also, two vials of liquid. One able to staunch blood and see wounds knit the sooner and another to be blended into a sleep-encouraging tisane. Though her mother hadn't taught Anya the Druid chants to enhance these potions' healing powers, she had taught her daughter the mundane methods for putting them to work.

Anya's bag also contained the much prized crystal which she had begged from Evain years past. Though he'd given it to placate a winsome child, well Anya knew that through such tangible symbols a Druid could call upon the spirits of nature. Since near the day it had been placed in her small hands she had been striving to summon those same forces. Perhaps —it was a faint hope—her failure thus far was due to the fact that her white stone's angles, having not been smoothed by rolling between palms through many consecutive lifetimes, had barely begun to lose their roughness.

Irritated with herself for wasting precious time in

consideration of the matter, Anya sharply pulled the bag's string tight and shifted her attention to more immediate concerns.

"Oh, I near forgot the satchel of dresses I've outgrown that I offered the miller's oldest daughter. As I have only little brothers and they are in need . . ." Anya shrugged, praying Llys wouldn't see a rosy tint born of the lie which she could feel heating her cheeks.

Fortunately for Anya, Llys was lost too deep in worry over her husband's health and hope for his safe return to notice the younger woman's unease.

Anya concentrated on restraining her steps to a normal pace as she moved to reach inside her chamber door and lifted the satchel's strap to lie crossways from right shoulder to left hip. Laden with the satchel, she carried one sack of foodstuffs in each hand and departed with a cheery smile for Llys, her tiny daughter, and the boys dawdling over their morning meal.

The bright shades of dawn were fading into the pale blue of early morn as she made her way to the sorely depleted stable built against the keep's backside. Her father and his men had taken Throckenholt's great war-horses, leaving behind only the oxen at work in the fields and one mare too short and plump to be of use either in farming or battle. But though useless for arduous labors old Blossom was just right for Anya's designs.

The gloomy stable's door creaked as Anya pushed it open, and the dappled gray horse's head came up and stretched over the gate of her stall toward the source of many treats. Anya laughed and put the sacks safely aside. Reaching into one she withdrew an apple and offered it to the gentle beast. While Blossom contentedly munched, Anya hoisted a saddle to her back and affixed a sack of foodstuffs to either side. After being led from the stable, the mare patiently waited while her mistress closed the stable door. Filled with a mixture of anticipation and sternly repressed apprehension for the unknown, Anya mounted the docile creature and did her best to urge it into a semblance of haste—to little avail.

Under Blossom's plodding pace it took far longer than Anya had expected to reach the miller's home on a curve of the stream originating at the spring behind Throckenholt Keep. Consequently she gave the bag to the middle-aged man with less good humor than was her wont. She must hurry else the entire plan would be lost for missing Evain's passing at the junction where the path from his cave-home in Talacharn met the southwestern route from Throckenholt. Without knowing Evain's destination and aware how unlikely he was from that point to travel any well-marked track, Anya realized all would be lost were she too late to surreptitiously follow him.

A full day out from his haven in the Welsh mountains, Evain again attempted to shrug aside a continuing sense of Anya's nearness. The fading light of late afternoon further darkened his shadowy path through a forest filled with pungent odors and thick foliage—a bleak vista which only increased his self-contempt. It seemed certain that his thoughts of Anya and their intrusion on normally well-honed perceptions were nature's punishment for his having fallen to foolish actions when last they'd been alone.

The unnatural sound of a branch snapping beneath a heavy footfall jerked Evain from dangerous preoccupation. In one swift, smooth movement he whipped off the satchel whose strap lay sideways from shoulder to waist and his sword hummed as it rose to the ready. Whirling with powerful grace, Evain leaped into the gloom of the unmarked path he'd only just traversed.

Another sword slid free of its sheath but because its owner was far too hefty to lightly evade the quicker, younger prey abruptly become predator and bearing down on him, he was unexpectedly left to defend himself.

The violent ringing of forcefully wielded blade clashing against blade reverberated through the woodland. It pierced the peace of a maiden happily tracking a sorcerer's route down a narrow, crooked path not intended for a horse and one which Blossom had difficulty following with any speed. Anya dismounted. Diving into dense undergrowth, she rushed directly toward fearsome sounds.

Anya's headlong dash came to a sudden halt just behind a rawboned man whose drawn arrow was aimed straight at Evain's broad back. After the briefest of pauses, with a loud cry she instinctively launched herself at the archer. The loosed arrow's path was knocked askew while Anya and her quarry crashed to the forest's leaf- and grass-padded floor.

Though in the midst of deadly battle, Evain heard both Anya's distinctive voice and the zing of an arrow passing all too near. They knocked him off stride long enough for his opponent to take startling action. The stocky man turned and fled as rapidly as his bulk permitted.

Evain was forced to choose between pursuing his foe or going to the aid of the delicate maid who it seemed was at the heart of grunts, wild thrashing, and male cursing. In three strides he passed between

massive trees and through layers of tangled foliage to
thrust a flimsy bush aside. Blue ice eyes gazed into a
small glade created under the two crushing long green
blades and abundant ferns with their struggle.

His petite but amazingly fiery protectress sat straddling a prone man whose feet were caught in the
twisted remains of a fallen tree. Moreover, Anya's
fingers were so tightly entangled in her captive's dust
brown locks that she had pulled his head back to rest,
doubtless painfully, on bony shoulders. Although the
man flailed against the slight weight, Anya's fierce
hold complicated his struggle to free himself of her
clutches. His frustration spewed forth a stream of
vicious threats and curses. All in all it was a curious
sight and Evain melted into laughter.

"Hold, Anya. You've wrought sufficient mayhem
upon your pitiful victim." Evain tamed his amusement into a broad white grin. "Leastwise release the
poor man's hair."

Anya's normally serene face was rosy with exertion
and her green eyes glowed with determination. They
lost none of their fire in lifting to the laughing man
who appeared to find humor in her brave, lifesaving
feat. Her temper flamed! But after a few moments
beneath Evain's steady blue gaze, she took a deep
breath. Reminding herself that he'd been trained from
youth to use odd mood shifts to disconcert others, she
forced her unruly spirit back under its usual bonds.

Both startled and charmed by this glimpse of a fiery
nature seldom revealed, Evain soothed, "The man can
go nowhere but that I allow it."

As he spoke, Evain bent to scoop up arrows scattered from the defeated man's dislodged quiver. Over
an uplifted knee he wordlessly broke their shafts in

twain and then did the same to a forlorn bow. Next, taking a dagger from inside the man's boot, he cut the bowstring into a multitude of short pieces.

"Now we must permit our 'friend' to stand and face his captors." Evain held out a hand to aid Anya in rising and moving to his side while the erstwhile assailant, all big joints and skinny limbs, struggled to free his feet from twisted branches. Beneath two pairs of unwavering eyes, at last and with great difficulty he managed to heave himself upright.

"Tell us who you are," Evain calmly demanded. "And what sorry whim led you to cross my path."

"I am Claud of Aberstwyth." The one humiliated at the hands of a dainty female grudgingly answered but in shamed defiance added, "I meant to rob you."

Evain's crooked smile did nothing to warm his icy gaze. "You are far from proficient at your calling."

An unattractive brightness flooded Claud's gaunt cheeks as with a grimace he uneasily mumbled, "'Tis a trade new to me. And, aye, my skills need honing. Thus, when I saw you and the other fighting, I lingered near thinking whoever won was like to be so weary I'd have a fine chance for making off with his goods."

"If your intent was to rob, then why was your arrow aimed to kill?" Anya's question revealed a heat the antithesis of Evain's chill demeanor.

Their opponent's ruddy color deepened. "As I watched, it came to me that should I succeed in bringing one man down, the other might reward me with food . . . and mayhap a coin or two." Claud's shaggy head bent toward the man infinitely more intimidating than he'd appeared from behind. "He was the one with his back toward me. If it had been t'other way about . . ." He shrugged.

"And all begun in a ploy to make off with what was not rightly yours?" Disgust coated Anya's words while Evain studied the clumsy man in silence.

"Already have I confessed it so," Claud stated, apparently annoyed at having not only his ineptitude but his wrong emphasized yet again. "I have given you my name," he irritably argued, "and you ought do the same for me."

Despite handsome face held impassive, a dark head nodded an acknowledgment of the logic behind this complaint—no matter the attempt on his life.

"I am Evain." The widening of his hapless captive's eyes proved the man familiar with the name and its holder's reputation as a sorcerer.

"I didn't know 'twas you." Claud fairly quaked in terror. "I swear upon my mother's bones I didn't."

Again Evain nodded without a flicker of emotion.

Focus of a hard blue glare, Claud shifted uneasily and bent an accusing scrutiny upon the dainty beauty who had brought him, a man full grown, down so low.

"I am Anya." She ignored her rumpled state, squared slender shoulders, and proudly tilted her chin while adding, "And great-granddaughter of Glyndor, another famed Druid sorcerer."

Evain was amused to see that the girl's claim further frightened their defeated foe. No doubt he would eventually find solace in this fact for a maiden's ability to thwart his attempt and see him caught in this predicament.

"Now that you know who we are . . . begone with you!" Evain's command was quiet yet it rumbled like thunder.

In an instant Claud went white as new fallen snow and his Adam's apple plunged with a fervent gulp. "I fear I'm not—" He abruptly dropped to the patch of grass crushed by the earlier struggle. Sitting amidst the scattered remains of a broken bow and multiple arrows, his haggard face sank into his hands' spread fingers.

Wordlessly acknowledging their defeated opponent utterly overcome by his plight, Evain addressed him again. "Stay in this grove if you wish or move on as you please. But be warned: Follow you our path and I will see your action end in a reprisal well to be feared."

Taking Anya's small fingers in his hand, Evain turned to lead her away but paused to address Claud once more. "With a diligent search you will find your dagger in the undergrowth on your right. It's there where, once beyond your sight, I mean to toss it." The pathetic man was so lacking in the skills needful to survive that Evain found himself unable to leave him in the midst of the forest without a single tool for self-defense.

Evain motioned Anya to follow closely while he laid a purposely zigzagging path back and forth through woodland shadows and verdant greenery. Betimes he retraced their steps to lay false trails to nowhere, the better to befuddle trackers almost certain to come after them.

Anya was aware of her reluctant escort's purpose. Gaze steady on shiny black locks brushing the broad back ahead, a smile once grim warmed to pleasure. Whether Evain welcomed her or no, she had succeeded in joining him and had won the time alone in his company which she sought above all else. To her mind the latter was a fact worth whatever personal cost might be called forfeit.

At length, Evain paused beside a clear, bubbling brook. As he sank to his knees on the moss cushioned bank, he gently tugged Anya down to join him in sipping refreshing water from cupped hands.

Peeking sidelong at the stern-faced sorcerer, of a sudden Anya realized that since leaving Claud behind he had yet to speak a single word directly to her. An inevitable confrontation loomed near and beneath a serene facade she frantically sought to bolster her belief in the virtue of her cause so as to meet Evain's displeasure unflinching.

"The time has arrived for you to explain." Rising to tower over Anya, arms crossed over a powerful chest, an expressionless Evain spoke to the petite maid who had seemed oblivious to him as she slipped off her shoes to cool overheated feet in the stream's gentle flow. "Tell me what witless impulse drove you to become a burden complicating my quest."

"Burden?" Anya had expected reproach but not this scorn of her worth, not after what she had done for him. She leaped up and despite her bare feet's uncertain hold on a mossy bank not only soft but slippery, shock broke the tight bonds she'd wrapped about her temper. "Saved your life, I did!"

"Really?" With a mocking half smile Evain looked from tiny toes peaking beneath a green hem up to the emerald fire in wide eyes. They dominated the delicate face framed by the golden tendrils which her valiant struggle on his behalf had freed. "In reality 'tis nearer the truth to say a rescue of you prevented me from pursuing the man more surely a threat to me— and the successful completion of my mission."

"Hah!" Anya sputtered, fingers curling into

clenched fists resting on slender hips. "The arrow aimed at your back would've *permanently* prevented you from succeeding at that or any future goal!"

Behind Evain's emotionless mask, he was host to a disconcerting and dangerously seductive pleasure in the fire of his elfling maid. This further view of the burning heat at her core threatened to entice him into investigating what deeper, forbidden flames he might arouse.

Held immobile by an unwavering blue gaze, Anya learned that being the focus of Evain's disdain was a new and horribly unpleasant experience. Worse still, she felt certain he was determined to view her as an errant toddling. Suddenly aware that her frustrated vexation would only seem further proof of her child-ishness, thick lashes dropped to lie against soft cheeks while she forced her hands to relax and drew a deep breath. To disabuse him of his misapprehension, she could and would exercise more self-control than ever before.

Anya willed the return of her expression to its usual lines of serenity and sought to divert their collision course. Turning a sorcerer's weapon back upon a sorcerer, she abruptly shifted her mood from anger to curiosity and the subject of their talk from her heated action to a quiet questioning of others' intents.

"Were both of our opponents forest brigands? The sort whose wicked deeds are so oft fodder for the tales visitors repeat in the keep's hall?"

Evain recognized Anya's strategy but shielded his amusement behind an unyielding mask. "So, as you heard, the last admitted." He chose not to increase Anya's apprehension by revealing that the first just as certainly wasn't a simple bandit. The man's clothing and weapons had been too fine to be else than those of a professional warrior.

Deeply regretting his sweet Anya's involvement in the recent violence, Evain meant to shift her attention away from that savage scene.

"Whatever the truth of the deed exposing your presence, you've effectively trapped me into taking you with me on a dangerous mission." His words bore the sharp edge of an irritation renewed by bleak reality. During the rite performed in Throckenholt's oak grove he had learned of the dangers assuredly hovering over this journey and crouching in shadows on every side. To defeat all those who would see him fail, he needed his wits unmuddled and senses unclouded. But the simple fact of his wrongful love of Anya complicated that objective. And now her nearness made it almost impossible to achieve. His expression remained as emotionless as carved granite and his eyes seemed shards of blue ice as in the deep tones of doom he added, "Your company increases the peril yet I dare not waste the precious time required to see you safely returned to Throckenholt."

Anya had taken pains not to appear until 'twould be too late for him to send her home. Yet in this moment that fact increased her devastation over the dark shades lending his deep velvet voice a myriad of textures from faint resentment to clear condemnation. She had wanted to aid, not to hinder. And that she had already done, no matter his discounting of her feat. But if he could not see it was so . . . If he found her presence a trial . . .

The intrusion of a long silky nose between the pair

blocking a narrow path newly laid broke the confrontation's tension.

Despite Blossom's plodding gait and their twisting path, the mare had somehow followed and overtaken her mistress. Evain's soft laughter greeted the gentle beast's welcome interruption. And yet, fearing human pursuers might do the same, he immediately aided Anya in mounting the plump animal and then began leading the way on another convoluted path through uncertain danger toward an urgent goal.

Chapter
3

Night had settled its blackest shroud over the forest where Anya lay curled under her dark cloak with head resting atop joined palms. Surrounded by the fresh scent of foliage spiced with the tangy fragrance of honeysuckle, in stillness she listened. But all she heard was the soundless echo of Evain's deep voice earlier chanting gratitude to nature. This he had done before gathering lush grass to add to piled leaves fallen the previous autumn and formed for her a soft bed. The remembered song sent a warm thrill through Anya.

He was stretched out across the dying fire's dwindling flames opposite from her pallet. The thought of his powerful form so near revived exciting memories of their embrace in Throckenholt's oak grove . . . and strengthened her earnest wish to share that closeness again. The painful fact that he had made it abundantly clear he did not share her wish sent a single forlorn tear to trail down a soft cheek.

Anya knew what she must do, had known since their confrontation hours past. Though Evain lay unmoving, Anya had sensed his wakefulness for what seemed an endless time to the anxiety simmering beneath her serene facade. After leaving the inept Claud, they had traveled through the forest in silence. Evain had spoken only the barest minimum of cryptic words while signaling the end to the day's journey and building their evening fire.

In a gesture of contrition, she had offered him one of the round loaves of bread from her bag of supplies as a supplement to his own provisions. He had thanked her with icy politeness but nothing more. That action had shown Anya how foolish she'd been to believe herself able to win a mighty sorcerer's welcome.

Only now as the last glimmer of pale moonlight fled the sky had his breathing settled into the steady pattern of sleep. And only now could she risk embarking on another daring plan on Evain's behalf—one to undo the wrong he deemed done him.

Thankful that she'd had the sense to let fat braids remain plaited, Anya rose with caution. Leaving her bag of foodstuffs behind for Evain, she carefully lifted her satchel of clothing and took pains to make no sound while stealthily moving to attempt a more ticklish feat—the silent rousing and leading of Blossom into the forest.

Determination strengthened by the unhappy knowledge that Evain found her a burden, Anya reached into the small pouch still fastened to her belt and withdrew the rough crystal. This she slowly rolled between smooth palms while silently chanting the spell of shielding. Leastways Anya hoped she had the words aright. She had only heard it twice and both times as a child.

Anya nearly yelped when for the first time in answer to her call the white stone between her hands began to glow. The crystal's pale light was weak and flickered, yet glow it did. Fearing any abrupt motion or a cessation of her triads would endanger this small success, she carefully cupped the stone in one palm while turning to face Blossom.

Despite the mare's placid nature, Anya feared it too likely that in being roused to embark upon the return trail Blossom would make noise sufficient to wake Evain, a warrior-sorcerer trained to sleep light. Anya possessed no formal training in these matters but thought—although she could not be certain—that under the spell of shielding, all beasts as well as humans standing within the crystal's circle of light were invisible. And of greater import at this moment, she hoped it ensured the sounds of their passing would go unheard. Were it possible to pause in her chant she would pray that the latter be true as well.

No matter the answer to her questions, it seemed 'twas so as all continued smoothly while by the crystal's wavering light Anya picked her way around pebbles that might rasp together and over sticks that assuredly would crack if stepped upon. Moreover, when she reached the bush to which Blossom had been fastened, she was pleasantly surprised to find the mare standing and watching her mistress's approach as if awaiting her coming. Together they began retracing their day's trail.

Anya hesitated to end soundless chanting long

enough to mount Blossom until they'd traveled a distance beyond the camp and sleeping Evain. When at last she halted her lyrical litany, the crystal went immediately cold and dark. Offering a quick triad of gratitude and prayer of thanks, she carefully returned it to her pouch before swinging up onto the horse's broad back and prodding the slow beast forward.

Deep within a woodland where the branches of close-grown trees met to block even faint starlight from falling to forest floor Anya could see nothing and was left to trust Blossom's instincts. Barred from occupying her mind with the logistics of the journey, Anya could not suppress an unexpected apprehension. It was not a discomfort with intense darkness nor, yet, of forest creatures. She had absorbed too much of her mother's love for all natural forms to fear these things. Rather she experienced a prickling sensation as if subject to the watching eyes of an unfamiliar human.

Don't be the witless child Evain thinks you are. Anya silently berated her fears. *Even forest bandits must sleep through the night to be alert when daylight travelers venture near.*

Wishing she believed her own comforting words, Anya struggled to stifle her apprehensions beneath the shell of serenity practiced for years. This while Blossom—lacking mankind's imagination—plodded onward bothered by neither the deep shades of night nor the possibilities of unseen wild creatures or lurking human watchers.

After hours smoldering on a dying fire a log cracked and disintegrated, sending a flurry of sparks into the night sky. Stirring, Evain turned his head toward the

sound and sight of fleeting beauty. Tiny lights ascended to dance and glitter for brief shining moments
before abruptly fading to cold ash and drifting to the
ground. Ground. Empty ground!

Evain instantly rose with the lithe grace of a sleek
black cat. Anya was gone. He should've known she
would flee. Aye, in his fear for her safety amidst this
certain danger and even more in concern that his own
restraints might be insufficient to withstand her innocent temptation if too long alone in her company, he
had been too hard on her. 'Struth, by his cold manner
—lacking any shred of the warmth she was accustomed to receiving from him—he had as well have
ordered her to leave.

While snatching his stave from its resting place,
Evain's voice dropped into shivering depths. He
chanted powerful triads that brought a brilliant glow
to the crystal orb atop his staff and by that eerie light
strode down the path earlier covered.

His acceptance of responsibility for Anya's flight
was also an admission of responsibility for any harm
that befell her as a result of his foul mood. The rebuke
he'd delivered on her folly in trailing him into the jaws
of danger had been justified but badly mishandled.

Of a sudden a terrifying prospect loomed. It was the
vision of Anya, like one of the golden embers sent to
dance in the night sky, brightly glowing through the
darkness of his life only to fall into cold ashes at the
hands of predators into whose snare he'd sent her
fleeing. Under this bleak thought, his pace doubled.

Fortunately Blossom's slow steps made it possible
for him to catch up with the mounted girl. Exercising
the considerable self-control of a sorcerer he steadied

his breathing and suppressed the urge to reproach her for this further perilous action.

"So now you would desert me?"

Evain's gently mocking reproof washed over a melancholy Anya like liquid velvet. Though fearing the voice naught but the product of wishful thinking, she reined Blossom to a halt. Still she refused to turn and glance behind.

Evain strode forward until he reached Anya's side. Then, resting his staff against a low-hanging limb of one of the massive trees through which their path wound, he reached up to urge the dainty rider down into his strong arms.

Gently cradled like a babe in mighty arms she'd no doubt were able to crush any foe, Anya's heart raced wildly. She melted against the man she loved, refusing to question what whim of fate had brought him to her.

Under the feel of her sweet form—soft and yielding —curled in the circle of his embrace, Evain's worst fears were confirmed. His powerful body went motionless while the bonds of his good sense and honorable restraint showed themselves to be as insubstantial as chains of twined straw. Blue flame eyes caressed the delicate face of the innocent seductress with a gaze of green mist and petal soft lips whose nectar he remembered too well. Those lips were now parted and lifted in silent entreaty for his mouth. His face went rigid against the desperate need to taste them again.

Thoughts of their previous embrace filled Anya's mind—searing, exciting. . . . With her hand pressed against his chest she was achingly aware of the hard muscle and heavy heartbeat beneath as she studied Evain's mouth with the intensity of a kiss.

While cursing himself for his weakness where this one tender maiden was concerned and despite the inevitable guilty anguish sure to follow their forbidden embrace, he drew her closer. His delusion of her as a child, though carefully reinforced, was destroyed for all time as his arms welcomed the maiden who nestled generous curves so tightly into his strength that she irrefutably demonstrated herself a woman full grown. He wrongfully surrendered to the enticement of lips that had never known any save his. Brushing his mouth slowly, sensually across hers, he lied to himself that he could safely steal this much, truly only this much of her innocence—a morsel of sweetness that would always be his and belong to no other. A fool he was proven when, like wildfire through a dark forest, the kiss raged out of control.

As his tongue initiated a seductive dance of advance and withdrawal, Anya's world was swept into a whirlwind of fiery delights spinning ever higher. It burned through her body with helpless pleasure and she gasped at the darting, hungry pressure of its invasion. One heated kiss followed another, leaving her oblivious to anything save his desire and her own growing need. Anya's arms clung desperately around his neck and her fingers tightly twined into thick black locks.

Evain lifted his mouth to draw a ragged breath and, seeing her passion-swollen lips, drowsy eyes, and breathlessness, knew his action for the folly it was. And yet 'twas only by the strength of a sorcerer's will that he was able to tame his own staggering need and gently disentangle her fingers from his mane. Anxious not to further deepen the distress of his earlier rejection of her company, assuredly responsible for her flight through the night forest, he gifted her with a reassuring smile even as he slowly lowered her feet to the ground. Then he lay a chaste kiss in each soft palm before releasing her hands and stepping a brief distance back.

When Evain withdrew his support, Anya felt a chill far deeper than that lent by cool night air but she could not turn her gaze from eyes the same blue as the hottest flame.

Flashing a teasing smile, Evain abruptly asked an utterly unexpected question. "Has my hair gone white?" He deemed this the most appropriate of times to employ a sorcerer's disconcerting tactic of a mercurial mood shift. 'Twas a Druidic habit Anya would assuredly see through but not one she would challenge.

Although Anya's attention instinctively lifted to a mane as dark as the surrounding night, her eyes narrowed with annoyed recognition of the strategy behind his peculiar question. She warily gave her head a slight shake and the colorless glow of the claw-held globe of the staff still resting against a sturdy limb to one side made a bright halo of pale gold ringlets easily freed from braids by their play.

"It ought to be so after all the barbs of fear you've loosed upon me this day." These rueful words were spoken by a mouth curled into a devastatingly potent smile.

Despite Anya's certainty that after viewing both sword fight and arrow aimed at his back she would be justified in charging him with the same, she put annoyance aside. Her feelings for Evain were too deep to be shaken by the slight pique roused by his purposeful loosing of a sorcerer's skills upon her.

"You've been raised by loving parents, cradled in

the physical protection of a powerful father and the mystical guard of a sorceress." Evain bent his head toward Anya and softly spoke of unpleasant realities. Though he had far rather Anya remain his innocent elfling wrapped in ethereal fantasies and warm dreams, he knew he must see her forewarned and prepared. "Thus, I understand your difficulty in comprehending the depth of danger in the world beyond Throckenholt's borders."

Anya drew a deep breath and straightened with the intent of heatedly defending herself against his insinuation that she was naught but a spoiled child unable to fathom the world of man. Then she paused as cool restraint, like oil poured over boiling water, calmed her words into a measured response merely tinged delicately with sarcasm.

"You would warn me of forest bandits . . . again? I had thought we covered that subject following the aid I lent you in their defeat—and aid you I *did.*"

Irritated by this proof that he'd failed to open her eyes to looming perils, Evain plowed the fingers of one hand through raven hair as if the action might succeed in restoring his rarely threatened calm, a calm only Anya could consistently disturb. He was frustrated by the quandary of how to convince her of the ominous dangers lurking on all sides without completely shattering her sweet serenity. Still, having begun he must finish.

"Forest bandits are the least of our worries." Even as he spoke Evain recognized this as a statement able only to further widen the gap demanding explanation.

"Do you think," Anya quietly asked, "that I have forgotten the stories recounting the dangers my mother, you, and Llys faced in putting an entire army to flight? Do you doubt me capable of comprehending the perils later defeated by you and Llys in order to end yet another threat to Throckenholt?" Anya's own frustration grew. His determination to view her as child lent a sting to Anya's next query. "Or do you simply believe me so overprotected that I am weak and unable to bravely meet a challenge of any making?"

"By your parentage alone I know you to be no coward." Evain's eyes darkened in a reflection of Anya's pain as he hastened to reassure her of his trust in this certain fact while at the same time the quagmire created by her unfortunate presence and his need to keep her safe deepened. How could he explain that, in truth, he did suspect that the tales oft repeated as heroic epics in countless halls had given her a false sense of invulnerability?

"Merely do I fear your familiarity with past victories has misled you," Evain continued at length, "into an inaccurate belief that every conflict ends justly." He paused and his eyes hardened to ice. "They could as easily have resulted in our defeat."

Anya turned sideways and began fondly rubbing her patient mare's nose. 'Twas clear that—despite or mayhap because of their passionate embrace—Evain refused to see her as else than a troublesome child. Plainly he thought her too immature to understand the depth of the peril entailed in either past or current quests. Doubtless he deemed her useless for any fray. Though the fire of her temper smoldered, she curbed it with the reminder that it could hardly be elsewise for a powerful wizard who believed her lacking in any small spark of such gifts as he commanded. But he was wrong! The glow she'd called from her rough crystal proved it so. Absently biting a full lower lip, Anya gave her head a slow shake.

Seeing bright hair shine with her negative motion and thinking it a rejection of his explanation, Evain firmly stated, "'Struth. Where there is a winning side, there is also one that loses. In the 'challenge' now faced it may be *my* turn to fail." As if with a will of its own, his hand stroked one soft cheek. "And regret for your presence here begins with my fear that you may become a part of it."

"But don't you see," Anya earnestly argued her case, curling small fingers over his and pressing her face into his caress, "I have come to help you safely succeed with your mission." She saw his jaw go taut in rejection but still she met his hard glare without flinching. "'Tis what I've vowed to do and do it I will."

In her steady silver-green eyes Evain recognized the impossibility of inducing her to even admit the folly of her initial choice to slip away from the keep and follow him. But folly he was certain it had been, one that lent fervor to his determination to ensure she not pursue her ardently stated goal into far greater jeopardy. Having watched her from childhood, Evain knew that at his quiet elfling's core simmered a willfulness difficult to deflect. And his familiarity left him all too aware of how likely she was to risk her own life for the sake of the promise given.

"You've sworn to see the deed done but I swear my willingness to risk the pressing goal of this mission by forfeiting the time required to escort you back to Throckenholt . . . fail you to give me the promise I demand."

Anya was startled when Evain moved to stand directly in front of her while the hand once stroking her cheek lifted his staff upright.

"An oath given by the power of *this* crystal." Holding the gaze of the tender maiden, Evain moved his staff to stand betwixt them and directed her attention upward by raising his own eyes to its bright orb.

At the prospect of so grave an oath, Anya would've backed away but for the mare who in shying from the moving ball of light had moved to stand close behind and block any such action. To break a vow sworn by even her small crystal would be to shatter it and any hope for a bond with the powerful spirits of nature. But the thought of failing in one given upon a sorcerer's mighty globe was terrifying.

Despite Evain's certainty that Anya's presence could only complicate his path with unavoidable worry for her safety and strain his willpower with enticements to taste forbidden delights, she was here and here she must stay. However, to see her remain as protected as possible throughout the trials ahead, he was forced to take this most extreme of safeguards.

"Swear by the power of my staff's glowing crystal that you will neither seek to again flee from me nor to join in any battle against foes intending to hinder our course."

Thick lashes, shades darker than her gleaming braids, momentarily settled on Anya's creamy cheeks while she nibbled a soft lower lip and her mind raced. 'Twould be a pledge more easily given than at the first expected. Steadying a melodious voice, she began.

"I give my oath by the power of the glowing stone

that I will not flee from you." This Anya gladly promised. As for wielding the arms of war, she was not so foolish as to think it even possible to heft their weight. Never would she have tried. There were other ways better suited to her talents—such as the ability he chose not to believe her capable of possessing. "And, too, I swear that I will not raise any weapon in battle."

Her simple pledge ended with a pleased smile so warm it rightly roused Evain's suspicions. A fact so obvious that Anya blinked in confusion when he chose not to answer but rather, with his staff in one hand and Blossom's reins in the other, motioned for her to walk at his side as he silently began striding toward the abandoned campfire. They moved down a path now so well worn by their repeated passing that his day's attempt to mislead likely pursuers was wasted.

A stocky man huddled amidst a thicket, concealed by the plentiful leaves of surrounding bushes. His brows were drawn in disgusted bemusement. This would be difficult to explain, this strange experience wherein Rolf had seen a fat little horse and petite feminine rider move past him as clearly as if openly watched across a sunlight meadow. The next instant they were gone. Just gone. Completely gone.

Only Bishop Wilfrid might accept his story for truth. A fact reminding Rolf of an apology owed the bishop for having misdoubted his warnings. He'd hosted only disdain for a leader in the Christian church who scoffed at the gods of the heathen Saxons he sought to convert yet warned his henchman against the powers of a Cymry sorcerer. But now . . . now

Rolf had seen the unbelievable. Cynicism pulled thick lips down. More precisely, 'twas what he had not seen.

Aye, Bishop Wilfrid might believe . . . but then again he might not. Vivid memories of the supposedly pious man's temper weakened a never strong intent to add news of this odd scene to the report duty demanded.

Chapter
4

The hooves of several huge steeds thudded over Throckenholt Village's single lane. The usage of years had pounded its dirt and pebbles into a hard surface that lent distinctive sounds to the comings and goings of different people and a variety of animals. This heavy, drumming pattern had become rare during the months since outright war broke out between Northumbria and the Saxon kingdoms to the south. It might herald the descent of foes upon a virtually unarmed town. Or it could mean the longed for return of loved ones long absent.

A mixture of fear and hope filled anxious hearts as people scurried to peer from the humble cottages and small shops lining the narrow road. Glad cries, laughter, and happy tears greeted men splitting away from the small mounted company to be enveloped in welcoming arms. Only their lord continued down the path toward the wood frame keep at its end.

"Papa! Papa!" A black-haired child caught sight of the lone rider and raced toward his much-missed sire, forgetting the warning that this was a dangerous misdeed he must never commit.

Fortunately the huge beast, able to stand steady amidst the fury of clashing swords, battle cries, and the smell of blood, obeyed its master when reined to a halt and stood unmoving despite the madly dashing Edwyn.

Wulfayne shared his errant son's happiness, and the emotion brushed aside any thought of rebuking his folly. Instead he dismounted to sweep Edwyn up into a crushing hug. No sooner had he eased his hold on the younger boy than his older son arrived to fervently clasp his waist. Together the three climbed thick plank steps into the keep's hall. The heavy oak door scraped loudly as it swung open. But when, despite the frown Brynna cast toward the offending noise, the babe cradled in her arms slept undisturbed it was apparent that neither the noisy door nor the boys' welcome had been as loud as he'd thought.

At the sight of her beloved lowering Edwyn to the floor, a glowing pleasure instantly wiped Brynna's frown away. She lost no moment laying Cenwulf in his woven basket and hastening into inviting arms opened wide. Only after a passionate kiss and fervent embrace did the realities of time and family intrude.

Though sensing in Wulf a frustration mingled with anxiety that cast doubt on her question, Brynna forced a note of hope into her voice as she asked, "Is the conflict at an end?"

"Nay, merely is there a lull in the onslaught. Our opponents have pulled back from the border and our line of defense, yet it is near certain to be merely a respite while both they and we reinforce our positions. It may last as little as a sennight or it may be that they intend purposefully withholding their assault much longer in the belief that the strain alone will go far to wear us down." Wulf slowly shook his head and the fading daylight slanting through an unshuttered window glowed on thick hair still bright though now more silver than gold. "Whatever their reasoning, King Aldfrith proclaimed this our best opportunity to visit families and check on shires . . . and to gather all the additional supplies we can procure."

Brynna's gray eyes, soft with love, went mistier still in response to the regret darkening her love's expression. Were it not a dire need, she knew neither he nor their king would take more from the limited stores of those struggling with inadequate labor to keep shires productive.

This oblique revelation of the depth of their army's desperate plight left Brynna glad she hadn't immediately spoken of the one matter at the heart of her most urgent fears. Apparently in the excitement of their father's arrival, neither son had spoken of an absent sister. Now she hesitated to burden Wulf's bleak horizon with additional gloom. Eventually he would ask and she would tell him all. But until that moment came Brynna meant to gift him with the time of peace and comfort he so clearly needed.

Purposefully turning her thoughts to practical matters, Brynna began enumerating what little was left of supplies already winter- and war-depleted. "You know we had a plentiful apple harvest last autumn. A fair array of bushels remains in the cellar. And we can assuredly provide large rounds of cheese. But our salted meats are near consumed, leaving us to rely upon the joint hunting efforts of extreme age and youth." Brynna cast a mock glance of despair toward her oldest son.

"We're doing a fine job of meeting that challenge!" Cub instantly defended himself against this hinted slight, in the process moving a step closer to parents still wrapped in each other's arms. "Why just three days past old Ulford and I brought down a big deer. And Edwyn, with some of his friends, has snared a goodly array of squirrels, pheasants, and other such small creatures."

"Seems I am no longer needed here." Wulf feigned sorrow while suppressing a grin.

Still hosting the gullibility of a child, young Edwyn believed his father's pretended anguish and with balled fists assaulted his crestfallen older brother.

"Nay." Wulf laughed, a welcome sound missing too long. "I but jest with you!" He ruffled the dark hair of both boys, an action that gentled into a loving caress. "In truth I am proud of you both, pleased by your worthy labor to fill in the gaps left by we who are absent on the king's business."

Though Cub brightened under the praise, it was Edwyn who puffed with delight and staked his own claim to good deeds. "I've even taken over Anya's task of gathering eggs now she is gone."

"Gone?" Brows still dark gold furrowed as Wulf turned toward his wife with the question whose answer he instinctively knew would be unpleasant to hear.

The moment foreseen had arrived and nowise could

Brynna prevent the distress caused by worry for her daughter from deepening her eyes to storm cloud darkness. However, she exercised her years of practice in a Druid's emotional control to begin quietly revealing the whole in a calm and methodical order.

"I will start with positive tidings received at the outset." Brynna slipped her fingers into the crook of her husband's arm and tugged him toward a sturdy chair by the central hearth. The boys quickly settled on stools drawn near, but she chose not to continue until after Wulf was seated and relaxed—despite his obvious expectation of the cheerless news to come.

"Days past Llys received a cryptic message, one which first must surely have passed through an untold number of hands." Brynna calmly stood directly in front of her impassive husband. "'Twas unsigned yet there is no question but that Adam was its source."

"Are you certain?" Wulf sat forward, frowning. Before the disbelieving question faded into silence, he took Brynna's small hand into his much larger one and asked others lacking any hint of skepticism. "How did you learn about this message? And how did you determine the writer's identity?"

Brynna gave him a grim smile. "Upon receipt of the missive, Llys sent word to Evain, asking that he meet her here at the keep. We gathered around the high table to discuss this development and agreed that the scrap of parchment appeared to have been sealed with Adam's ring." Brynna saw a question flash in Wulf's silver-green eyes but raised her hand to prevent it from reaching his lips. "We were not so foolish as to discount the possibility that the same foe who took his armor and weapons had also taken the ring with the intent of misleading us." She paused, peering closely at her handsome husband's stern face for some hint of his response.

Wulf nodded his understanding of the three Druids' concern. Knowing better than to interrupt, he restrained his impatience for an explanation of his daughter's absence and gave Brynna an encouraging smile.

"The three of us took the ragged paper into the oak grove. There together we chanted the eternal triad of balanced power."

Dark gold brows arched. Wulf well knew the potency of this spell. Only great danger would justify its use. Thus, plainly, they who sang its triads sensed a serious though mayhap nebulous challenge to be overcome. That they had felt the need to perform such a mighty incantation seemed a harbinger of ill and raised his tension. Beneath his expressionless mask, he struggled to tame a growing anxiety.

Brynna had paused for a moment to give Wulf time to take in the unspoken import of this action but then continued. "In answer we each received a revelation which when joined one with another were sufficiently enlightening to send Evain off on a quest to win Adam's freedom for his sister."

"What is Evain's destination?" Wulf quietly asked, thinking of the reports received by their king only the day past, reports with information on enemy movements and new alliances.

Brynna gave a slight, helpless shrug. "He would say only that Adam's prison was a stone palace surrounded by forest and sea."

Leaf green eyes closed tightly against the uselessness of this description, one that characterized a myriad of structures built by legions of ancient invaders all across coasts on three sides—southern, eastern, and western. Pushing aside his frustration with this answer that was no answer, with growing apprehension Wulf firmly returned their talk to the daughter whose absence seemed more ominous by the moment.

"And Anya? Did Evain take her along on this quest?" The arctic depth of his tone made it clear how badly such an action would be received.

"Nay." Brynna shook thick black locks even as she reached out to lightly brush her fingertips over Wulf's clenched jaw. "He left during the night hours after our spell was wrought. Anya was here the next morn."

"Then where is she now?" Wulf's question was logical but asked through gritted teeth.

"Llys watched as Anya packed bags of supplies and departed to fulfill a promise made to see the miller and his family fed while his ailing wife recovers."

Wulf's expression remained unchanged when Brynna paused again. Such an action was the rightful duty of a lord's wife and daughter and thus assuredly no more than an additional happening leading toward what he waited to hear.

With her husband's eyes narrowed upon her, Brynna hastened to finish her account of events that unfortunately explained very little. "One bag Anya left with the miller but then to his surprise, rather than turning back up the path toward Throckenholt, she rode into the western forest."

"She went to meet Evain." Wulf's words were matter-of-fact but icy cold. He respected Evain for both his physical strength and mystical powers. Indeed, Wulf loved the younger man for the foster son he was to him. And yet Evain knew as well as Wulf's family—particularly the infatuated Anya—that the thought of a Druid sorcerer as spouse for his golden daughter was unacceptable. Now it seemed that not only would they defy a father's wishes but were bent on a course that would take them down a path of fresh and uncharted perils.

"Nay." Brynna firmly gripped Wulf's broad shoulders with both hands. "Never would Evain willingly have permitted her to dare such danger."

A grim Wulf looked unconvinced.

"Truly he would not! Only think how rarely he visits and of recent months never but that he is beseeched to come." Brynna's voice softened to an aching appeal for his acceptance of the truth in her plea. "I believe he does cherish our daughter . . . and you must see he cares too much to risk seeing her suffer the pain of a doomed love."

What Wulf clearly saw was Brynna's distress. And aware that there was nothing she could do to change a deed already done, he merely asked, "How long have they been gone?"

"This is the third day." She paused to control the glittering tears threatening to fall. "I *pray* that Anya has indeed caught up with Evain. He is our best hope for seeing her safety protected against all the dangers lurking in the forest."

A startled Wulf blinked. Never had he heard his wife speak of even the possibility of danger in any natural form.

Brynna recognized the source of his surprise and wryly smiled. "I am able to commune with the spirits of nature. They and the beasts of the wild are my friends. Had Anya that same bond I would not fear for her but . . ."

Sweeping his beloved into a comforting embrace,

Wulf rested his cheek against the cloud of dark hair atop her head. He could not deepen her distress by sharing the news that the southernmost Cymry princedom—through which he feared Evain meant to travel—had joined Mercia and likely soon Wessex to see Northumbria and its allies destroyed.

Anguished voice muffled against a wide chest, Brynna spoke. "The moment I realized that she'd gone I wanted to immediately chase after Anya and bring her home. But with our boys and the people of Throckenholt dependent upon me, I knew I could not leave."

Wulfayne shared Brynna's sense of powerlessness. It was a feeling the mighty warrior had rarely experienced. The urge to instantly set off in search of his daughter was strong. However, two unalterable facts restrained him: duty to his king twined with the lack of any certain path to follow or destination to be reached.

Lifting Brynna's chin, Wulf bent to brush his lips over hers. "We'll both put our trust in Evain to find and protect Anya." With the words Wulf forced a reassuring smile to his lips, hoping Brynna's distraction would serve one good end in preventing his normally perceptive wife from noticing that it failed to reach his eyes.

Anya stretched, slowly coming to full wakefulness amidst the green gloom of the haven into which Evain had led her as the first bright gleams of a rising sun touched the eastern horizon. The gracefully draped branches of a willow provided shelter and protection from the elements, and while curving boughs trailed over the thick grass on all sides she felt safe in nature's embrace.

Following the halt Evain had put to her flight during the darkest hours, they'd returned to their abandoned camp. There they reclaimed supplies left behind before journeying on through the gloom by the light of his staff's glowing crystal. Not until the sky had taken on the dull gray of predawn had he begun looking for a stopping point to seek refreshing slumber. While forming for her another soft bed of grass and leaves, he'd shared a wee bit of his plan. Their previous day's battle with forest bandits had convinced him 'twould be best were they to sleep through each day and travel by night, the better to elude humans lacking a sorcerer's skills.

Lying on her back, comfortably wrapped in a dark cloak, Anya suddenly realized she was alone. Her heart raced. Had Evain left her behind? A bright smile instantly quelled that witless fear. He hadn't gone to such lengths to prevent her from leaving him only to desert her. Nay, wherever he'd gone, she'd no doubt he would soon return for it must surely be nearing twilight.

Anya loosened the cloak's hold and rolled over. Reaching the short distance required, she carefully parted the willow curtain to peer out and find her assumption well-founded. Gentle evening mists had settled their cool kiss over day-warmed earth while the sweet scent of night flowers which blossomed only for the moon wafted near, providing further proof of the late hour.

To savor last moments of relaxation, Anya moved to one side the swathe of hair unbraided and combed before lying down hours past and then rested her cheek on joined hands. She found simple pleasure in listening to the quiet sounds of small creatures moving in the undergrowth, likely journeying toward the stream whose peaceful babble she could hear.

Her enjoyment of nature's soothing aura was rudely broken by a crashing noise in the bushes not far distant. Without pausing to consider possible peril to herself, she impulsively rushed toward the snarls and grunts of a violent conflict.

Anya nearly stumbled into the midst of the thicket where a huge wild boar held a fox in its jaws, viciously shaking the limp auburn form. 'Twas a soft whine that called Anya's attention from the gruesome sight. A small fox pup huddled forlornly under a fern's thick fronds.

Tempting the charge of a wild boar would be folly in the extreme and yet Anya was determined to do something. Although too late to aid the mother, she thought to rescue the frightened pup from the violent brute. With the memory of her recent somewhat limited success she devised a plan.

Anya hastily pulled the rough crystal from her small pouch and rolled it between her palms. Lacking complete confidence in her powers, she was wise enough not to risk drawing the boar's attention by singing aloud. Instead, it was again in silence that she chanted the simple triad of shielding. After the stone began to glow, she held it in one hand while with the other she reached down and lifted the quivering ball of silky red fur. It never occurred to her to wonder at the ease with which the small wild creature yielded to her clasp.

Once she'd succeeded in calling forth light from the

white stone, her confidence in its shielding powers was strong. However, she was not certain how long the spell would last and hastily backed from the site of carnage. It proved a wise choice as she learned a new lesson—worry dispersed concentration. Her chant faltered and the stone went dark. She quickly ducked through trailing willow branches into the haven, over which she was certain Evain must've cast a spell of protection.

"So, you haven't fled from me again." Evain's words completely broke Anya's preoccupation with the tiny creature in her arms.

"Of course not!" She was vexed that the darkly frowning sorcerer would even suggest her to be so dishonorable that she might do such a thing after giving any oath, let alone one as powerful as he had demanded.

"Of course not." Evain's soft velvet laughter filled the willow's small enclosure as thoroughly as his flashing smile brightened it. By tilting his staff toward her, its crystal unharmed, Evain proved from whence his certainty came.

Anya gritted her teeth against his display of anger swiftly followed by laughter. Many a time had she watched Evain work his mood altering trick to disconcert the Saxons who crossed his path, but only during these days since their "adventure" began had he bothered to turn it on her. She didn't like it. Didn't like it at all!

The flash of temper in green eyes only seemed to make Evain's laughter deepen, and he absently lifted his staff again. An action which earned an unexpected response.

The fox cub stiffened in Anya's arms and snarled at

the man seemingly lowering a threatening club toward his savior.

"What ho?" Evain was startled and not only by the presence of the small creature gone unnoticed in his determination to convince Anya the wrong of wandering alone in the forest. Nay, the greater surprise lay in the animal's response to him. As a master of Druidic powers, never before had he known his mastery challenged by any creature of the wild.

Anya was as shocked by the fox's defense of her as Evain. And she was grateful for the distraction provided by the task of quieting her small defender with gentle strokes through downy-soft fur and a soothing murmur of words that made no sense at all.

"I see you've found a fierce beast to stand as your guardian." Evain spoke only half in jest. Although the young fox was hardly of such size as to offer any physical defense, the creature would be an effective guard for her virtue since it seemed the cub would not permit him to come so close to the maiden as to be a threat to her innocence.

"Then you permit that I carry him with us as we continue our journey?" A sweet smile accompanied Anya's plea. She was relieved that he had not asked her how she'd come to possess the creature. Though far from the narrow view she'd taken on the matter, Anya suspected Evain would see her rescue of the cub as interference in the natural balance of nature and a deed testing the intended boundaries of the oath against conflict which he'd extracted from her. Moreover, she had far rather not be called to explain how she had besought nature's powers to accomplish the feat. That a sorcerer as powerful as Evain hadn't sensed her tapping into the flow of nature's forces must mean her skills were nearly infinitesimal. The thought stole the pleasure Anya had felt in her accomplishment, and she buried her face in soft auburn fur.

Her latter assumption was wrong. Evain had sensed a ripple in the current of Druidic powers but thought it merely a result of his unwise awareness of Anya's proximity. He felt the gloom overtaking her nature's natural brightness and feared his actions—though necessary—were the cause.

"Aye, take him if you choose. . . ." Evain permitted a measure of the emotion he felt for her to warm his voice. "So long as we waste no further moment, for 'tis time and past to move on. Thus, we must eat with haste and resume our travels."

Again Anya provided a round of hard rye bread but this time added healthy orange slices cut from the block of cheese she had packed into her sack of foodstuffs. To these Evain joined strips of salt-dried meat and a horn of fresh water newly retrieved from the stream that could be heard nearby. Under a steady sapphire gaze, Anya shared a measure of her portion of meat with the fluffy ball of fur in her lap.

Hunger appeased, they began repacking their supplies. With the ease of long practice Evain soon had his goods neatly tucked into an ever present satchel. Anya required a brief time longer to stow her things inside the bag that would again be attached to Blossom's saddle. While she rushed to finish, Evain took up his staff and began a low, eerie chant which rumbled from his chest as thrice he repeated poetic triads. It was not a spell of shielding, for to maintain it for extended periods of time required a level of power such as would drain him of physical strength, a dangerous prospect while perils of many forms hovered near. Rather, he entreated the forces of nature to guide and guard their way.

With a glowing crystal to provide direction through descending darkness, their journey resumed. To his audible chant, Evain added an unspoken plea for strength to avert an overwhelming awareness of the dainty beauty whose closeness he feared presented a threat to a Druid's all-important concentration.

Cradling the fox pup while riding Blossom a few paces behind Evain but not outside the crystal's ring of light, Anya studied his powerful back and abruptly ached with desolation. Despite his physical nearness, it felt as if she'd been deserted by the one so important to her, the man so long her shield against unhappiness.

On and on from falling dusk through midnight darkness they continued without a single word or moment's pause.

Chapter
5

With Evain and his crystal to lead the way Anya had
no reason to fear the darkness of cloudy night. Indeed,
as time passed she found solace in the gentle arms of
nature. Its soft breezes whispered through thick leaves
overhead and carried to her the fragrance of shy
flowers peeking through lush undergrowth. Attaining
a measure of peace almost equal to that of the dozing
fox, Anya reminded herself that she had secured what
was to her a most precious gift—the blessing of time
to be spent in her beloved's company. And, despite
Evain's reluctance to share this journey with her, she
was determined that her intrusion would prove to be
of value to his cause.

Evain fought to contain his frustration over the
need to restrain his stride and match Blossom's
plodding pace. It was a task made more difficult by the

disconcerting feel of the green eyes rarely shifting far from his back. Her constant alluring nearness was too dangerous. He feared the forbidden temptation she embodied had so thoroughly disrupted his ability to sense anything beyond her presence that he would fail to recognize hidden adversaries lurking about until 'twas too late to foil—

The rapid beat of wings fluttering upward incited Blossom into a terror-stricken, panicked thrashing that roughly sundered the bleak path of Evain's thoughts.

The fox cub's yelps joined desperate neighs, and Evain whirled to find Blossom risen up on her haunches, pawing the air in apparent defense against the improbable menace of a frightened bird protecting her nest. Having not thought the old mare still agile enough for so strenuous a deed, surprise curled Evain's lips into a wry grin.

"No-o-o!" Anya's cry was as soft as the thud of her falling body.

Evain's amusement instantly disappeared. Beyond the spooked horse a dainty figure now lay crumpled, wedged between two large rocks. Worse still, she wasn't moving.

Rushing to Anya's side, Evain felt as though his heart had been seized by the hand of a giant intent on squeezing it in punishment for a sorcerer's inattention. Aye, it was his distraction which had permitted this wretched price to be paid by a maid innocent of any wrongdoing—a maid guiltless, too, of the conscious wielding of a natural allure for which he had blamed her. He could only implore the spirits to spare his pure elfling rather than demand that she forfeit a cost which ought be his own.

Evain drove the bottom tip of his staff into the earth a handsbreadth beyond the golden pool of Anya's hair, loosened by her violent tumble. As oft was true of wild creatures, the little fox had landed on his feet but then, whining and on haunches, he crept forward to nuzzle his injured patron. Fortunately, unlike the last time Evain had drawn near and earned a vicious snarl, the animal seemed to sense the human's intent to aid and did nothing to hinder his approach. A boon that saved time which elsewise would've been wasted in dealing with the cub.

Shrugging free of a satchel whose strap crossed from shoulder to hip, Evain sank to his knees. He was oblivious to the sponginess of ground cushioned by layers of the previous year's vegetation which remained beneath lush grass and ferns. Gently he probed beneath her wealth of shining tresses. Anya quietly moaned when he found the ominous lump already forming. Though not as learned in the healing arts as either Brynna or his sister, Evain had been taught and often called to exercise fundamental measures to treat injuries from accidents such as this or—due to mankind's endless rounds of war—battle wounds.

Forcing his agitation to subside beneath bonds of serenity, Evain cautiously lifted the maid from the cleft between the pair of cruel rocks and laid her flat upon a carpet of green blades. Next his fingertips lightly ran down the forest-hued wool of her gown where it covered the curve between arm and hip on the side that had taken the brunt of her fall. Even unconscious she cried out in pain.

Evain sat back on his heels. Ribs were either broken or badly bruised. Whichever the case, he must see them both to some safe haven where the mending process could begin. A goal made the more important by the possibility that the injury to Anya's side, though alarming enough, might not be the biggest danger. He feared that the blow to her head would prove infinitely worse. Anya must be closely watched until she awoke—and he would plead with the spirits of nature to see that she recover her senses.

Fortunately the mare he'd had no time to quiet had resumed her usual calm. He shifted his satchel to Blossom's back, and she stood placidly watching while he chanted triads of veneration and a plea for guidance. As the eerie words passed through firm lips the crystal atop his stave flared until the darkness beyond was pierced by a beam brighter even than the glowing circle of light which had remained steady since the beginning of their night's journey.

Gently lifting the tender maiden to lie cradled in one strong arm, injured side protected, Evain took up his staff and followed the beacon's path back over ground already crossed. He was aware that both fox and mare would trail behind. When the beam shifted to the right, he immediately obeyed and made a sharp turn. Within a few paces he faced a wall of sheer stone—or so it at first appeared.

Evain was unfazed by this seeming impasse on his quest for a refuge. After a moment's quiet study, he ducked sidelong through an area of deepest shadow and into a cave invisible to the eyes of those lacking his acute senses. Blossom balked at the narrow entrance but the fox stayed close to his heels.

Once inside Evain was surprised to discover signs that, although empty, the cave had earlier been used by a human and quite recently. There were few who'd the ability to find such havens. But someone had. As evidence there were the cold embers of a central fire, an empty and battered pot, and a tattered blanket folded against the furthermost wall—also a stack of bones from small prey. Proof their stalker lacked either a mature hunter's skills or weapons . . . mayhap both?

Unwilling to waste thought on the matter, Evain rested his staff with its still glowing crystal against a rough stone wall and with the hand thus freed unfastened his black cloak. After whirling it out to float down and lie in a full circle on the stone floor, he settled Anya upon it with all good care. He'd a potion that might wake the maid, were she not too deeply lost in unnatural slumber. But she needed rest to mend and that would be more easily accomplished if not conscious of discomforts.

Whether bruised or broken, her ribs must be bound. He acknowledged the necessity but hesitated. It would best be done without the discomfort of her kirtle and undergown bunched between flesh and bandage. This task would require him to remove her clothing . . . and to accept the danger of sights too alluring, visions of which were certain to plague him for a lifetime. What option did he have? For her sake, none.

Unbuckling and setting aside his sheathed sword, he again sank to his knees at her side and began to loosen the side-lacing of her kirtle with an unnatural clumsiness. In unfastening the belt riding narrow hips he encountered the small pouch attached. Black brows furrowed slightly. He was curious about what tokens and potions would be carried by the winsome elfling lacking a Druid's knowledge but set it aside to investigate after dealing with more urgent matters. By reminding himself of how desperate Anya's plight might yet prove to be, he forced into abeyance his discomfort with the intimacy of deeds about to be performed. Only after succeeding in that mental exercise did Evain gently lift and shift Anya while removing her clothing.

When she lay bare to smoldering sapphire eyes, even Evain's powerful control could not prevent him from drinking in the beguiling sight. Her pale gold hair flowed in shining ripples over the spread folds of his dark wool cloak while the warm cream and petal pink of delicious curves proved to be the forbidden enticement he'd feared. In truth, 'twas a sight far more exciting than even the fantasy images of her that had long haunted his dreams.

Evain groaned. Drawn by a natural power stronger than those which he as a sorcerer wielded with such mastery, Evain bent to brush a whisper-kiss across Anya's cheek. He meant to seek nothing more but despite her unconscious state, Anya turned her face and joined her mouth to his. Evain froze. Nectar-sweet temptation trembled on her lips. Falling to her innocent lure, he moved his mouth over hers, cherishing its tender contour.

A soft growl intruded. The small fox crouched less than a hand's span from Anya and the man leaning above her limp form.

The animal's timely warning weakened the bonds of Evain's growing hunger, a task finished by the stinging lash of his conscience. He pulled away, self-disgust flowing through him like a burning poison. The kiss had been purely wrong under any circumstances but incredibly so while the girl lay helpless and unaware. Taking several deep breaths, he attempted to soothe

the ache of guilt by reassuring himself that Anya was under no danger from him.

'Struth, Evain realized with humorless sarcasm, he was not a threat to the maiden trapped in unnatural sleep. Rather, with her instinctive reaction to his kiss the responsive maid had demonstrated herself a greater threat to him. As clearly as if seen in a chant-summoned vision, he acknowledged a daunting truth. No matter what distance he put between himself and his lovely elfling, never again would he sleep but that her image would appear. An image as potent as the flesh-and-blood reality of this woman he must not love . . . but did.

Over Evain rolled a consuming fury with himself for stealing a kiss from an unconscious Anya while her health was so precarious. But disturbing desire and fury aside, he purposefully turned his attention to the task for which he had divested her of clothing. He rose and moved toward the cave's entrance. A few steps beyond he retrieved his satchel from Blossom. While slipping back into the cave, he rummaged through his bag until he found the rolled bandage he sought. He had been called upon to tear whatever cloth was handy into narrow strips in order to treat people's injuries so often that he'd begun carrying a prepared roll whenever he traveled.

With gentle but determinedly impersonal motions he firmly wrapped Anya's ribs to provide support and protection against further injury. Then, seeking a reprieve from sweet temptation, he turned aside to lift her cape. Thankful for the shield it would lend, he spread it to cover Anya's beauty from pretty toes to chin.

Intent on shifting his thoughts from both the

enticement too near and the uncertain state of her recovery, once more Evain lifted the small pouch earlier attached to her belt. Spreading cord-drawn edges wide he upended the bag above one palm and shook it.

The flint which was first to fall into Evain's cupped hand was no surprise. Nothing could be more basic. Two vials quickly followed and earned a wry smile. Considering her mother's healing gifts he should've expected them as well. Only an oddly shaped and somewhat bulkier object remained caught within. He carefully deposited the first three objects on the floor, freeing the fingers of one hand to probe inside and release the item.

Evain's eyes warmed to blue smoke—'twas the crystal which he'd given to the persistent toddler Anya had been. He was certain this was the same white stone although its rough shape had been slightly altered. This fact blunted the pleasure brought by discovering she kept his token near with distress. Sharp edges had begun to smooth. By experience Evain knew how much constant rubbing was required to accomplish such a state, and he recognized this as evidence of her efforts to duplicate the skills of a Druid. Evain was saddened by his certainty that Anya's mixed heritage rendered her attempted feat futile at the outset.

"I dreamed that while I slept you kissed me."

The faint but steady sound of Anya's voice caught Evain utterly unprepared—as no sorcerer ought ever be. Still cupping her crystal in one hand, he shifted his attention to wide misty green eyes full of a lingering wonder.

By the uncommon sight of dark color staining

Evain's cheeks Anya recognized her dream for truth. A warm smile bloomed on lips that could almost taste his. Having feared that she'd trapped him into previous embraces, Anya was so delighted with his secret kiss that she could easily forgive him the deep frown that had instantly darkened his expression.

"You tumbled from Blossom's back, fell between two boulders, and soundly struck your head. The blow was so fierce I worried it might permanently rob you of your senses." Evain paused while remembered worries threatened to weaken his control. "I am truly relieved that you've come back to me."

The moment this heartfelt statement left Evain's mouth he recognized the error in permitting his relief to speak it. Though not dishonest the words were most poorly chosen, and his failure to consider more wisely in the first instance deepened Evain's annoyance with himself. Thrusting the items released back into her pouch and absently tucking it inside his own, he hastened to attempt a diversion. "I will thank all the powers of nature for permitting your return to wakefulness."

Anya's smile deepened into a grin so bright it could near rival his staff's glowing crystal. She knew he regretted the inference both that she was his and that he had wanted her back for his own sake, yet she would treasure words she consciously chose to believe escaped from his heart.

"So our bait has been taken, hmmm?" Bishop Wilfrid fair beamed but his satisfaction had a biting edge. "I worried that 'twas too well concealed. Thus, I am pleased with this proof that my first instinct was accurate. The greater the challenge and toil required, the more importance it gains in the sorcerer's sight and the more earnestly he will seek its resolution."

Not blessed with sharp wits, Rolf was uncomfortable with the bishop's riddles and restlessly shifted his bulk from one foot to the other. "Truly it seems to be as you say." Though not sure he understood the man's meaning, Rolf was certain that this was what his listener wanted to hear. "As already I have said, I came upon him traveling southward a day's walk from his home."

"Came upon him?" Wilfrid pointedly questioned this bulky minion's wording. The orders he had given all those sent into the forest to watch for this prayed for response from the sorcerer had been to do only that—watch. He had made it abundantly clear that any interference in the much desired action would be unacceptable and earn the doer a nasty retribution.

"Aye." Greatly ruing the alliance which had caused his king to put him at the bishop's command, Rolf took a deep breath. He struggled to devise a believable explanation without tempting the bishop's fury by confessing the sword fight into which he'd been drawn. "The man I tracked turned and saw me . . . but only briefly."

The bishop growled his disgust with even a limited encounter—if in truth it were only that. He did not trust this guardsman who'd shown himself brave in battle but weak in the lesser conflicts of daily life which lacked the fire of a physical fight.

Although his mind was dull Rolf's instincts were acute enough to keep him from deepening his plight by mucking about in the bog of his initial error until he drowned. He stood still as stone and met the other's suspicion with a bland smile.

Wilfrid's hands came together in a clap that reverberated against stone walls. "No matter your likely misdeed, my strategy has earned the response I sought and I will win what I seek."

The prospect that a decade of contacts made and alliances earned in several Saxon kingdoms would come to fruition soon brought Wilfrid a delight whose wickedness he refused to acknowledge. He felt justified by the fact that not only would it see the end of two ealdormen and a line of Northumbrian kings who had cost him sorely, it would bring the obliteration of heathen Druids who had humiliated him. And—he rubbed his hands together in self-righteous glee—the deadly aim of the latter was surely justified as the goal of a holy war, one surely aimed to the greater glory of God.

It was plain to Rolf that the bishop was filled with smug pleasure, and yet he sensed that beneath it lay a personal vengeance with a core of cold malice. Grateful not to be the focus of such viciousness, Rolf was glad he hadn't further complicated matters by speaking of his peculiar experience involving a maiden and horse that had disappeared in the blink of an eye.

Chapter
6

A long, thin sliver of sunlight fell through the cave's indirect opening to cross the stone floor and climb some little distance up a rough wall. Anya concentrated on that bright beam while seeking escape from hazy, distinctly unpleasant dreams. Before winning her valiant struggle the focus of her mind's eye narrowed upon two vastly different scenes which she realized were not dreams but memories.

Anya remembered a terrified Blossom frantically rearing back and the sharp pain which immediately followed. Those dark images flowed into a fearsome void wherein she floated hopelessly until rescued by the gentle brush of Evain's kiss. Anya couldn't explain how she knew it was so yet she was certain that 'twas the sorcerer's wordless, possibly unintentional call which had pulled her from the black abyss and returned her to the world of waking thought and natural rest.

Shifting a small distance, Anya gazed toward the man leaning against a rock wall, thick black lashes lying in crescents on strong cheeks. His feat in saving her should be no surprise considering it was not the first time he'd worked such magic on her behalf. When she was a child Evain had saved her from the stranglehold of a deadly sleep.

Evain's eyes snapped open in answer to the faint stirring sounds of the injured woman. Toward his intent of monitoring Anya's progress he had allowed himself to sink no deeper into slumber than to doze just below the surface of consciousness. Now he quickly moved to her side.

"How do you feel?" The concern audible at its core deepened the soft burr of his question.

Despite a throbbing head, Anya forced a brave smile to her lips and tried to sit up. She cried out at the unexpectedly sharp pain in her side. Anya dropped back and the cloak spread over her started to slide down in a movement which shocked her with an even more disconcerting discovery.

She was nude! Completely nude! Gasping, Anya hastily jerked dark wool up and gripped it chastely beneath her chin. A tide of crimson flooded soft cheeks and she tightly closed eyes gone to flashing emerald.

"Lie still." To urge compliance Evain put a gentle hand on Anya's shoulder while a wry half smile pulled one corner of his mouth up. Anya's modesty was laudable . . . but hours too late. Wrapping her ribs had been the only physical comfort he could provide and for that deed he would pay dearly over a lifetime of hopeless memories of a forbidden delight.

Shortly after Anya's first awakening the previous night, she'd dropped into a more natural rest. And yet Evain had worried while watching as she fitfully slept, doubtless disturbed by the pain of an injured side and aching head. Were it not for the blow to her temple Evain would've given Anya a dose from one of her own vials, the one containing a potion he knew able to alleviate a measure of pain and provide untroubled slumber. But, aware of the possible danger in such a remedy, he had instead taken his staff to the cave's entrance and there earnestly beseeched natural powers to grant the sweet maiden peace and health restored.

In answer to Evain's words, Anya did hold perfectly still. Though rarely one to accept another's command without an inward questioning—considering her embarrassing position—for once she gave no thought to circumventing Evain's order. Indeed, it required all her powers of concentration to divert her awareness that it was assuredly Evain who had removed her clothing. Wishing to postpone facing that disconcerting fact until she felt better able to deal with it, Anya bent her full attention on the mental search for a subtle way to locate her missing garb. Subtle? Impossible, none existed. She'd no option but to boldly ask.

"Where, pray tell, are my clothes?" Despite the rosy tint of a lingering blush, Anya strove to sound calm and confident.

Evain ruefully shook a dark mane but his broad white grin ruined any possibility of feigned solemnity. "Where they'll remain safe until you are completely recovered."

Anya's thick lashes dropped to conceal the temper flaring in green eyes while she fought to don leastways her invisible shell of serenity. It was a task more difficult than expected. Seldom had she been goaded to such anger, not even by this man who had so oft gently baited her willful nature.

Sensing Anya's turmoil, Evain repented . . . but only so far as to soften his statement's hard edge with an explanation. "Truly, your healing will be best speeded by not moving far from your bed."

During the hours of night a pleasing thought had presented itself to Evain. He'd been permitted a small compensation in return for the price to be exacted over many lonely years for the terrible pleasure he'd taken in the beguiling visions and sweet feel of forbidden flesh while disrobing Anya. That cost itself could nowise be lessened yet the fact of absent clothing would leastwise provide a fine guard to restrain the quietly headstrong girl certain to attempt too much too soon. Asides, he'd known something had to be done about the mare. If Blossom were seen lingering at the cave's entrance, its secret might be revealed.

To deal with both issues, during the darkest hours Evain had rolled the green garb removed from Anya into a neat bundle and gone out to lead Blossom into a deep and heavily forested valley. Along the downward trail he'd unquestioningly followed a silent admonition to drop the bundled clothes into a patch of bushes. Then, once on the valley floor hidden by towering trees but blessed with abundant forage and falling water which pooled on one side, he freed Blossom of saddle and bridle. Realizing Anya's pouch still resided in his own and preferring to avoid any need to confess his curious review of its contents, he quickly buried the small bag inside the satchel packed with her change of garb and laid it next to the saddle. The sack of foodstuffs he'd carried back to this cave, pausing only to rinse himself in the cool waters of a spring not far from its entrance.

Anya recognized his ploy's intent to build a prison without bars and silently fumed while Evain carefully tucked the cloak about her with mocking concern before standing to tower above her.

Anya wondered at Evain's unusual lack of perception. He must truly be worried for her health elsewise he'd surely have taken into account a fact he was more aware of than most any other: Her long-cultivated patience would quietly submit only to so much and then no more.

An aching body could nowise dull the sharpness of Anya's mind, and after a moment's consideration she restrained a satisfied smile with difficulty. Some things there existed over which even a sorcerer had no control. It could be but a small victory yet one she meant to gleefully claim.

"No matter what elsewise is true, I *must* be permitted to answer nature's call." Holding the cloak near to protect her modesty, Anya again sought to rise, although this time with a caution prompted by the knowledge of a pained side and throbbing head earned by her first attempt.

Evain wordlessly admitted the validity of her claim. Moreover, he sensed Anya's embarrassment over the view lent him by the treatment of her injury. To lessen the possibility of further awkwardness, Evain fought an urge to help the physically suffering maid likely fearing to inadvertently reveal a further glimpse of bare flesh. Instead he turned his back while small gasps and rustling cloth proved Anya had not only gained her feet but moved into the cave's far shadows to adjust folds of dark wool into a semblance of decent covering.

While Anya's companion faced light streaming sidelong through the entrance, at the cave's back she rearranged the cloak with as much haste as possible while hampered by the awkwardness of an injury hurting more with each passing moment. At last the garment flowed from shoulders to floor. Yet, rather than using her brooch to fasten it at the throat as was her habit, she continued shifting the garment until it opened over her right shoulder. It was there that she securely closed it with a pretty circlet of silver inlaid with tiny pearls. Then by lifting the hem of the cloak's back opening and folding it up over the front side to be clasped by her left hand she was covered—only just—while at the same time leaving her right hand free. Doubtless Evain would deem this arrangement adequate for the limited purpose intended. The irritating thought earned a faint growl from her.

At that sound of disgust Evain's wry smile returned. He sympathized with Anya's frustration but refused to relent. Though she had oft demonstrated an ability to play upon his emotions as easily as upon the strings of her beloved harp, he would not allow her to strum over them now. Particularly not in this instance when her goal would assuredly be to pick out a tune leading him into permitting actions best denied.

As Anya moved to stand between him and the entrance, Evain kept sapphire eyes averted and sank down to kneel atop the cloak still spread over the stone floor. From its outer edge he pulled two gold pins. Each was the length of his hand with one end sharp and the other a swirl in whose center rested a large, bloodred garnet. When done with the task, he glanced toward Anya.

"I see that you've put your brooch to good use." He absently nodded toward his gentle elfling, a lovely vision even swathed in deep brown. In truth, her garb merely made the contrast of moon-glow hair seem the brighter. "However, if you would appreciate additional guards for propriety's sake, I will gladly donate these to your cause." He rose and on one palm held the two pins out for Anya to take or leave as she chose.

"I thank you for the generous offer." Anya made as elegant a curtsy as possible under the constraints of her odd garment and the sharp pain in her side. "One pin to fasten the back edge to my left side and the other to prevent a gap at my knees." She lightly claimed the two items and put them to the uses suggested while attempting to hide any sign of the unavoidable pain involved.

"And before I return . . ." An imp inside Anya just couldn't let Evain think it so easy to have everything all his own way. "I think I'll seek out the source of the rushing water I hear. A bath would be a welcome pleasure." She knew full well the impossibility, nay, the danger of such an action. And no matter how delightful the prospect, had no intention of carrying out her threatened plan.

"Nay! That you will not do!" Evain took a long step forward, blue fire flashing from his eyes. "Your need for private moments in the forest I understand, but if you have not returned within a short span of time, I promise that I'll come and—no matter what you are about—fetch you back again."

Anya heard the further unspoken warning of an unpleasant retribution which would terrify many, but she flashed a wicked smile and departed without an answer.

During Anya's absence Evain realized that he had yet to see her fox cub this morn. Plainly the small animal had slipped away while human companions slept—a natural action for the wild creature but an absence sure to dispirit his tenderhearted elfling. It meant leastways one fortunate thing had come from the complications Anya had faced so far this day. Their distractions had kept her from missing the cub's presence.

To thwart an impatience borne of dark concern for Anya's safety in the forest alone, Evain stepped from the cave. However, sensitive to Anya's need for privacy, he ventured only so far as to gather armfuls of lush green grasses to soften the place where he would insist she spend the day resting. Several trips were required to finish the chore to his satisfaction. Anya had not returned by the time it was done, and he wondered if it would be necessary to follow through on his threat to fetch her back. Standing in the entrance, he intently studied the woodland's green shadows for a sign of movement.

Although certain she'd been gone for naught but a brief while, Anya's bright spirit had dimmed by the time she stepped past the handsome man near blocking her way back into the cave. Even the limited exercise undertaken since opening her eyes to morning light had turned the ache in her side to a misery that made the notion of lying down again a welcome prospect. But still, irritated with her untimely weakness, she moved to scowl down at the waiting bed clearly padded in her absence with the intent of seeing she remain long upon it.

Evain smiled in relief as Anya appeared, but it soon faded. The furrowed brow marring her lovely face seemed like to indicate annoyance at the prospect of a confinement he meant to enforce until her injured ribs were much improved. Thought of the need to linger longer in this cave reminded him that he'd as much reason to be displeased by the prospect as she. Not for an instant did he resent the commitment of time required to render the tender beauty all good care, but 'twas a dismal truth that waiting for her recovery meant a delay to urgent plans—and possibly a threat to their success.

As Evain turned and stepped toward her, in eyes gone dark and hard as shards of black ice Anya recognized the source of his wintry expression. It was disheartening. She had hosted only the purest of motives in hatching the scheme undertaken to land him with her unsought company. The very last thing she sought to do was complicate his task. But she acknowledged again, as on the night of the flight he had forestalled, that was precisely the ill effect of her design and there seemed no good deed she could perform to mitigate the wrong.

The sound of a cheery voice whistling the melody of a familiar children's rhyme wound its way through gloomy silence. Faint at the start, it grew louder and drew the attention of the pair within to the cave's entrance. It was there that the tune ended on a gasp and the soft thud of a half-filled sack dropping to the stone floor.

"Who are you?" A towheaded lad of mayhap ten years stood in the rectangle of sunlight falling through the opening. His fists were clenched and chin was lifted in a show of bravado too clearly backed by fear. "And what are you doing in my cave?"

Evain's white smile flashed. "Ah, then this was your fire and pot. And that your blanket?" Carelessly gesturing toward spent coals, battered bronze container, and folded homespun, he answered questions asked with others of his own. 'Twas a ploy experience had taught him was as effective with adults as with Llys and Brynna's children. "And who are you?"

"I am Keir—" The response came to an abrupt halt. The boy was vexed with himself for so readily offering any information, even less an answer to the same question he'd asked but to which the man had not responded.

"'Tis an honor to meet you, Keir." Evain continued with the easy tone of a host greeting a welcome guest. "I am Evain and my companion is Anya—a sister of sorts."

Beneath her customary shell of serenity, Anya bristled against Evain's unwelcome description of her— their heated embraces had surely disproved it.

The boy's mist gray eyes shifted from the ebony-haired speaker to the woman whose locks were as fair as his own, then back again. He frowned and flatly stated, "You can't be brother and sister."

Shrugging, Evain's smile widened into a rueful grin. "Her mother and father stood as foster parents to me."

A cloud of skepticism cleared, turning gray eyes to pale blue. This explanation Keir understood, although it could neither smother all suspicion nor earn his trust for either the dark and intimidating man or the oddly garbed beauty at his side.

"Anya fell last eve and badly injured her side. 'Tis what brought us to your cave." Evain was pleased by the guileless boy's quick nod. That easy acceptance of his less than forthcoming explanation smoothed an awkward moment.

"What have you there?" Evain amiably shifted the topic, waving toward the boy's fallen sack.

Again the boy's eyes darkened, not with confusion but with a pain that also strained his voice. "A few items of no value to others yet treasures to me." Keir swallowed hard. "Things salvaged from the ruins of . . ." A shaming dam of tears blocked further speech.

"Your home?" Anya sensed the depth of the boy's emotion and as if a candle had been lit in the dark of night she realized that this was how a child his age had come to be in the wilds of nature alone. "Your family?"

The boy's single brief nod ended with his face lifted and eyes blindly staring into the shadows overhead while commanding brimming tears not to fall.

Anya was reminded of Cub although Keir was fair where her brother was dark. Thinking of the pain she and Cub would suffer were any ill to befall their parents, Anya shared this boy's pain as if 'twere her own. Forgetting her physical pain in the face of Keir's emotional torment, she wordlessly moved forward and with her free right arm reached out to stroke solace over pale hair.

Keir had held strong for weeks since those awful hours during which his peaceful life had been destroyed. Even had he held his composure while taking the risk of returning to the burned-out shell of the abode where he'd been born and happily lived. But beneath this woman's gentle comfort, he crumbled. Whirling, Keir buried his face into the thick woolen folds of her cloak.

"They came in the night and burned everything . . . everything." Each word was a sob. "Our house . . . the barn . . . even the pigpen's fence."

"But you safely escaped." Anya's heart ached for the anguished child whose tight voice went on as if he hadn't heard her speak, as if once begun he must release every pent-up word, confess the full extent of his terror and impotent rage.

"My bed was in a loft above where my parents and little sister slept. I woke choking on thick smoke but saw moonlight where there used to be a wall. I panicked and jumped through the hole burned by fire." Keir paused while a renewed bout of strangled sobs revealed more of suffering than any spoken words ever could. Taking huge gulps of air he recovered his composure enough to add a further damning memory.

"From my landing site I looked up and the whole house seemed one big flame." Again Keir paused, small hands twisting in the dark folds of Anya's cloak. "And all the while horses circled around as their riders *laughed!* But they didn't see me . . ." A bitter hurt curdled by loathing filled the words.

Evain empathized with the lad's helpless anger and frustrated desire for revenge. These were piercing emotions whose pangs he had once suffered. Keir's description revived in his mind graphic images which were not spawned by imagination but rather were memories of childhood events too real. Though Evain had sensed rather than witnessed his parents' murder by a frightened mob unable to comprehend unseen powers, he and Llys had both watched just such a scene when their grandparents were slain by the minions of a vicious and greedy prince.

Carried along on a flood of misery overflowing its banks, and unaware of the man's approach, Keir took another big gulp and leaned far enough back to gaze up into the woman's compassionate smile. "I should'a stayed and made some attempt to save my family." The words ached with an unspoken plea to be denied.

"Once fire takes control, no mortal's weapon can defeat its power." Evain spoke quietly from behind the hurting child. "You did right to wrest yourself from the flames' deadly hold."

The boy warily turned a tear-stained face toward the dark man speaking prosaically of *mortal weapons* —as if he possessed knowledge of otherworldly powers. Nay, Keir inwardly mocked his foolish moment of hope. Only because he wanted it to be so had he heard what was not meant.

At the same time Anya silently gasped. This was as near a statement of Druidic powers as she'd ever known Evain to offer any Saxon. And yet she suspected how it had happened. During years spent quietly listening while others spoke, she'd heard vague references to a similar event in his life. And that one had ended with the twins in the custody of Glyndor and her father. Doubtless such memories had weakened his barricade against making even an oblique mention of things never revealed to those unworthy of being taught.

"By the saving of your own life you've denied your

foes their victory." Evain sought to reassure the boy, and the conviction of experience lent his words a sincerity which won a measure of Keir's trust. "Take heart in the certainty that every breath you take is a triumph over the wretched men who lit the blaze."

The emotional outburst which had drained Keir's store of energy had also weakened his self-confidence. But in the dark man's reasoning he found a measure of courage and strength renewed. Tugging the remnants of his tattered pride together, he released his grip on Anya's cloak and again stood alone.

"You must be hungry." Evain was impressed by the gallant spirit of the boy whose pitifully thin condition made it safe to assume this subject offered a safe path to take in diverting unhappy thoughts. "I know I am."

"Yes." Anya warmly smiled. "Come, join us in a morning meal." The invitation was issued with mock formality while at the same time she sought to inconspicuously adjust her uncertain covering further disarranged by the boy's hold. She nodded toward the place where a sorcerer's cloak lay spread over the stone floor, padded with fresh grasses, indicating it was there Keir ought take a seat. "We've bread . . . and cheese . . . and apples."

Keir's hunger promptly sent him to the waiting cloak. He'd eaten nothing since the fire save the few wild fruits and edible greens he'd scavenged from the forest and three hoards of acorns stolen from the same luckless squirrels he trapped and roasted.

Evain saved Anya from the daunting struggle of maintaining her modesty while distributing portions of food. It was he who reached into her sack for bread, apples, and a round of cheese. And while she awkwardly settled beside the boy, unable to hide a grimace of discomfort, Evain distributed portions before taking up his own bag and pulling forth strips of salt pork for each.

Silence reigned while the three devoted their attention to the meal. Eating was a challenging task for the woman who had the use of only one hand, but despite the difficulty she succeeded. Even was she able to block nagging physical discomfort by watching the youngster attack his food with the single-minded earnestness of his age. Evain had clearly given the boy a more than generous amount. In this action she saw yet another demonstration of the care he consistently gave innocent children—further proof of the gentle nature at the powerful sorcerer's core.

Brushing aside bread crumbs, which were all that remained of his meal, Evain reached for the silver-capped drinking horn leaning against his satchel. He offered it first to Anya, who took a long drink, and then to the boy, whose expression closed once more into a diffident mask.

"I've a misliking for the taste of ale." Keir shook his bright hair, embarrassed by the admission of a distaste which earned him the scorn of most adults. "I'll go to the spring or stream it spawns. They're not far distant."

Anya stifled a smile and gently restrained the boy, who made to stand. Keir responded to her action with a deepening scowl that left her wishing 'twere possible to share forbidden truths. If only she could explain that sorcerers rarely risked muddling their minds and thus their powers with fermented drink—and certainly never when, as now, dangers hovered near and important feats waited to be performed.

Evain sensed Anya's struggle and quietly intervened. "I, too, prefer the refreshment of nature's pure liquid. 'Tis why I carry only springwater in my drinking horn." With the flash of a white smile he again held out the ornate vessel given him by a grateful king.

This time a wide-eyed Keir accepted the offer of an unexpected beverage and swallowed a healthy measure.

Gentle amusement lingered as Evain reclaimed the horn to sample its contents for himself. He then asked of the boy a question whose answer he suspected would be of import. "Since this is where you now live, why were you not here when we arrived last eve?"

With a brief negative shake of his head, Keir cryptically denied Evain's initial assumption. "Don't mean to make this cave my home nor to remain here always."

Dark bows arched in wordless query.

"I have plans." The mulish set to the boy's mouth made it clear he'd not willingly say more. Evain easily granted the young Saxon his right to silence on this matter. However, he sensed that to aid in attaining the greater goal of his quest he must have answer to the question he had asked and repeated it once more.

"But why were you not here last eve?"

Keir's face remained solemn but he did not hesitate to explain. "Wishing to salvage whatever I could from the ruins of my home I set off early yestermorn to make the attempt. 'Tis a fair distance yet I thought it possible to complete the task as well as make the journey to and fro and still return by nightfall."

"But then you discovered the task required more time than expected and that the distance was greater than you believed between here and the home situated on the border between Northumbria and Mercia?" Black brows arched again, making Evain's statement a question, while his wry smile was backed by a warmth that tamed the possible sting of a weakness revealed.

Suspicious of the man's apparent knowledge, Keir nodded, pale hair catching the distant glow of sunlight slanting through the cave's darkness.

The lad unwittingly confirmed an unpleasant fact. He and Anya had covered far less ground than Evain would've been able to travel alone. In truth, they had surely spent near as much time retracing their steps as moving forward. Yet Evain possessed sufficient strength of will to never punish another, let alone a child, for his own frustrations.

"'Tis nothing so dramatic as you fear." Evain soothed Keir's apprehension, permitting a soft burr of mocking laughter to escape his throat while cynically wondering if the boy might not find the truth of his visitor's identity as a Druid to be even more fearsome. "Merely am I aware that war between the two Saxon kingdoms burst into flame after being ignited by cowards who beset the border and strike unarmed farmers with fire in the night."

Feeling driven to make clear the actual happenings on his previous day's quest, Keir resolutely spoke. "My home sits where you say—just within the shire of Throckenholt. But our western border also butts against the point where meet the Cymry princedoms of Talacharn and Gwyll."

So startled was Anya by this news that Keir had lived within a day's ride of her home in the keep that she failed to immediately question the boy's knowledge of her parents. And Evain quickly intervened with a query meant to prevent any shift from the subject whose explanation might be of great import. "Surely 'twas more than distance alone that prevented your return last eve?"

"Aye, had it only been the length of ground to be covered I'd have made it back afore full darkness claimed the forest. 'Twere another hindrance that blocked my way." Remembered disgust tinged Keir's words.

"As I made my way into the woods I heard curious noises and peeking through bushes discovered unfamiliar warriors making a careful search. Fearing they might be the same wretches who burned our farm I hid where surely they'd least expect anyone to shelter . . ." Puckish delight danced in eyes now bright blue and glancing between two adults. ". . . In a briar patch."

The soft thunder of Evain's unrestrained laughter provided unspoken congratulations for the ingenuity of this choice. It pleased the boy.

"And I was right. They didn't look there." Keir's pride in the feat soon changed to a rueful grimace and slight shrug. "But neither did they move away from my prickly haven and permit my escape. Instead they camped near within arm's reach and left me trapped the whole miserable night long."

Evain tempered his amusement into a compassionate smile. At the same time he was relieved that they'd finally come to the point when the information he hoped to learn might be revealed.

"How did you elude them this morn?" Tilting a dark head, he gently probed for details important to the course to be taken in coming days. "Did their path diverge from yours?"

"Aye, thank the saints it did." Keir's response was

heartfelt. "They arose early and departed on an eastern path. Thus I was able to have quit of my uncomfortable perch and with a measure of safety set off on the westward climb to this place."

As the fair-haired youngster talked of his adventure, with one hand he rubbed across the top of the other and then shoved a loose sleeve up to do the same to his forearm. The action drew Anya's attention to the thin, interlaced scratches marking his flesh.

"Growing on the left side of the cave's entrance is a short, broad-leafed plant." Not for a moment did Anya pause to consider the boy might think her suggestion odd or wonder at the source of her knowledge. "If you break a leaf in half and rub its juices over your skin, it will ease the discomfort."

Evain saw the boy's brow furrow in confusion and, to deflect questions that were best left unasked, broached a sensitive matter with less tact than was his wont. "During the brief time spent at your home had you the opportunity to bury your family?"

The baldly stated query instantly summoned to Keir's mind images of the scorched scene and gruesome remains. He fiercely bit his lower lip and in fear of a renewed bout of tears merely shook his head.

"I understand." Evain clasped a slight shoulder in a heartening gesture. "Such a serious chore requires a strong back and more than a single pair of hands."

Keir responded to the raven-haired man's steady encouragement with a crooked smile. Anya, too, was warmed by Evain's patience and offer of an aid doubtless of greatest value to the boy.

"Then come, you and I will go and see the deed honorably done." Evain rose to his feet. "If we depart now, we'll be back afore the midnight hour."

Just as Keir stood up to join Evain at the entrance, a blur of auburn fur streaked into the cave and landed in the still seated Anya's lap.

Green eyes blinked several times and yet she gingerly hugged the small fox's weight despite a stab of pain. "Welcome, little beast," she crooned into soft fur. "I had thought you rewarded my rescue of you by deserting me after I came to harm."

Finding he'd been wrong in thinking Anya so distracted as to be unaware of the cub's absence, Evain felt compelled to deny her unhappy assumption by revealing the truth of the animal's actions.

"Your wild pet, small as he is, remained at your side as fierce protector until we both drifted into dreams last eve. I didn't realize the fox had disappeared before you stepped out earlier."

Anya's smile was as warm as the summer sun. "Proves even fox cubs need time alone, but he returned, and now I'll have his company while the pair of you are gone."

Evain went still, feeling struck to ice by the thought of his injured Anya alone and unguarded. He inwardly cursed himself for having failed to consider that prospect. Considering the promise given Keir, what choice had he but to perform the deed he'd suggested?

Anya sensed her sorcerer's turmoil and sent him a bright smile of potent sweetness, one containing every grain of confidence she could glean. "I'll spend the day resting in hopes that the action will speed the healing process and see our quest resume with all possible haste.

"Noddi is here and will serve as my protector." Her gentle fingers stroked auburn fur. "So be off with you, the better to return before the night is done." She made a shooing motion with both hands to hurry them on their way.

Though amused by the name Anya had given the fox—the Cymry word for protection—Evain was torn between the conflicting duties he felt owed to his two companions. Looking considerably less than comfortable, he reluctantly turned to lift his satchel and depart, motioning the blond lad to follow after. For the first time in a decade he would travel without the aid of the crystal-topped staff that could only confuse and likely frighten the Saxon boy whose less than direct route he chose to trace between thick-grown trees and through dense foliage.

Chapter
7

Beneath the heat of the midday sun two figures toiled to dig a joint grave at the forlorn site of a home reduced to cinders. The healthy green of surrounding fields intensified a desolate pall of death. While Evain wielded a shovel which had miraculously escaped hungry flames, Keir steadily worked with what remained of a hoe—its iron head. During their labors the boy began to reveal how by virtue of a battle wound his father remained on the family farm whilst every member of the fyrd was summoned by King Aldfrith to do battle with Mercian foes.

"The knave's blow shattered my sire's leg. Mama did all she could, yet his leg healed so crooked he couldn't walk—merely hobble with the aid of a young oak's sturdy branch." Keir drove the hoe's head deep into the earth with the pent-up fury of long seething anger. "'Twas me who worked to plow these fields and why, as you can see, their furrows are none too straight."

What Evain saw was that in the brief span of the young Saxon's life already had he endured an over-measure of life's unhappiness. The lad would no more view the grievous injury which had crippled his father as a boon that kept the man home at time of war than had the crippled man. Evain knew enough of Saxons to know that to be so restrained would have eaten on the man's morale like vile acid on flesh until it threatened to destroy him from the inside out. The man would assuredly have preferred an honorable death in battle. With this knowledge of Keir's history, Evain felt it small wonder that the boy so hated the culprits responsible first for crippling his father and then for returning to destroy the man's family and possessions before claiming his life.

Wanting to help the boy turn the corner on this sad portion of his life, Evain immediately shifted attention to the final act in this mournful duty. "Come, help me put our work to its intended use." He led the way to the place where a blanket badly singed but still all of a piece lay atop a plot of herbs and bright flowers. Doubtless the tiny garden had once been tended with care by the woman now gently laid out beside her mate.

Clearly the couple had soaked this blanket with water from a ewer found lying in the ruins not far distant from bodies which had plainly huddled beneath its folds while the structure burned about them. The condition of their bodies proved they'd not perished by flame but rather had been smothered by foul air black with blistering smoke.

Keir was determined to be as much a part of this

task as in the toil of digging his loved ones' final resting place, so when Evain picked up one corner of the blanket, he took another. Together they gently dragged the blanket and its burden to the grave site. There Evain accorded the couple all good respect while carefully wrapping them in folds colored by smoke and lowering them into the pit prepared in honorable measure by their grieving son.

The dirt was more easily replaced than removed. A task immediately followed by another which saw mounded earth soon covered by stones meant to protect the grave from desecration by scavenging animals.

After placing a final rock atop those already piled over mounded dirt, Evain straightened and looked toward the boy standing stoically at the head of the joint grave. Clearly Keir was waging a war against emotion, intent on willing away the brimming tears in misty eyes. No matter Evain's sincere belief that what came after the step through death's portal was a better existence, his sapphire gaze softened with sympathy for the boy's aching loss.

"Do you wish to offer up Christian prayers over their resting place?" Evain gently asked.

Though warmed by the compassionate suggestion, Keir was struck by renewed discomfort over the morn's lapse of control and flood of tears. It was a shame deepened for having done so before Evain, who by his actions had proven himself a man of strength beyond physical might. Forcing a measure of composure to curb his feelings, Keir gave a brief nod that called the bright rays of an early afternoon sun to dance over blond hair.

"For the sake of my father—" Tight words came to

an abrupt halt which Evain wrongly ascribed to an understandable lump in the youth's throat. In truth, Keir caught himself to prevent speaking of things his mother had warned he must never confess.

While Keir signed the cross and bowed his head in silent prayer, Evain respectfully stood motionless. He had experienced the same anguish both as a child mourning parents and grandparents and as a man suffering the absence of a revered mentor.

Once this last farewell was complete, blue eyes clouded by stifled grief lifted to a black-haired companion. Keir struggled with a final unanswered question. "Why couldn't we find Sian?" Although he daren't tell why he thought it a possibility, Keir gave voice to his deepest concern. "I worry that she lives but has been stolen away."

"How old was your little sister?" Evain quietly asked, seeking facts that would help him ease the boy's fears despite his own curiosity for how it was that the couple hadn't held their baby near in the desperate bid to survive the flames.

Keir grimaced, fairly certain what the man meant to imply was that a being so tiny had been as utterly destroyed by the blaze as were so many purposely given to the fire for final rest. "She was born three summers past."

"Because your ancestors practiced consigning their dead to flames, you know that any human form can be consumed by their heat and a body that small . . ." He gently left the obvious unsaid.

Keir more firmly bit his lip while one shoulder lifted in apparent acceptance of a fact he couldn't question without explaining his reason for doubt.

The bleak moment was interrupted by a squawking

chicken. Startled, Keir whirled to find his prized hen madly flapping wings to scare off some uncertain creature daring to draw near her haven in tall grass.

"Cyw! Always knew you'd outlast us all." Fears thrust into abeyance and view brightened by this discovery of another survivor, Keir rushed toward the bird, who greeted his enthusiasm with a bigger fuss.

Black brows met in a faint frown. *Cyw*—the Cymry word for chicken and the second time in one day that words from his native language had been used to name an animal. Anya's naming of the fox he understood. Her mother was as purely Welsh as was he. But this Saxon boy? How was it that Keir had done the same?

Excitement left Keir oblivious to his companion's curiosity. He halted his headlong dash and exercised caution in moving gradually toward the bird. By quietly clucking he calmed the hen enough to reach out and gently pull an egg from beneath her, once and then again and again until he had several eggs stored in a makeshift container formed in the hollow of his tunic's upturned hem.

"Only see what good old Cyw has provided." Keir turned a brilliant grin to the raven-haired man, who met that warmth with a half smile, cynical but lacking bite.

"Aye, looks like our next challenge must be to find some method of transporting your booty back to the cave all of a piece."

Slender shoulders sagged. 'Twas a complication unforeseen, and it stole a measure of Keir's pleasure in the discovery.

Wanting to restore leastways this small bit of joy to the hurting boy, Evain sought and found an answer.

"Aha!" Mocking humor sparkled in sapphire eyes. "I believe I have the solution."

Evain moved to the charred stump of a tree which once must have towered above the leveled abode. It was there he'd left his satchel while they toiled. Bending to delve inside, he pulled out a square of folded cloth. This he shook out, revealing it to be a sack of a size to hold the contents of a medium-size basket.

"What say we fill this with grass and then gently tuck your treasures inside. Then if you carry it with care, they'll be as snug as if still in Cyw's own nest."

Pulling up an abundance of green blades, Evain set the pattern which Keir followed with gusto until the sack was so thoroughly stuffed its sides bulged. Grinning with a determined youthful glee, Keir cautiously nestled one egg after another into its waiting softness.

The boy had the chore of carrying the sack of eggs on the return journey and willingly fell into place behind the handsome leader proven to be that rare, admirable figure: a man who joined strength with understanding. Fearing to fall into useless melancholy for deeds that could not be changed, Keir refused to look behind at the home forever lost to him. Instead he stared blindly at the broad back of the man in front wending down a path into the woodland that had become dangerously well marked.

Of a sudden Evain's sharp-honed senses detected a looming peril—but to them or to his sweet elfling? In an attempt to defeat its threat he cast aside precautions meant to prevent any person unworthy of possessing secret knowledge to see it at work. He sharply veered from their expected course and led his young friend over hidden pathways ascending the steep, heavily forested mountainside in a direct route which to others would seem impenetrable. By this means they would return to the cave with far less time and toil than expended in their descent.

'Twas a fine plan but one across which a foe unknowingly stumbled. Hearing the movements of a bumbling oaf crashing through nearby bushes, Evain promptly whirled. In a single motion he pushed Keir into the cover of a tiny thicket and unsheathed his broadsword. Then standing, feet spread and sword at the ready, he squarely faced the noise's source. As a stocky warrior stepped through the wall of greenery Evain began a low chant whose words a wide-eyed Keir strained to hear even as they dropped into shivering depths. . . .

For the second time in the length of a single day Anya awoke to rays of light slanting through the cave's offset entrance—the first from a sky tinted by dawn and these from the setting sun.

Naught but halfway through the journey between slumber and wakefulness, without forethought she yawned and stretched. The motion brought a realization that the discomfort in her side had become more a dull ache than the sharp pain of before. Plainly her ribs were not broken but merely bruised. Heartened by this assurance of a quick recovery certain to please Evain, she sat up. As Anya's position changed, her attention was caught by a stray beam of sunlight flashing against the crystal orb atop the staff a sorcerer had left in shadow. That glimpse sent a flood of worry through her.

In trepidation Anya had watched as her devastating beloved led a Saxon boy from the cave and ventured into a forest where foes likely lurked. Though Evain doubtless thought her too young and protected to be aware of such dangers, she was not so naive as to believe that the departure of Keir's erstwhile assailants meant no others remained. Aye, Evain had walked into unsafe paths and, for the sake of avoiding a Saxon boy's questions, had departed without the staff he wielded with magical powers. All she could do once the oddly matched pair were well away was fervently chant a spell of protection. That she'd done despite a sinking feeling that while trapped abed inside a cave and without even the small crystal carried away with her clothes her words were woefully inadequate for the task. She had promptly backed her chanted plea with earnest prayers for the same boon and added a request to be healed for the sake of her dear sorcerer's justified impatience.

Through the memory of those deeds struck a fear intensified fourfold. She jumped to her feet, oblivious to the discomfort of sudden motion. Not for a moment did she question the compelling urge to take immediate action. A sacred time of in-between was upon the land and either she move now or lose the potency it might lend her uncertain chants. Moreover, desperate to do all she could to protect Evain, Anya conquered a longstanding terror that so much as touching a sorcerer's powerful emblem without his leave might be to defile it and—the most dreadful possibility—break its orb.

Wasting no instant in anxiety over the temerity of her action, Anya reached out to take Evain's staff from where it rested against the rough stone of the cave's wall. In the possession of one powerful enough to command them, this staff could aid in wielding forces able to control the heavens and demand that incredible feats be done. She was not such a one but surely as her call would be made on a sorcerer's behalf . . .

Moving two paces beyond the haven's portal, she faced a horizon drenched with the setting sun's glory. While the fiery ball slowly sank into the band of rose laying its blanket across the earth's purple hues she lifted the staff with both hands and in a sweet voice trembling at the outset began singing a simple but heartfelt chant.

It seemed her best efforts were to no good purpose. Then, just as Anya felt destined to meet defeat, the stave's crystal flared into a brilliant white light. Her song grew stronger and its notes of unearthly beauty soared into the heavens until a warm sense of calm swept over her, washing her concerns into peace.

Certain of her success and Evain's safety, Anya stood quietly gazing into the lavender mists of twilight when a silvery murmur wound its way into her awareness. 'Twas the stream she knew passed nearby and which now seemed to beckon her to its cool banks. Through Anya's mind floated the words Keir had spoken of a spring and its outflowing brook. It posed too great a temptation to withstand.

Her companions would be absent until, by Evain's own estimate, the midnight hour. Thus she would have privacy for a welcome bath. And, too, from the fresh waters of the spring she would fill Evain's drinking horn and once back in the cave use Keir's battered bronze pot to cook up a batch of porridge. Although the air still held the heat of a summer's day, by the time her companions returned 'twould be chilly and the warm meal welcome no matter the lateness of the hour.

The prospect of her plan filled Anya with pleasure, and she dipped back into the cave to pull the leather strap of Evain's silver-capped drinking horn over her head before departing again with the reassurance of his staff firmly clasped in one hand. She refused to be disconcerted by her lack of either towel or fresh clothing. Warm air would dry her flesh with reasonable speed and the cloak, loosened to flow from shoulder to ankle, was covering enough for the trip there and back.

A few steps into the verdant woodland she paused and closed her eyes to the beauties all round, the better to hear rippling waters. Following the gentle sound, she promptly turned to the left, ducked under a low-hanging branch, and picked her way around near hidden stumble-holes until she reached the mossy bank of a narrow rivulet of water. Tracing its flow back to the spring, she filled Evain's drinking horn and then hung it over the same limb against which she rested the stave. Next she allowed her cloak to drift down and pool about dainty feet before stepping into the clear liquid's welcome embrace.

"Anya's not here." Alarm strained Keir's young voice. The gentle lady's absence seemed proof that he carried the plague of ill fortune to all whose path he crossed. And the thought that the wolves of violence stalking his path had turned their claws upon this friend newly made was horrifying.

As if the signal of a gathering storm, black brows scowled. Evain's heart, too, had plunged in dread of wicked peril overtaking his sweet elfling but he comforted himself with the certainty that had harm befallen Anya he would have felt her pain. However, seeking confirmation for that hope, he closed his eyes while forcing clenched hands to open and serenity to smother the last shreds of unease. These actions enabled him to exercise senses well-honed and particularly receptive where Anya was concerned. His effort was rewarded by a feeling of peace surrounding her. She hadn't been attacked although he felt murky danger hovering over them all.

"Calm yourself." Evain turned toward the boy whose unjustified guilt he heard as clearly as if it had been spoken aloud. "Anya is well."

Keir looked to the man, expressionless but for eyes which flashed with blue sparks as if struck from hard flint.

"I know where she is." Evain was thankful that he hadn't already divested himself of the sheathed sword belted at narrow hips. "And I will fetch her back again if you promise to lessen my burden by remaining here in safety."

This oblique inference that the man was concerned for him did more to soothe Keir's anxiety than any direct words of comfort could have done.

In a dark temper over the woman absent from the cave where she ought to be, Evain stomped into the rapidly deepening shades of twilight. And yet, believing her in no immediate danger and considering what he expected to find, Evain made a slight detour on his path to the stream. He headed first to the hidden glade on a deep valley's floor where he'd concealed Blossom with her saddle and the satchel containing Anya's belongings as well as the bundle he'd made of garb removed before binding injured ribs. With Keir about, Evain much preferred for the gentle beauty to be fully clothed. Toward that end he meant to restore garments to the maiden busied by the bath he'd forbidden.

Evain paused at the unexpected ravine's brow and through an oak's branches peered down over the treetops below. An unwelcome impression of things gone awry rose to greet him. He lost no moment in descending the rock bestrewn hillside, only to confirm his initial unpleasant suspicion. Blossom, her tack, and the satchel attached were gone. Certain the placid mare would leave neither the valley's protection nor its waterfall and abundant grasses—and even less willingly embark on the steep upward climb—he realized she'd been stolen. It was possible the thieves were scavenging forest bandits but more likely that they were Mercian warriors. Considering his repeated encounters with lone men, Evain had come to believe them a group divided for the sake of widening the scope of ground covered in their hunt for him.

Sapphire eyes narrowed on the empty space beneath the tree where Blossom had been left. If foes had found Anya's mount, then they surely knew that their prey was near and would intensify their search of the area—but not till the morrow. Despite the Mercians' habit of night raids on defenseless farms they'd never been known to meet any prepared foe in the dark. 'Twas a fact which made it the more important to fetch Anya back to the cave. From there, as Anya's actions seemed proof of a measure of returned health, they must take the boy and immediately resume their journey in order to be well away before the sun brightened the eastern horizon.

Evain quickly turned his attention to one further task, thankful for the odd impulse which had caused him to hide Anya's bundled clothing in a thick patch of dense-leafed bushes. Even in daylight her rolled garb's green hues would blend with its surroundings, a fact which could only have aided in seeing it remain safely concealed. Moving rapidly, he retrieved the bundle. Although Anya's satchel of spare clothing was gone, he was grateful she would leastways have the clothes worn in her tumble from the horse's back.

In the uncertain chance that it offered a faster path to his destination, Evain briefly considered climbing the wall over which the stream dropped in a glittering rush but discarded the risky option. He retraced his downward path until he came across a faint trail.

Even were he unfamiliar with the spring's location, the marks left by dainty feet crossing long blades of grass were easily followed, a passing confirmed by twigs broken at intervals along the way. The marks so easily tracked forcefully reminded Evain of her imprudence in wandering alone through the wilds of the night forest. It roused his temper with fears for her safety as he neared the point where the spring's water formed a small pool before rushing away in a quick flowing stream. Ire burned brighter at the renewed and unpleasant realization that she would be garbed in a cloak and nothing more and flared into a torrent of words before he stepped from the cover of trees whose branches met overhead.

"What wicked imp prodded you into a deed of such folly? Have you so soon forgot the black toads who would see us captured or dead?"

Shoulder deep in the spring with masses of pale hair freshly washed, loosely piled, and precariously fastened atop her head by the precious ivory comb most oft used to anchor braids, Anya froze. She looked toward the black-clad man standing nearly invisible amidst twilight shadows intensified beneath the trees' joined limbs. How could she begin to explain the magic wrought by one not only untrained but of mixed heritage; even less explain how she'd accomplished it with the aid of the staff he seemed not to have noticed propped against a trunk within his reach. Evain's next words showed her mistake in underestimating a sorcerer's innate skill at detailed observation.

"Knowing far more of Druidic methods than any Saxon Christian ought, you must be aware that my staff alone holds no power to protect you?" He motioned toward the long, use-smoothed stave with its dark crystal resting against the sturdy branch from which hung his drinking horn, but did not shift his penetrating gaze from the silent beauty.

Anya heard Evain's description of her as a "Saxon Christian" as the insult it was meant to be—never mind that it was true, although only one half of the whole.

The distress Evain knew he had caused Anya poured oil on his boiling ire even as a low growl demanded his attention. He looked down to find her fox menacingly crouched at his feet. Regret for having permitted the lash of his temper to fall upon her softened his next question. "Surely you cannot think this tiny creature fierce enough to frighten away any determined assailant?"

Of course, she hadn't expected such a thing of Noddi! Anya's own temper rose. She bit her lip to contain it. Her only weapon was to turn a Druid's trick against the sorcerer by doing the deed least unexpected—answer his attack with another but with an air of unconcern sure to irritate him the more.

"How is it you've come back so soon? I hadn't expected you till the midnight hour—by which time I'd be in the cave with a kettle of hot porridge waiting."

Evain was not so easily disconcerted and with a potent, one-sided smile accepted her challenge. At this game he was the master and she would lose.

"You must be cold. I know, I earlier bathed there myself. So, come out and dress. I brought your clothes back to you." He shook the folds from bundled garb like an enticement.

At the prospect of walking nude from the spring beneath his steady gaze Anya could feel the heat of a blush rise in a bright tide from her throat to her hairline. Her first instinct was to simply sink into cold waters. But, to avoid the difficulties involved in again soaking a thick mass of hair already washed and nearly dry, she quelled the initial desire. Instead she buried her face into the welcome chill of liquid lifted in cupped hands.

Instantly regretting the "game," Evain found himself bothered that Anya seemed sincerely horrified by harmless banter suggesting such an event. She'd known him her whole life. He had taken time from important training to play silly games with the child she'd been, and from her first steps she had followed him as ceaselessly as a shadow—the same habit that had brought her into their current path of danger. No matter, the fact remained the same: She of all people ought to trust him.

"Why are you so fearful of me seeing you as I have many times since the days when I bathed you as a baby and watched over you as a child?"

Anya heard the distress at the core of a question

phrased as another teasing jest, yet she wouldn't so easily let him escape the price for his victory. "'Tis *not* something you've been a part of since I left childhood behind. And I am not a child now."

"Mayhap you think that last eve your clothes were removed by elves? But no, you've left childhood tales behind and must surely realize it was I who did my best to treat your injured side."

Another tide of heat threatened to flood over Anya at the image of Evain performing so intimate a deed for her. With the certainty that the action had been undertaken for the purest of motives she calmed an embarrassment twined with annoyance over having been observed while lying unconscious. To completely eradicate resentment, Anya reminded herself that she would willingly give whatever Evain sought of her. To prove this truth to him, Anya began moving through the pool toward him with a bravado hastily bolstered by a less than certain belief that he would turn his back rather than watch.

Despite the warnings his conscience screamed, Evain couldn't look away from the ethereal vision of loveliness rising from moon-silvered waters. Her breasts were full and firm with uptilted tips hardened by cool water while her waist was tiny and hips narrow. She stole his breath. The renewed reality of her was devastating and his body tensed with poorly timed desire.

Anya knew she ought turn away from the blue fires burning in the depths of his eyes, ought to find shame in the blatant pleasure he took in her nudity. She ought yet could not deny the fiery attraction which had steadily built since the first kiss given her as a man to a woman. The undeniable hunger in his expression stole her shyness and left her certain that coming to him this way was the most natural action she'd ever taken.

Evain's jaw tensed as she drew nearer—lips parted, green eyes misty with need, and breasts rising and falling with unsteadily drawn breaths. Even while naming himself a witless fool, he absently dropped the green gown and reached out to brush his fingertips lightly over satin curves and taut tips.

She gasped and that response lifted her breasts toward the teasing touch that tantalized with a promise of delight yet did nothing to satisfy the hunger they created. Following her instinct for more, she reached up to wrap her arms about his neck and twist urgently against his broad chest.

Feeling the heat of lush breasts like a fiery brand even through the fabric of his tunic, Evain shivered and locked her against his powerful body. Once she was inside the circle of his arms, the feel of his muscular body overwhelmed Anya with burning sensations and drove the last tendril of rational thought beyond her reach.

As Anya's fingers twined in his thick dark hair Evain's hands slid down the satin of her bare back to clasp her hips nearer still before moving lower to cup her perfect derriere and lift her into the center of his need. In the reckless desire of that moment he forgot her injured side while she, lost in the thrall of aching pleasure, was oblivious to its hurt.

With the unexpectedness of a thunderbolt from a clear sky, Evain was abruptly struck by the unlikely but ghastly possibility of unseen men watching his incredibly exciting virgin, nude and wrapped in an intimate embrace. With a harsh groan he tore himself free. He stiffly bent to retrieve Anya's carelessly dropped cloak and swirled it about her shoulders, shielding tempting flesh before sweeping her up into his arms. Intending to provide Anya with privacy to dress, he carried her into a seclusion provided by large bushes thickly covered by honeysuckle vines.

When Evain gently set Anya on her feet within the circle of flower-laden bushes and immediately backed out, she knew he meant to see their love-play at an end. But, still lost in the fire storm of desire, she ached for more and put maidenly inhibitions aside to lure him back to her. She refused to let pass this rare opportunity for time alone with the devastating man who was the center of her world and spread her cloak over nature's carpet of green blades. Pulse pounding in the heavy rhythm her sorcerer had taught it, she settled atop the dark cloth.

In rapidly deepening shadows beyond the honeysuckle wall, Evain drew deep breaths, and by thinking of the North Sea's icy waves attempted to cool the heat of molten blood rushing through his veins. For once he wished his drinking horn contained something more bracing than springwater as he took the dangling item from the branch where it had been left. Then, gathering up the green dress haplessly discarded, he moved to step again through the wall of bushes—and froze.

"You're taking risks, child." Though assuredly an innocent, she didn't look like a child while the moon's luminescent glow kissed the luscious enticements of her alabaster body where it lay in stark relief against the dark cloak. Neither barrels of ale nor an ocean of ice water could quench his desire for her.

"I'm not a child—you only wish that I were." Anya trembled with the unhappy truth of her claim. "You wish it but I am willing to dare any risk." As if to prove it she gently arched her body in an untutored invitation while softly moaning, "Evain . . . kiss me again."

Evain's jaw clenched against the tempting vision of green eyes darkened and drowsy with new desires, of soft lips swollen and yearning upward, but still he held back. 'Twould be madness! This permitting himself yet another taste of forbidden ambrosia which would haunt him for a lifetime and likely beyond.

Fearing a loss in his hesitation, Anya took Evain's hand and pulled him down until she could wrap her arms about broad shoulders and sob in his ear, "Please!"

The will of a sorcerer could not be so easily buckled were its result not so surely an answer to his own longings. Evain fell to her enticements. Mouth opening and crushing down on hers, he told himself he would take the pleasure of only one kiss, only this single long, endless kiss.

The heady scent of honeysuckle drifted around them as Anya, her body on fire, tugged Evain nearer until he gave her both his full weight and the unrestrained passion of his devouring mouth. These gifts she welcomed with a headlong urgency that threatened to steal every shred of his noble intentions.

Only by wielding the powerful control of a sorcerer —despite the hurting tautness of his body and the fever in his blood—did Evain pull away and stand up.

Feeling bereft and, as the moments passed, humiliated by the fact that he had regained his control so easily while she suffered an aching emptiness—it was this difference which reminded Anya that Evain, unlike herself, had experience in these matters. The thought intensified her distress. Folding arms over her breasts, she shivered with shame while lowering eyes from which crystal teardrops escaped.

"Don't cover yourself." Evain's deep voice held all the gentleness of a warm summer's midnight hour.

Against her will, Anya glanced up to the stunningly handsome man now towering above.

"Not now." Almost did Evain reach out to brush his fingertips over silky hair and satin flesh. Almost . . . "Let me look at you a few moments longer, and take consolation in knowing that's all I can do." Even as Evain said it, he knew the possessor of eyes now emerald wells of pain would find no more consolation in that fact than did he.

"Don't you want me?" Her soft voice ached with desolation.

Cynicism twisted Evain's smile. He wouldn't answer a question proving just how innocent she was when the physical proof was all too obvious. Once again blue-flame eyes moved over the silk-soft, shining hair flowing in glorious disarray around her delicately flushed face and the pale ivory of her lush body—a sight so enticing it could near break the will of a sorcerer. Evain desperately wanted to touch her again yet his hands did not reach for her. Rather, against the temptation they clenched upon the green cloth in his hold. His gaze accepted no such bonds and moved over her slowly, thoroughly, as if imprinting in his mind for an eternity this vision more dangerous than even the one stolen the previous night.

Anya trembled beneath its power. "You could take me." She brushed away a forlorn tear of hopeless love. "I belong to you as I have always and always will."

"No. That cannot be—cannot ever be. I am no more than a memory from your youth who will fade into the past when one day you belong to another man as his wife and the mother of his children." The words, though assuredly true, burned on Evain's tongue with the acid of regret. "I must leave you pure for him."

"I can never belong to another man." In a calm, quiet voice Anya firmly denied Evain's description of her future. "If I am not yours, then I will be forever alone."

In this statement Evain, who knew the willful maid so well, recognized a heartfelt conviction impossible to alter. While meeting the deep green pools of sorrow that her eyes had become, inside him rose such a wave of grief for what could never be that he nearly cried out against the Druidic destiny barring their happiness. Instead he froze all emotion and dropped the forest hued clothing beside her before stepping from the honeysuckle scented haven.

Struggling to stem the flow of tears she feared Evain would deem childish despite the anguish of their source, Anya repeatedly dashed them away between the motions required to don her clothes. It was clear that she'd driven her beloved further away by actions pleading for what he viewed as a threat to the fulfillment of his overriding debt. This debt was the core of her mother's oblique but oft repeated warnings that Evain owed unswerving loyalty to those of his heritage throughout ages past and yet to come. But she was *not* a threat! To prove it Anya knew she must demonstrate herself to be as truly a part of that heritage as he. With the fires of determination she banished silent tears.

While Anya dressed, Evain sought to restore control over his emotions and regain the imperative serenity of a Druid. Waiting in the peaceful glade, he contemplated the spring ever bubbling with fresh waters and in its eternal renewal found a measure of comfort.

Chapter
8

Moving through the velvet darkness of night by the light of the staff's globe, which Evain had chanted to brightness, he and Anya made their way to the cave while the fox cub trailed behind. On the journey Evain shared with Anya the news of Blossom's taking and the loss of her satchel of clothing. She was saddened by the theft of her aging mare. But upon reaching the cave the unhappy news was leavened by Keir's great relief for her safety and excited recounting of a peculiar event which had occurred as he and Evain returned from the day's sad duty.

"Peculiar! Truly!" Keir nearly danced at her side. "I was fortunate that Evain pushed me into a thicket and even more fortunate that during the fall I succeeded in protecting a treasure." With the words he waved toward a delicate cache of precious eggs carefully laid atop a grass padded bag.

Anya's initial thought was that she was fortunate the boy, with the single-mindedness of a child, gave no notice to her change of garb. But with a single glimpse of his *treasure,* her attention was thoroughly diverted. Aye, his eggs had survived intact and in sufficient number for each person to have several.

Keir's tale was interrupted by Anya's glee over the treasure and nothing would do but that she must immediately see them prepared for eating.

While Anya happily toiled, Evain turned to Keir. "I must make haste and soon depart."

Keir gazed at him with an unspoken question which Evain chose to misinterpret.

"A quick leave-taking is necessary to elude the same foes who struck your home."

Eyes gone misty gray dropped to the stone floor. The man had made no mention of Keir's place in coming events—must mean he had none.

There was no doubt in Anya's mind but that Keir would go with them, and upon hearing Evain's limited explanation, she thought that for the boy's sake he ought to have more clearly defined the task ahead. However, in consideration of all that had so recently passed between them she chose to leave Evain's methods unchallenged. Asides, boiled eggs were ready for eating.

While night's black mantle rested heavily upon the earth three people gathered around the cave's fire to partake of a meal prepared with unusual speed. It was not the steaming porridge Anya had envisioned but rather, despite the haste of its making, one even more welcome to people whose limited diet of recent days had included no eggs. Now boiled and divided among them they made up the bulk of the meal although supplemented by hunks of cheese and the last crusts of her hard bread.

A fair amount remained of Anya's food, while with the appetite of a growing boy Keir wolfed down his. This feat accomplished even as with a determined brightness he resumed the dramatic story of a sunset confrontation between Evain and an armed stranger. In summing up the adventure, admiring blue eyes lifted to the dark man.

"Guess you frightened the fool who stumbled into our path to death with the threat of your strength . . . and inexplicable deeds?" Keir's statement ended on a question's up-note, plainly in hopes of learning the reasons behind his companion's odd conduct.

Evain was not so easily drawn into saying anything he did not wish to tell. "The *fool* is not dead, merely in the deepest sleep he is ever like to experience." Even his chill half smile of mockery disappeared when he added, "In the end he will awake."

As Evain shared that small morsel of curious truth with the Saxon boy, it came to Anya that the sunset confrontation of Keir's vivid description had surely taken place at the very moment she was struck with a fierce urge to chant the spell of protection. It must've been Evain's desperate need which had given her the courage to take the daring action of claiming his staff and imploring its aid to guard his safety.

Anya's attention returned to companions so different in coloring when Evain took a new tack in sailing the boat of their conversation into waters he deemed less treacherous.

"This morn you gave us to understand that you hadn't meant to make this cave your home." Sapphire eyes met a pale blue gaze with the gentle demand for answers. "Where did you think to go? Have you family elsewhere? Or do you mean to seek aid from Throckenholt's lord—your lord?"

Keir drew a deep breath. Because Evain had not suggested his inclusion on the journey about to resume though he was host to an earnest desire to go with them, Keir knew the time had come to speak plainly. At least insofar as to confess his original plans. The prospect was eased by a certainty that these two were worthy of his trust. He would only pray they wouldn't discount his hopes as naught but the silly dreams of a child—just as his stalwart but utterly unimaginative father assuredly would have done.

"My mother was of Cymry blood. She was born here in Gwyll and from her father learned tales of a man in the mountains of Talacharn. She repeated to me those same tales of how that man rescued a boy left all alone—like me. Rescued him and his sister, too."

Keir didn't hear the contradiction in his claim that a boy with a sister was alone. Anya did but, aware of his prickly pride, hid the amusement it roused in her. Evain understood the meaning behind the boy's words very well, grasped it with the ease of a memory which caused him to listen the more intently.

"The man in the tales is a sorcerer." Awe filled Keir's voice. "A Druid known as Glyndor and who possesses incredible powers."

Evain's face went blank while Anya held her breath. Nowise could Keir know that before him sat a central character in the story he continued to tell with an expression of wonder. Nor could the boy possibly suspect that the sorcerer of whom he spoke had played important roles in the lives of both his companions.

Keir sat unaware of his friends' stillness. He was caught up in the pleasure of sharing the tales of near-mythical people he admired and of feats performed from children's rescue to "the great death of birds."

"And more—" The two words almost glowed with hope. "Mama told me the tale of how Glyndor passed on to the rescued boy all the mystical spells and great powers he possessed."

Once Keir finished speaking there fell a silence so deep and long that he began to glance nervously from the dark man on his one side to the sweet lady on the other. Although Evain so oft seemed full of mockery, no hint was present now on his impassive face, and Anya seemed stunned. But why?

At last Evain spoke to quietly ask a question the answer for which he suspected—nay, nearer to feared —he already knew. "What had those tales to do with your search for a home?"

In the face of this emotionless reception for the tale Keir had taken care to spin with all the magic his mother had given it, he squared his shoulders and defiantly lifted his chin. "I meant . . ." Keir boldly announced his initial intent, "to go in search of Glyndor and offer myself to him as another willing pupil."

"Glyndor is dead," Evain flatly stated. "Has been for nigh on to a decade."

"No-o-o." Keir's single word was a wail of anguish intertwined with disbelief. "Were that so I'd have heard it long ago."

Evain was certain that as Throckenholt landholders his parents had been aware of this fact. Likely they had found no worthwhile reason to give such a final end to the thrilling tale treasured by their child. For them 'twas an understandable decision, although one which would make acceptance more difficult for the boy first robbed of family and now asked to bear yet another unhappy circumstance.

"'Tis a sorrowful reality that Glyndor is gone." Seeing the continued mutinous set of the boy's chin, Evain gently but insistently spoke again to drive home a truth meant to save Keir the useless flight toward an illusion. "Although one I deeply rue, I assure you 'tis an unalterable fact.

"Glyndor was my mentor—" Despite Evain's impassive face, the depths of dark blue eyes held the ache of loss. "I am the boy whom he rescued and taught to follow after him."

"And I am Glyndor's great-granddaughter." Anya calmly added as Keir struggled to assimilate the unpleasant blow to his dreams. "Did you not know that the wife of your lord, the Ealdorman of Throckenholt, is Glyndor's granddaughter?"

"Lady Brynna?" Keir looked confused.

Anya nodded, compassion warming her eyes to silver mists. "Lady Brynna is my mother and Glyndor my great-grandfather."

Keir straightened and twisted his face away from these bearers of unbelievable news. This pair had made too many claims of things he felt sure he'd have heard before—were they true. "Nay, I'm certain my mama would've told me if 'twere so."

Met with Keir's stubborn disbelief of her honest words, Anya was shocked into silence.

Evain reached out to take Keir's stiff shoulders in both hands and firmly turned the boy to meet him face-to-face. "Do you believe me when I tell you I am Glyndor's protégé?" Evain solemnly asked.

"You must be." Keir slowly nodded despite the shadow of doubt in his eyes. "I saw you stop an enemy with your spell. The strange words that you sang were a spell, weren't they?"

Unwilling to further bend the bonds of secrecy so important to Druidic ways, Evain refused the preciseness of a verbal answer to this Saxon child's question. And half or whole, Evain firmly believed that Keir's Saxon blood made him utterly unworthy of a Druid's knowledge. Yet, because to remain safe the boy *must* be made to sincerely believe, Evain accepted the necessity to *do* something. Thus it was that to avoid putting into words matters best left in the shifting mists of the unspoken he skillfully wielded a sorcerer's ploy of mercurial mood shifts.

As his dark head fell back, the deep thunder of a sorcerer's laughter echoed against stone walls. Leaping to his feet, Evain took up his staff and strode to the cave's entrance. There he began chanting quiet words. The eerie melody dropped lower, growing in intensity until it seemed to shake the heavens and rumble with the ability to command nature's submission. As if in proof Noddi crawled forward on his front paws to crouch at the sorcerer's feet.

In the fox's movement Anya recognized the purpose of Evain's chant. Rising, she took the wide-eyed boy's hand and led him to stand behind a broad back while all manner of untamed creatures from squirrels to deer and even a wild boar heeded the sorcerer's call.

Continuing to hold animals compliant to his will and gathered within the brilliant ring of light flowing from the globe atop uplifted staff, Evain's night-dark gaze moved to the boy. Keir was lost in an awe bolstered by a fearful respect well justified.

"Chants are not a game," Evain cautioned. "Never would I use my skill in communing with natural forces for such a frivolous display did I not deem it important that you accept all that both I and Anya have said for the truth it is."

Evain turned again toward his extraordinary audience of diverse animals and waved his staff in a slow, broad sweep that sent them scurrying into the shadows as quickly as they'd appeared. Drawing close the staff with its crystal gone dark, Evain shifted his solemn attention to Keir.

"If you are to travel from this place with us, your life may depend upon it."

"You mean to allow that I go with you?" Keir's blue eyes flashed with delight. His enthusiasm earned a slight smile from Evain—until the boy added, "And will you teach me to be a sorcerer, too?"

Evain's face instantly became an expressionless mask and his thick mane of ebony hair brushed wide shoulders as he slowly shook his head. "You travel with us only because I cannot lose the time required to escort both you and Anya to the safety of Throckenholt Keep."

Exercising her long-practiced skill in quiet listening, Anya recognized the statement as a Druid's lament for being saddled on this important mission with two half-Saxons able only to be unwelcome complications. And yet, that he did so rather than leaving them here to fend for themselves until he returned—an assuredly justified action—deepened her admiration and love for him.

At the same time, Anya could almost find his disesteem of a half-Saxon's aid amusing considering that it was she who this afternoon had wielded his staff at the moment he most needed aid. It was plain that were she to tell him of her deed, he was most like to view it with the gentle but condescending amusement given the antics of a child mimicking its elders. He wouldn't believe her attempt of value. Thus, Anya wouldn't reveal to him what she had done. Asides . . . if he whose bond with natural forces was undeniably strong hadn't sensed her calling to the same powers, then mayhap his low opinion of her worth in such matters was correct. That demoralizing thought left Anya grateful that she'd not spoken of her attempt to wield his staff.

While these thoughts rushed through Anya's mind, Evain continued speaking to Keir.

"The goal of my quest is to free my sister's Saxon husband from the hands of men doubtless allied with those who burned your farm." With calm, dispassionate words Evain gave the explanation Anya had earlier wanted him to speak. "'Tis too important to risk further delay. Do you understand?"

Gilded hair glowed in firelight as Keir immediately nodded.

"And will you give me your solemn oath to obey whatever command I deem necessary to make?" Evain felt he must have assurance of this important requirement.

Again the boy nodded his earnest willingness to accept whatever Evain commanded.

As Anya watched the exchange she was struck by an uncanny likeness between her two companions, despite the fact that Keir's hair reflected the golden

brightness of noon and Evain's the darkness of midnight. Shaking her own silver-blond mane to dispel
surely imagined fancies, Anya turned her attention to
the task ahead.

While his two new friends set about organizing
essential items for the journey, Keir comforted his
grief over all that was lost with the knowledge that
leastways deeply rued events had given him this
opportunity to join a sorcerer's quest. He smothered
any hint of despondency over the implied denial of his
dream to become a sorcerer with the weak hope that
by lending aid on the trip ahead he might prove
himself worthy of being taught. And prove it without
having to confess more of what he'd sworn he would
not.

"So the girl-child we sought has been taken to Isca?"
Bishop Wilfrid nearly gloated. His substantial girth
required that he sit farther back from the high table
than either of the guests flanking him and yet it was
that very size which proved how little an impediment
it was to his enjoyment of any meal.

Torvyn deemed the dangers risked in the abduction
of a single toddler unworthy of the effort required to
see her delivered to the old Roman fort built of stone.
But he restrained the sneer of contempt he might have
permitted were it not for the identity of others present
here in the Mercian Abbey of Eadben—a Cymry
prince and his own lord, King Ethelred of Mercia. All
three were seated at a table burdened with an abundance of amazingly diverse dishes. The meal's savory
aroma alone would be enough to rouse any man's
hunger, and after a day's hard ride Torvyn was so

famished his attention was easily beckoned by the feast.

"Be you deaf?" The bishop resented being forced to ask a simple question again and again. He'd little respect for Torvyn in the first instance but at the moment the man standing below the dais seemed to have gone completely witless. Using the slow, sharply defined syllables required to communicate with the feebleminded, he repeated his query once more. "What of the boy?"

Torvyn couldn't prevent dislike from glittering in his eyes and he took delight in further frustrating the pompous oaf by shrugging idly while giving the answer sought, although assuredly one unwelcome. "There was no boy."

"But they had a son." The plaintive cry came from a man on the bishop's left who was near as heavy as his host. "I've had the family watched for years and I *know* they'd a son!"

"I do not doubt your claim, my lord." Torvyn turned a face schooled into respect toward the aging Prince Mathru of Gwyll. "I merely state the certain fact that when the farm was raided, no boy was found."

The stolid and battle-hardened king seated on the bishop's right shared his thegn's low opinion of the other two men. However, Ethelred forced broad, scarred hands previously clenched to flatten atop a tabletop covered with white cloth. Ethelred subdued annoyance by reminding himself of the good use he intended to make of their festering hatred for men he also wished to see brought low—although his motive was callous ambition.

"No boy? What matter that?" Breaking in to halt growing dissension, Ethelred tempered his usual booming voice into an uncomfortably quiet tone while he sought to placate fractious cohorts. "You have the little maid as well as the captive ealdorman, and they surely ought be sufficient to achieve your planned retribution."

Both bishop and prince hosted a bitterness over personal grievances that with passing years had fermented into poisonous acid. Their joined schemes to avenge the variety of wrongs each deemed committed against him had initially been devised as an aid to Ethelred's cause. But not for an instant did the wily king forget that the acrimony so useful to him could also be a danger to his goal were careful controls loosed. However, such a threat to his long-standing objective of conquering Northumbria he would never permit!

Wilfrid swelled with indignation. Ethelred knew full well that a successful end for the plan shared with Mathru would be difficult with only the Cymry child and Saxon man. A fervent denial burned on his tongue but remained unsaid as the Mercian king continued with a soft but potent warning.

"Beware you don't make the mistake of thinking a willingness to permit *my* warriors to do your bidding might indicate a weakness in me. I have not forgot nor will I allow you to forget the payment promised for my men's success in securing your captives—and secure them they did."

"But . . ." Mathru's hesitant voice faded as Ethelred leaned forward to glare around the portly bishop with the full force of his dominant personality.

"And, Your Grace . . ." Ignoring the aging prince,

who was as weak as his fading eyesight, Ethelred again addressed a man he better understood, the bishop, whose greed matched his own. "You've demonstrated a fine gift for commanding men not under your rule. 'Twas a boon willingly given but now 'tis my turn to make a demand. I would have an accounting of what progress you've made to fulfill the grave oath you gave. When do you mean to perform the deed promised me?"

"King Cadwalla has been occupied of late with quelling an uprising on his own lands and had no time to consider our proposition. But I leave on the morrow for Wessex and will meet and negotiate with him for the alliance we seek. From there I will send you a message and then come back some distance to the monastery at Ecley."

Ethelred nodded a head completely bald on top but blessed with a long, thick gray fringe around the bottom. He was not pleased by news of an uprising's delay. But there was a measure of satisfaction in the prospect of action soon to come on this final piece in his broad-based strategy for victory in a conflagration for which the small forays waged to date were but the tiniest spark.

Feeling certain the king's rumbled grunt of satisfaction with his planned action justified a renewed questioning of Torvyn, Wilfrid turned to the raw-boned thegn.

"Where is the warrior Rolf?"

Torvyn had expected, anticipated this question and took wry pleasure in responding. "Rolf remained to continue a closer observation of the area where we came across the mare ridden by the sorcerer's companion."

"Companion?" Wilfrid was startled by this statement as few things had ever startled him. It couldn't be true and he said so. "Since the old sorcerer died, the younger never travels in the company of another."

"No men, mayhap." Torvyn's smile was a leer. "But, as you say, he *is* a young man. And it has now been proven he's not above taking with him a tender beauty."

"A woman!" Wilfrid's surprise sank into deep concern. Were the sorcerer to have sons, they, too, would assuredly be trained as Druid sorcerers—and further the spread of what must be stopped!

"A Cymry woman?" The bishop asked the question of Torvyn but looked to the Cymry prince, who had claimed he would certainly know if any such danger loomed.

"Nay." Torvyn's pleasure grew.

At the thegn's cryptic answer Wilfrid's attention snapped back to him.

"What do you mean?"

"I mean what I say." Restraining a laugh with great difficulty, the youngest man in the room could not stifle a grin and went on with the exaggerated words of a lovelorn fool. "The maid has hair like moonbeams and eyes of gleaming emeralds lost in twilight mists."

Wilfrid's jowls settled into a frown. Not one of anger. Rather, it was a sign of the depths to which he sank in careful consideration of how best to exploit this unexpected news to their advantage. After long moments while others watched him, he barked out a decisive order.

"Capture her. Whatever else is lost or gained. Capture her and bring her to me at Ecley."

Ethelred sat impassive while Mathru clicked his

tongue in disgusted certainty that the bishop had gone mad. But Torvyn was the most disconcerted . . . and unhappy to find it was so.

Wilfrid's eyes stared blindly at the chamber's door while in a voice sharp as any bared dagger he spoke again.

"She is the single most important weapon we could secure. Anya, the great-granddaughter of Glyndor, daughter of Brynna, and—as you heard—Evain's beloved." Wilfrid had not thought the Druid sorcerer would link himself to one not of pure Cymry blood but . . . "She is the only person for whom all the others will do anything, give anything to save."

"Then, Torvyn, you must see our friend's wish fulfilled." Ethelred emotionlessly confirmed the order while sending his thegn a meaningful glance.

Dust brown hair brushed angular shoulders as Torvyn nodded. "I will carry the order to Rolf myself."

With a slight smile Ethelred nodded his understanding of the oblique agreement.

But Wilfrid didn't understand and argued. "Why do you not do the deed yourself?" He took as an insult the thegn's intent to pass this most important responsibility on to a less than sharp-witted underling.

It was King Ethelred who answered. "Torvyn has methods all his own and as they are generally more effective than any other, I trust him to take whatever actions he deems most likely to win the end besought."

The disgruntled bishop could hardly dispute a king's command of his own man.

Wilfrid settled back in his chair, rotund belly pressing tight against the table's edge as he reached for a chicken leg dripping with juices and gilded with precious saffron powder. Aye, the bishop acknowledged while meticulously wiping an excess of juice from the corner of his mouth, it was impossible for him to interfere between Ethelred and his man. Not when the Saxon king's support had been and doubtless would continue to be so necessary to his personal well-being. Yet there were ways and then other ways to teach the arrogant thegn, Torvyn, a much needed lesson in humility. And what chore could be more appropriate for a bishop than to thus minister to an erring member of his flock?

Chapter
9

The dull gray of coming day lessened woodland gloom for a trio who had spent the remaining hours of one night, the length of an entire day, and most of the night that came after journeying over secret pathways. Following a sorcerer's lead, Anya and Keir had wended through the ancient forest's towering trees and dense foliage. In an unthinking display of trust to cross rivers they had duplicated Evain's exact footfalls over rocks near hidden by rushing waters and stepped across the gleaming ripples of small brooks.

Evain realized that although his companions had demonstrated a willingness to continue trudging onward without complaint, they'd gone so long without sleep exhaustion was imminent. In truth, after two days and now two nights without rest, even he was weary to the core. He comforted himself that the southwest path he'd chosen had brought them much nearer his destination. And when bright streaks of rose and gold gifted the eastern horizon with proof of coming day, he abruptly turned. Evain moved a few paces into seemingly impenetrable vegetation before sweeping aside and lifting a curtain of dangling ivy.

Anya immediately dipped below the shiny green drape. An unquestioning but bewildered boy followed. Keir halted, surprised by what he found—a natural refuge with near-solid walls of foliage and a roof created by limbs joined overhead. In the center lay rocks encircling a small pile of cold ashes.

Evain offered a brief but potent chant of gratitude to the providers of shelter before lowering his satchel to a carpet of lush grass.

Anya, too, inwardly praised the source of this gift. Then, while their leader began to unbuckle his sheathed sword, the other two thankfully lowered their own burdens and wearily sank upon a cushion of green blades dotted with tiny yellow flowers.

"Are you going to light the fire?" Keir asked, propped up on his homespun bag of items salvaged from the ruins of his home.

Feeling the strain of his unfinished quest like a weight on his shoulders, Evain shrugged against its tension as he absently answered. "We've no need for its warmth."

"But to ward off wild beasts . . ." Keir's voice trailed into silence.

Both of Keir's companions grinned. However, Evain gave his attention to carefully placing a sword to one side of his satchel, leaving Anya to answer.

"In a Druid's company, Keir . . ." The words were as gentle as the sweet smile she turned to the boy.

". . . There is no danger from creatures who know him as master . . . and friend."

Even before Anya spoke, Keir felt foolish for suggesting it could be elsewise. After he had witnessed the incredible spell wrought by a sorcerer able to command those very beasts to his will, the question was an addlepate's deed.

An embarrassed Keir busied himself awkwardly resetting a bag already well positioned. He had been truly amazed by the sight of untamed animals answering Evain's summons but shouldn't have been so surprised when his mother's tales had implied such mystical powers. The thought of her stories revived in Keir's mind an image of the disapproving frown their telling had ever brought to his father's lips. And yet his sire's response had borne not disbelief but rather an odd tinge of guilty regret.

Anxious to waylay hurtful memories of parents he'd lost, Keir pulled up a handful of grass and spoke without judicious forethought. "I pray that someday I, too, can be a friend and master to wild creatures."

In the act of spreading his black cloak on the ground, Evain went still. He'd a choice to make, an unpleasant one which for Keir would end either in an ache now or a greater pain later—a choice much the same as the boy's parents had faced in deciding not to tell their son of Glyndor's death. Aye, Evain could allow the boy's words to remain a hazy dream or dissipate its insubstantial mists with the gale winds of truth. The former course was the easiest and for Keir the most pleasant. Yet, the fervent but impossible longing at the heart of the Saxon boy's words prodded the sorcerer to regretfully pursue the latter. His intent was to save future anguish at the lesser expense of the present moment of unhappiness.

"Keir, I am of pure Cymry blood, as was Glyndor and as is his granddaughter, Brynna, and my sister, Llys. We four are all Druids by virtue of our heritage." He peered through the grove's green shadows and searched the boy's expression for some sign that his message had been understood. The youthful face showed a dismaying ability to become as impassive as so often was Evain's own.

"Both Llys and Brynna are wed to Saxons." Fearing Keir would refuse to accept an indirect explanation, Evain forced to his tongue the manner of specific words a Druid despised in speaking with one unworthy. "And by that choice they know that their children cannot share the destiny which now I alone must see continue."

Keir's expression did not change but his hands crushed together. He saw too well what the sorcerer implied but refused to acknowledged it any more a fact than that Evain alone could continue the destiny of mystery. How could it be so when such magical figures existed as the witch of Illsdene Wood who, 'twas said, saw visions of both the past and future?

"By mixed bloodlines," Evain quietly spoke a brutal fact whose truth he was certain could never be changed, "they cannot hope to share a Druid's bond with the forces ensouling all natural forms."

Evain's words drove a piercing pain into Anya's heart, and she quietly pressed clenched fists against soft lips to prevent an escape of the anguished moan she could feel rising from her depths. Always had she known her beloved shared the two sorceresses' belief that mixed bloodlines barred any bond with nature, but she had suppressed an awareness that his acceptance of that rule would ever prevent him from taking her to wife. Instead she had blamed Evain's obvious reluctance on her father's unhidden disapproval. Now his blunt statements made it impossible for her to continue down that lane of self-deceit. It was all too clear that for the sake of a grave destiny he seriously believed his children *must* be of pure Cymry blood. Thus, no child she gave him would be acceptable.

Evain felt Anya's pain as if it were his own. Desperately he wanted to take her in his arms and comfort her woe—but could not. There were no honest words to ease her distress. He couldn't unsay what was true nor would he when it was a subject they should've frankly addressed long ago. He'd merely postponed the inevitable by hoping—no matter his desire for her—that in treating her as a child or a younger sister such a discussion would be unnecessary. Their heated embraces had made a jest of such hopes and after their first burning kiss he should've made her understand. It was a strike against his honor that he'd failed to do so because he couldn't bear the thought of a permanent break in their bond. That wrong admitted did nothing to lessen the regret for that very deed now belatedly done.

Anya wanted to flee from the green haven and find the darkest of caverns wherein she could release the boiling tears building inside, burning her throat and threatening to sear her cheeks with their fall. A willful nature came to her rescue, staunching liquid pain unshed with a refusal to accept Evain's rejection.

Her mother was wrong and Evain was wrong as well! Despite Anya's lack of confidence in her abilities, she *had* called to life not only her own crystal but the orb atop a sorcerer's stave, too. And before this quest was done Anya was determined to prove her Saxon blood was no bar to a Druid's powers . . . and no block to Evain's love.

"Evai—" The sharp cry came to an abrupt end but Anya continued struggling wildly against the fierce grip binding her painfully to a beefy chest. Barely had their journey resumed after a day's rest and already it was interrupted by men dragging her backward through a wall of green darkened by twilight mists. One hand remained clamped over her mouth while the man's other arm restrained hers. Her captor sank to his haunches just as a second man materialized to hold her legs immobile.

These fools, Anya realized, thought to outwit a sorcerer. Seemed they foolishly believed it possible to hide sheltered amidst Evain's own natural preserve— an untamed forest where few humans were welcome.

Whirling toward the sound, Evain's cloak swirled out like black wings. The path behind was empty. He froze. Dangerous blue flames flared in the depths of dark eyes as he turned his considerable powers of concentration toward the woodland in an attempt to penetrate its unnatural quiet.

"Anya!" Keir broke that silence. "Where are you?" Unfamiliar with a Druid's ability to learn by communing with voiceless forces, the boy dashed back the way they'd come until—even untrained—he was overcome with an awareness of his surroundings' utter stillness. The eerie absence of motion and complete lack of sound struck a deeper terror in Keir's heart than even the fierce nightmares of his burning home which had visited his sleep every night since.

After her initial struggle Anya went limp, knowing no good could be accomplished by furthering them. Though reduced to captured quarry, she had complete trust in Evain's ability to locate her foolish predators' lair. However, it was an amazingly fierce growl and the pointed face of a tiny fox that sundered the peace.

Anya was delighted. Noddi had trailed her every step since their brief journey from the cave began. Now here was proof that her little protector was not to be defeated even by the sudden end to the trail of her scent. Persistent Noddi had found his mistress and gave a long, ominous snarl.

Anya felt her captors stiffen in horrified disgust. The small fox was nowise large enough to present a physical threat to them but he made noise sufficient to be a very real danger. Lips curled in pleasure beneath a cruel hold. The motion was detected. In punishment for her amusement and the unwelcome fox, the hand became a vicious vise.

Exposed by a sorcerer's bond with nature, Evain had already begun striding toward the area where Anya was held prisoner, but Noddi's snarls pinpointed the exact site.

Realizing the animal's unabated growls exposed them to immediate peril, as if of a single mind Anya's captors rose and tossed the girl into a bush bearing sweet-scented flowers . . . and thorns.

Evain burst through dense vegetation to find the roughly handled maid lying amidst a patch of wild roses while a bundle of auburn fur stood protectively at her side. He ruefully smiled, relieved by the relative ease of her recovery but regretful for the discomfort of sharp barbs. Sparing a moment's thought and word of gratitude for the small animal proven a more literal guard for the woman than expected, he bent to carefully lift Anya from a thorny resting place and then lower her feet to the ground.

Burdened by guilt, Keir stared at the crushed bushes and bruised flowers left where Anya had fallen. Clearly the fault for her taking was his. Had he obeyed the sorcerer's directions—as at the outset he'd sworn to do—and stayed at the back of their small party to protect the rear while Evain led the way, the wicked oaf couldn't have surprised them or so easily taken Anya.

Sapphire eyes glanced toward the gloomy boy and recognized the source of his woe. "'Twas not your doing, Keir. I've been tracked for days."

Keir accepted that fact without pause but it neither explained their enemy's action nor excused his wrong. With a slight shake of his head, he asked, "Why Anya, rather than you or me?"

"Surely you've seen enough of wild creatures' ways to know that predators single out the smallest, weakest, or the one alone to prey upon. Anya walked behind and alone—"

"And is the weakest." Anya was less than pleased by his implied slight and sent the man a gentle glare. "Yet your analogy can be called into question by the fact that the weakest and smallest of our number was the first to arrive in my defense." She bent to gently lift into her arms a bundle of auburn fur.

Keir's eyes narrowed on the little fox who by standing brave against human foes had shown his loyalty—an steps that earned the boy's respect.

"I should've remained at the back." Keir's voice ached with guilty regret.

"Aye, you should have," Evain solemnly agreed.

"But we can never undo a thing done, and 'tis useless to so rue something past that it prevents us from moving forward and proving ourselves able to do better the next time."

Evain rested an encouraging hand on the boy's shoulder. And when gray-mist eyes lifted, the sorcerer responded with a smile of forgiveness.

Keir squared his shoulders with renewed determination to demonstrate himself worthy of trust and quietly asked, "What can we do to escape your trackers now?" He turned his head from side to side, peering into impenetrable shadows for men he feared still lingering close to their quarry.

Evain put a long forefinger against his lips to signal the need for quiet. Keir was right. Their foes would lurk near in hopes of striking again and more successfully. Evain took steps to bar them from any such action. He lifted his staff and began a low, deep chant.

Recognizing his words for the spell of shielding they were, Anya smiled her delight. Under this conjured veil of invisibility they could escape prying eyes. Yet, when she made to set off on the southerly route through the forest which had already been set by a sorcerer, Evain held out a restraining hand.

"Those we would elude assuredly know our destination and have watched us long enough to expect that we'll continue on in a direct line through the forest." Taking pleasure in the prospect of frustrating their pursuers, Evain's mocking half smile reappeared. "Instead we'll turn about and travel east to the edge of the Mercian border."

Anya frowned. Evain knew the destination; their foes knew it—but she did not and by that lack it was she who suffered frustration. Knowing less even than their enemies, she had no notion which way to turn, either on the literal path or on the road of her life.

Sensing his tender elfling's aggravation with its underlying desolation, Evain saw the downward curl to lips whose petal softness he remembered too vividly and sought to reassure her. Anya's breath caught when Evain's smile deepened into potent charm while an intense, heated gaze of blue smoke settled on her lips with the sweet power of a kiss.

Feeling himself drawn to make the caress a reality both ill-timed and forbidden, Evain abruptly broke their visual link. For Anya the sundering was painful. Between the dawn's devastating acknowledgment that Evain viewed any bond with her as impossible and this twilight loosing upon her of a potent charm, sleeping or waking, she had tarried in a muddled bog of despair and hope—vastly divergent emotions reinforced by these two events.

"Mayhap . . ." Evain forced himself not only to think but to speak of sobering strategies which must not be waylaid. "We'll take our enemies' own roads to the palace they *seem* intent on preventing us from reaching." Considering the number of times these foes had run to escape open conflict with him, Evain had come to believe it was more likely that they meant to drive them nearer. Into a trap? Leastways such had been his assumption until that pattern was broken by the foiled but doubtless honest attempt to steal away the maiden precious to him.

Anya forced herself to concentrate on the meaning of Evain's words. Recognizing his plan's offer of a plausible escape, Anya nodded. Shafts of sunlight penetrated their thick woodland cover to caress a cloud of hair the pale, glowing shade of moonbeams.

Keir saw his companions come to an agreement and frowned. Having no knowledge of the magic which had been wrought, he couldn't see how veering into the forest at the same point and in the same direction as their opponents would help in eluding those very trackers.

"You promised your trust and willingness to obey," Evain reminded the boy. "Do you mean to do better at keeping that oath?"

Further errant beams danced over another blond head, though this the gold of the sun itself, as Keir instantly nodded. How else when already once he had failed in answer to a trusted sorcerer's request?

Chapter
10

The setting sun's bright hues had faded into the purple shades of a summer's dusk. No clouds blocked the first glimmer of starshine overhead. Yet, as a sorcerer led his companions down the border between a quiet vale's tilled land and the forest, their feet were hidden by tendrils of ground mists escaped from the trap of the woodland's dense vegetation.

Evain was dispirited by the fact that though they had walked for another full night and day their zigzagging route meant they were now farther from their goal than when they'd set out. Under the certain fact of this necessary diversion's additional delay to his quest and the ogre of failure it roused, he didn't hear inner voices uttering fervent warnings.

"What ill fate brings you to my farm?" The challenge was issued by a sturdily built man standing as immovable as a rock in their path and holding a menacing pitchfork as if it were a spear.

"My husband and I," Anya quietly spoke while slipping her hand into the crook of Evain's arm, forestalling his reach for the hilt of a sword, "are making a pilgrimage to the Shrine of St. Ultred in Wessex."

Seeing suspicious curiosity narrow their human impediment's hazel eyes, Anya floundered for a moment in the desperate search for some reasonable purpose to explain such a journey. "There we mean to beg the saint's intercession on our behalf, in hopes that with his blessing our earnest prayers for a child will be granted."

The ceorl was father to a sizeable brood and so startled by this declaration of infertility made by a clearly young woman that he failed to see a similar confusion in her claimed spouse's expression.

As the man still looked unconvinced, Anya lost no moment in adding, "'Tis a blessing we have thus far been denied." Thick lashes drifted demurely down but not before their challenger had the opportunity to catch a glimpse of anxious hope in emerald depths. It was an honest emotion, though borne of a wish for safe passing rather than a child.

Despite having initially been less than pleased by Anya's implication that he lacked potency, Evain remained silent even when subjected to the farmer's cold scrutiny. Of a certainty the Saxon would expect an immediate denial from any man were so shaming a statement untrue. Thus Evain knew his wordless acceptance of her ploy nearly ensured that their passage would be allowed without a physical challenge—one he would win but a success which would leave too clear a trail behind. In truth, Evain was impressed by Anya's quick wits and the excuse that explained not only their presence here but the southeast journey they'd continue.

"Then the boy?" The still doubtful ceorl could not be easily contented. "Is he not yours?" This question was asked of the husband but the speaker's skepticism was made plain by the shifting of a hazel glance between the man's ebony mane and the child's golden hair—a contrast not even the color stealing shades of dusk could hide.

"Nay," Evain instantly answered, glad that by the light of dawn so many hours past, he'd packed mud about a sorcerer's crystal orb against the possibility of just such an encounter as this. "Keir is my dead sister's son. He is half-Saxon—as is my wife—while I am all of Cymry born. Indeed, 'tis in the Welsh princedom of Talacharn that we reside."

Evain hoped this statement would forestall any question as to why he had not been summoned to join the battle raging between Saxon kingdoms. Like a reverse image reflected by the smooth surface of a pond, this reasoning for his action prompted a question in Evain's mind. How, he wondered, was it that this ceorl was not so employed? The man was beyond the strength of youth but seemed far from being either feeble-witted or shorn of physical strength, as witness the threatening pitchfork. However, Evain was in no position to baldly demand answer to this question.

Keir watched the confrontation in silence while Anya most clearly heard Evain's claim of her as wife and took pleasure in the words despite their falsity. Fervently wishing they could be true, she gazed side-

152

long at her devastatingly handsome companion and was caught unprepared for the farmer's abrupt change of attitude—almost as startling as a Druid's mercurial mood shift.

"Then come, pilgrims." The human impediment's scowl was replaced by a broad, cheerful smile. "Lend me proof that you forgive my waylaying of your honorable mission with a threat of violence by consenting to partake of an evening meal in my humble abode."

With the dropping of a pitchfork's tines to stab only the outer edge of a tilled field, answer was given to Evain's earlier silent question of how the man remained at home in time of war. For the first time it was plain that the ceorl's left arm hung useless at his side.

"I am Durwyn and my wife, Mora, will gladly welcome you. Visitors here are rare and she is often lonely. Though children we have aplenty, each is grown with homes of their own and much nearer the village of Nestwood. So, I pray you will come, eat with us and stay the night in our home as well." He looked hopefully from Keir to the pair so different in coloring. "We've a loft with sufficient space for the boy, and we can offer the two of you the use of our eldest son's bed."

Anya stifled a gasp. In the first instance for the overwhelming prospect of spending all the hours of night so near her beloved. But, second and of more import than that, she well knew Evain's habits. As a Druid he had far rather not tarry in any man-made structure and yet the ceorl was certain to take any refusal of his hospitality as a personal insult.

"We thank you, kind sir." Evain immediately ac-

cepted the offer, as aware of the danger in affronting
the man as was Anya. Yet he refused to take the risk of
answering this Durwyn's implied request for his
name. It was too likely to be recognized even in the
kingdom of Mercia.

Anya sent Keir a telling look warning him against
inadvertently speaking what plainly ought remain
unknown. A head as bright as her own gave an
infinitesimal nod as their host turned to lead the way
across open, moonlit land to his home. Anya surreptitiously held back long enough to motion Noddi to
remain within forest shadows—for a time.

Following Durwyn's path between rows of grain,
Evain cast behind a lingering glance into the woodland's cool haven. Reluctantly he shifted his face
toward fields profaned by men lacking the wisdom
either to seek permission before harvesting nature's
bounty or to thank its spirits for such gifts. Rather,
without regard for the powers they drove into silence
by their actions, Saxons selfishly robbed the land of
every tree and crudely cleaved the earth with their
cold, sharp plows.

Evain watched as the feet of the man ahead, visible
to a sorcerer even in an evening's deepening shades,
sank into the softness of tilled dirt, and he suffered for
the death of deeply furrowed ground. He felt the
hurtful weakening of a Druid's bond with natural
spirits. That pain had not resulted from what every
Druid was taught to fear and warned to prevent—the
tragedy wrought by allowing voiceless powers to go
silent for lack of those able to commune with them.
Nay, 'twas caused by the Saxons' ever-widening grip
on the land. Despite those among their number who
were his friends and even—by marriage—his family,

Evain saw too clearly the cost of the aliens' presence. And, through an earnest search for answers, he'd come to realize that the flow of invaders was unlikely ever to recede or to again leave the land in peace. The fact of their ineradicable blight on his heritage and destiny saddened Evain to the depths of his soul.

Anya sensed Evain's melancholy, understood some small measure of its source, and ached for his sorrow. Unable to comfort or so much as mention the matter in Durwyn's company, she purposefully turned her attention to their destination.

The farmer's house sat on a slight rise in the midst of a field of ripening wheat. As they drew closer Anya's attention was drawn by the easily discernible sight of a small but well-tended garden of herbs and berries to one side of the goodly sized structure's door.

They stepped past the door Durwyn held wide with his good right hand and into an abode illuminated by tallow candles grouped atop a simple table and the central hearth's fire, which emitted more smoke than light. While disposing of cloaks where the host indicated by hanging them from pegs on one side of the door, with deceptive ease Evain also left his staff resting between their folds.

Mora proved to be an amiable woman of such girth as proved this farm must seldom fail to provide abundant harvests. Though it was with considerable difficulty that Mora waddled about her tidy home, the pleasure she derived from receiving visitors was unmistakable.

Mora also proved to be a most talkative woman and rarely stopped babbling while toiling to make guests welcome. Each visitor was provided first with springwater to rinse away travel grime and then with mugs of ale to quench the thirst their hostess knowingly stated was the inevitable cost of a summer day's dusty journey.

Between freshly washed hands Keir gingerly held the vessel of grayish brown pottery and watched as Evain quaffed a good measure. The boy reminded himself that—for the sake of proving himself worthy of training to Druidic power—whatever the sorcerer did, he must follow. Carefully restraining a grimace of distaste roused by the odor alone, he quashed his reluctance and took a sip. As the bitter liquid washed over his tongue Keir was thankful for having been given a lesser amount. He was even more thankful no one noticed lips that pursed against the taste.

"Come." Their hostess bustled about the visitors, shooing them toward the crudely formed benches flanking a use-smoothed table. "Sit or the meal will go cold."

Anya obeyed, sitting with Evain on one side and Keir on the other. Terribly aware of her supposed-husband's nearness, she gave unmerited attention to the woman slowly making her way to take a place on the table's opposite side.

"Had I known there'd be more than Durwyn and me," the woman chatted on, "I'd have made a wider variety of dishes."

"'Tis a bountiful meal and welcome to we who have survived on meager rations." Anya assured the woman while silently wondering what more could possibly have been prepared when already the table near groaned beneath the meal's weight. It was no wonder the woman was so large. Spread before them lay thick slabs of freshly roasted pork, berries from the careful-

ly tended patch seen on entering the house, near a loaf
of bread for each person, plus hunks of cheese and a
variety of salad greens and herbs.

"Aye, too true." Durwyn gave Anya a mock grimace
as he settled across from her, absently lifting a useless
arm to comfortably rest on his lap. "My Mora still
cooks in such quantities as to fill her whole brood—
though they've long been absent from our table."

"Not so." Taming a grin, Mora refuted her spouse's
claim with exaggerated indignation. "Our daughters
and the wives of sons off to the king's war visit often
and bring their own families. And since we never
know when they'll come, I like always to be prepared."

Durwyn looked to Evain and lifted his good shoulder in feigned resignation.

Earlier, while guests washed, Durwyn had told his
wife of their purpose in traveling to an abbey. Now
with the subject of children raised, Mora felt justified
in speaking on the matter to the young woman foolish
to be so soon worried. "If you would have a babe, you
must eat and put padding on them bones.

"To bear many children, you'll need a healthy
measure more." Though suspecting only patience was
needful, in sympathy and with the confidence of
experience, Mora reinforced advice she deemed cru-
cial. "I know. I've borne near a score and though six
we lost, thirteen still live today." Mora was proud of
this accomplishment.

Anya nodded acknowledgment of the justified
pride. Her mother, Lady Brynna, was a sorceress and
healer. And yet, it was from a sorceress's own experience and that of the women and children whose
ailments Anya had aided in treating that she knew

how common it was for babes to expire afore they'd lived a single year—and how oft either they or their mother failed to survive the birthing.

"Eat up—" Mora again motioned the slender girl and continued her urging until Anya obeyed.

Despite Mora's talk of visits by their children Durwyn felt he'd been isolated on this farm at the outer edge of Mercia's cultivated lands for an endless time with his wife as sole companion. Now given the opportunity for conversation beyond the scope of Mora's limited resources, he turned to his male visitor.

"You've done a deal of traveling, yes?" In his desire for talk on matters of greater import than the subject of his wife's chattering, Durwyn probed for news more directly than he might elsewise have done.

The central hearth's fire silhouetted the black-clad man, who cautiously nodded a mane as raven-dark.

"Then you must have news of how the war goes." Though Durwyn's meal was near consumed, his hunger for information was poorly hidden.

"Sadly, 'tis not so." Evain spoke untruths only under great need, and under current circumstances were unnecessary. Although Evain empathized with their host's wish to learn more of deeds threatening absent sons with mortal' peril, he honestly knew nothing of value to share.

"While fetching Keir from his home in the shire of Throckenholt," Evain quietly explained, pushing aside his empty wooden trencher, "Anya and I had contact with none save those left behind by warriors absent to participate in the conflict. All in that place were as anxious for news as you or I—and as lacking in any reliable source from which to obtain the information sought."

Disappointment dragged the corners of Durwyn's mouth down into a drooping frown while he nodded acceptance of that sad fact, a reflection of the circumstances which had spawned his own need to hear more. However, Durwyn willingly shared what he knew.

"We are not entirely outside the flow of information and on occasion hear a few interesting morsels, although little since came the news of our king's alliance with Prince Mathru of Gwyll. From that moment there's been naught but uncertain gossip of a possible bond with Cadwalla of Wessex—but only if Bishop Wilfrid succeeds with his negotiations between two royal benefactors."

Two royal benefactors? Evain restrained the fierce, dark scowl that had terrified many a man and froze his expression into a mask of polite interest. Whatever else was true, he was certain Wilfrid would not so name Northumbria's King Aldfrith. Rather, it was likely that if the bishop were to win his way, between them Ethelred of Mercia and Cadwalla of Wessex would see Aldfrith destroyed.

Anya recognized Evain's unaltered expression as a mask, and having felt him tense at the mention of this enemy of old, her eyes surreptitiously studied the stunning man so near. Though very young at the time of the bishop's shaming defeat, many a time she'd heard the tale repeated. Indeed, Anya had heard it so oft that she could never be certain where memory ended and story began. In either case it was an undeniable fact that Evain's sister, Llys, and her husband, Adam, had been the primary focus of those events. Moreover, they were deeds in which Anya's parents had participated and during which Glyndor died, leaving a mighty sorcerer's staff to Evain's care.

"Would that I knew if rumors were facts." Durwyn sighed his fervent wish but won merely a vague nod from the man to whom he spoke. The dark guest's obvious physical strength left Durwyn silently ruing the fact that the man was not amongst the Mercian army's ranks.

Evain heard words which neither offered answer nor possessed the power to draw him from a well of bleak thoughts. Long had he wondered what seemingly senseless purpose drove Mercian warriors to steal Adam away, breaking their normal pattern of attacking and killing all Northumbrian foes. He was pleased for Llys's sake. And yet, as months passed with no request for ransom, Evain's concern had grown over the deed's unknown but ominous purpose. He'd never doubted that the reasoning behind it would eventually be revealed, and now with news of the bishop's involvement, it had, although doubtless earlier than its perpetrators intended.

"What I cannot ken . . ." Durwyn made a further stab at regaining the ebony-haired visitor's attention. ". . . is the bishop's hatred of all things Druid. 'Struth, by the heat of his feelings 'twould seem the pious fool—" Durwyn bit back the word, plainly embarrassed at having spoken what could be interpreted as a blasphemy, then rephrased his wrong to continue. "The bishop actually believes . . . nay, he fears such powers as which, if ever they existed, must surely have long since been driven into darkness by the coming of Christian light."

Anya fought to restrain words that sprang to her lips. She badly wanted to lecture Durwyn with her certainty that the powers a Druid summoned from nature had as their source the same God all Christians worshiped. Yet without lengthy and likely dangerous explanations of how she'd come to be certain 'twas true, the ceorl would merely be shocked and deem her as unbalanced as the bishop.

While his elfling struggled, Evain lowered his gaze to shield the blue flames of anger earned by the suggestion that any Druid would flee like a whipped dog. It was the Saxon race's lack of respect for nature that would drive the earth into the darkness of those untaught. Evain concentrated on hands so tightly curled in his lap that they were white with the strength of their joined grip until he sensed the deepening curiosity roused in their hosts by a lingering silence.

To reduce and scatter the tension, Evain spoke in a carefully tempered tone. "Is this a matter on which you've heard Bishop Wilfrid speak?"

"Nay," Durwyn admitted, welcoming this end to the inexplicable tension of the moment past. "But King Ethelred assigned Wat, my eldest son, to the bishop's entourage, and Wat reports his temporary master is forever warning all who come near that such heathen beliefs are an abomination to God. And I ask you, how is it that a bishop can be so thoroughly consumed by fables and deceptions? Can you, can anyone explain the reason for his odd behavior?"

Black brows arched as Evain answered, speaking only the truth and yet certain 'twas safe to do so as he'd learned truth was seldom believed. "Surely you've heard tales told of Bishop Wilfrid's confrontation with such powers?"

"Aye." Durwyn's good shoulder shrugged dismissively. "But then they are *only* tales."

"Mayhap." Evain nodded, amused that Durwyn deemed the stories of the actual events naught but a fantasy created to entertain children.

Anya's breath had stopped when Evain risked suggesting the bishop's dangerous enmity borne of its very source. To forestall further fearsome exchanges, she feigned a yawn. It won the end she sought when Mora instantly spoke.

"Ah, you poor dears. You must be weary after your day's journey. I pray you will forgive we lonely fools for keeping you here at table so long and away from the rest for which you must yearn."

When his wife leaned her great weight on the table and rose to her feet, Durwyn had little option but to join her, although he would rather have continued his discussion of interesting matters with their dark guest.

Soon Keir was settled in the half loft above with Evain's unspoken hope that he would find a more peaceful rest than had oft proven true. And while Mora cleared the table and doused candles, their host banked the dwindling flames. In those moments the visiting pair stretched out on a narrow pallet against one wall. Evain then swirled his cloak out to spread over both himself and the maiden he'd claimed as wife for the length of this night.

Beneath a cover carrying her love's scent, Anya rested in sweet contentment. In the shadows left by a carefully buried fire she felt free from curious eyes and angled her face just enough to turn a loving gaze upon the center of all her dreams.

Evain sensed the whisper-light caress of misty green eyes. In need of their healing touch and certain of the protection from impossible temptations provided by the close company of strangers, he answered their silent appeal. His reward was the tender smile blooming on soft lips whose nectar he would taste forever.

Anya gloried in having summoned her beloved sorcerer with a wordless call even though he almost immediately turned his attention away. She closed her eyes, determined to soak in the warmth of his nearness, a blessing unlikely to be hers once this quest was done. She blocked the ache of that truth with a determination to enjoy the pleasure of this temporary bond for as long as it was hers.

Evain sought to bar further such exchanges with a review of important revelations newly learned. By knowing that Bishop Wilfrid was involved in Adam's peril the explanation for his taking was as clear as the reason why the same band had tried to take Anya as well. The bishop plainly blamed Druids for his losses. And how better to take revenge against those he deemed responsible for his having been shamed and driven from his see—and the consequent reduction of his wealth—than to imperil those whom the perpetrators loved? In the bishop's hatred for all who adhered to Druidic beliefs Evain recognized a personal threat . . . and a warning to take great care.

Serious thoughts and ominous dangers were important but even they could not indefinitely quash Evain's awareness of the sweet elfling proven to be a beguiling enchantress able to disturb his days and govern his dreams. Holding motionless and staring into the dark above massive beams, he clenched his fingers into fists to prevent them from reaching out to stroke luminescent skin and silk soft hair too well remembered. In truth, 'twas memories of their heated embrace by a moon silvered spring kept him from finding rest until long after her breathing gentled into the steady rhythm of travel weary sleep.

Though dressed in garb little better than a thrall's rags, Torvyn was a well-born thegn and Rolf but a peasant warrior. Still Rolf resented having been summoned to meet and report to this skinny man of strange habits in a hut on the outer edge of lands belonging to Torvyn's family.

"Had her in my hands, I did." Rolf's thick fingers clenched and bristling brows met in a scowl. "Had her in my hands . . . until her black companion appeared." He wouldn't mention the small fox.

"So you fled rather than face the sorcerer," Torvyn sneered. "Fled from him yet again."

"Claim you an ability to stand against a wizard's uncanny powers?" Rolf didn't for a moment believe it was true.

Torvyn shrugged. "I would not run from one who is only a man of flesh and blood, of hate and love— subject to the same perils as are we." Moreover, Torvyn silently affirmed, there were ways to do combat without the need to wield either sword or dagger.

Rolf refused to be drawn into a debate he would surely lose, a debate on a point doubtless intended to further denigrate him. Torvyn hadn't seen what Rolf had seen, and Rolf chose not to share his tale of a disappearing horse and maid with a man apparently determined to disbelieve such a thing could be true.

"No matter the circumstances," Torvyn continued after the hefty guardsman allowed the silence to lengthen. *"You* must go to Bishop Wilfrid at Ecley."

Rolf firmly shook his head.

"Aye, it must be *you*." Torvyn would not be gainsaid. "Our impious churchman knew the task to be yours to fulfill and you must be the one to explain a failure."

Rolf wanted to refuse the command more than he'd ever wanted anything but Torvyn's words were true. The failure was his doing and his to explain—he could only hope that the bishop, as a believer in the sorcerer's powers, would understand. This, Rolf knew, was a fool's dream.

"But with news of your unwelcome failure you can give good news as well." Torvyn made the offer with an impish smile that Rolf received with disgust. "Caution the bishop to patience with my assurance that, by waiting the length of two days, he will be presented with the maid. And as she is the lodestone, not long after more of those whom he seeks will follow."

Rolf glowered. Confessing his failure to the bishop would be an unpleasant deed but the act of admonishing the arrogant man to be patient would be too fearsome a feat. Asides, Torvyn's succeeding with the task he had failed to perform could only make him look the worse.

Give the message he must, but put a spike in the thegn's plans he also would.

Chapter
11

"Midday is past," Evain commented, gazing up through an opening in the leafy cover above. "We'll stop here for rest and a light repast." At the morn's outset Evain had recanted his jesting suggestion that they travel Mercian roads to reach their goal and instead led his companions back into woodland wilds, forestalling additional encounters with curious locals.

After leaning his staff against a huge trunk and dropping his satchel, the sorcerer lowered himself to rest on a soft cushion of tangled blades. The other two lost no time in doing the same. Before dawn's light arrived to do battle with a cloud-filled sky their small party had departed the farm and walked into a dense purple fog which soon hid them from the view of the ceorl and his wife.

Anya could not rue the circumstances which had gifted her with a night so near Evain, yet she couldn't help but be relieved by their return to the forest trail with its prevention of further tense exchanges. Now after hours of steady walking her feet hurt and back ached, and she welcomed this halt in a grassy spot beneath the widespread limbs of three oaks. Lying back and resting her head atop arms crossed behind, she also welcomed a young animal who promptly stretched out at her side. Having half expected Noddi's return to untamed ways, on reentering the forest she'd been pleased to find the faithful fox pup waiting.

"If we take a southwesterly route and travel in a direct line," Evain said as calmly as if of no more import than any trivial remark, "we'll be at the walls of Isca by the morrow's nooning hour."

"Isca?" Anya abruptly sat up, green eyes meeting the unwavering sapphire gaze of the dark man leaning against a massive oak. It wasn't the name, only vaguely familiar, which caught her full attention. Nay, 'twas the fact that this was the first time an actual end point to their quest had been unequivocally given. Since their journey's first day she'd longed for this answer but had known better than to ask it of a Druid uncomfortable with stating anything of a certainty one way or another. And though willing to challenge Evain on many matters, she was loath to ask anything of a sorcerer that would test the bonds of his Druidic training.

"'Struth." Evain nodded, a potent half smile gently mocking the intense curiosity of the maid he'd suspected frustrated by an inability to exercise her habit of learning by quiet listening. "We go to the ruins of a stone fort abandoned by ancient invaders long since come and gone."

Evain's gratification over the prospect of at last reaching his destination was tempered by a sober understanding 'twould mean the real challenge's start, the moment when he must undertake the difficult feat required of him. Determined not to burden the other two with problems they could nowise solve, Evain exercised a sorcerer's control to close his expression into an unreadable mask.

Seeing that the origin of one fragment of information was unwilling to give more, Anya dropped her gaze. She absently stroked auburn fur while studying an intricate pattern cast on the forest's uneven floor by what light of cloudy day penetrated branches tightly entwined overhead.

Slowly Anya became aware of a prickling sensation of being watched and shifted attention to her young companion. However, Keir's gaze was narrowed with singular intensity upon green blades being plaited by nimble fingers. In observing Keir, she realized that although she'd initially thought him like her younger brother—doubtless due to their similar ages—he rarely exhibited Cub's uncontrolled childish energies. Indeed, the ever quietly watching Keir more closely resembled herself at the same age.

While patiently sitting, Keir was filled with questions about their unfamiliar destination and what uncertain deeds were meant to follow but had quashed the great urge to seek explanations from companions sunk in calm pools of silence. Indeed, he'd learned enough to know the sorcerer resented being forced to state anything in definite terms. Yet when he realized Anya was looking at him he glanced up to meet the gentle warmth of her attention and opened his mouth to ask . . .

A cold smile curled an unseen watcher's thin lips with a pleasure rooted in the good fortune of having stumbled across his goal so near to where he'd begun the search. He had heard the words exchanged between the man and woman but from his vantage point saw only the two adults. So, when the woman turned to gaze in his direction, he feared himself discovered and purposefully blundered forward, making as much noise as possible.

"Claud!" Anya gasped, eyes widening upon the awkward man earlier encountered as a bow-wielding bandit of murderous intent.

"Thank the saints!" Pleased that the lady remembered the false name earlier given, Torvyn burst into the glade—and found himself facing a sorcerer's bared blade. It was a wordless threat to which he gave an unexpected answer. Bony hands came together in an odd, sharp little clap of delight. "I've found you at last."

"Found us?" Black brows met in a fierce frown echoed by the thunder of Evain's questions. "What daft impulse sent you my way . . . despite the warning I gave that to cross my path again could have deadly consequences?"

Torvyn dropped to his knees before the powerful figure. The man was truly a terrifying sight, what with strong legs firmly planted in a wide stance while one hand held a wickedly glittering blade against the background of a broad, black-covered chest and the other gripped a strange, fearsome stave. Almost could Torvyn believe him the sorcerer he claimed to be.

"Pray forgive me, gentle lord." Torvyn's well-honed acting abilities were little necessary to infuse these words with a fear honestly felt. "After our first meet-

ing I came to believe that the safest place in all
Christendom was to stand within your shadow. For
that purpose have I followed you since our first
meeting." Pausing, the speaker spread his hands wide
with vulnerable palms uplifted. "Leastways I did until
two days past when I heard your lady cry out and
thereafter found myself utterly alone. I've searched
ceaselessly until now I've found you at last."

Standing behind Evain, Anya grinned at Claud's
unspoken plea to remain in their company. The man
was clumsy but his reasoning was sound. She certainly
agreed that the safest place to be was in close proximity to Evain.

"I thought you aspired to be a forest bandit?"
Evain's each word was covered with a thick frost of
icy contempt.

"With naught but a small dagger?" Torvyn wryly
asked, lifting the same crude implement Evain had
tossed into the undergrowth when last they'd met.
"Asides," he whined, "as you rightly stated, my skills
are sorely limited."

"Then return to your home." Unmoving and with
eyes the coldest of blue ice, Evain counseled the man.
"Go back and harvest your crops." Evain was certain
he already had too many traveling with him into
waiting danger. And he was positive no rightful reason
existed for him to accept the company of this person
last met as foe and thus proven untrustworthy.

"My home is naught but a pile of cinders," Torvyn
announced with a wail of sorrow he hoped not over-
done. "And my land lies between two great forces
poised for battle."

Sapphire eyes narrowed consideringly upon the
abject figure. How was it, Evain wondered, that the

decidedly inept yet healthy man at his feet was serving in neither army?

Innocent heart believing he'd found another victim of such wrongs as he himself had suffered, Keir's sympathy was instantly roused. Without considering the wisdom of the action, he moved to the kneeling man's side.

"I, too, lost my home to flames . . . and my family as well. Have you family?"

Hiding a flash of excitement behind a feigned mournful expression, Torvyn gazed at the blond lad he hadn't earlier noticed and slowly shook his head. "My wife died with the birthing of our first child the summer last."

Torvyn realized that here was the missing boy whose absence had so upset both a prince and a bishop. Now with this discovery, the praise of both men could be earned. Oft had Torvyn been told he ought be a mummer, so great were his talents for dissembling. A fine thing that, for it was necessary to skillfully wield these gifts to conceal a deep satisfaction for all the possibilities opening before him. Beyond the others' well-earned praise and even beyond the valuable prize of his king's greater respect and goodwill, he could justly demand a worthy reward from the arrogant bishop. And he would.

"Then come, Claud." Anya deemed Evain unlikely to make the offer and quickly spoke. "Join our midday meal." Mora had insisted on sending with them large portions of the foodstuffs that remained from the past night's abundant repast and they could easily afford to share their bounty with this poor man.

"Thank you, sweet lady. Plainly your beauty is matched by your generosity." Claud took a dainty hand to fervently kiss its back, an action that earned Anya's shy smile—and an even deeper frown from Evain.

An overwhelming feeling of something terribly wrong settled over Evain. However, he found himself in the rare position of doubting his own responses, of fearing his judgment clouded by the sight of another man being gifted with his elfling's tender smile. Was Claud merely the presence he'd long sensed ever close behind? Likely so. And as Evain had felt no danger emanating from that presence, it was also likely that the only threat he suffered now was personal resentment of another man too near his beloved.

Jealousy Evain found difficult to admit. Such emotions, Glyndor had taught him, were for the weak-willed. And he assuredly was not that. Still, Evain coveted the maid and wished for the power to see her reserved only for himself. Sapphire eyes clenched tightly shut. Really, he must smother these feelings. Evain's destiny prevented him from claiming Anya. He must release her. The prospect brought a stab of anguish. Nay, worse even than that, he would have to stand by and watch Anya bound forever to another man.

Anya saw Evain's hands clench into mighty fists but misassigned his anger's source solely to the unexpected newcomer. To waylay any possible confrontation, she reached for her bag and pulled from it a loaf of bread, a big slab of cheese, and the smaller sack she'd coddled all morn. It contained fresh sweet berries.

Evain forced a smile that softened to gentleness as he stepped to Anya's side. He handed around strips of salt meat from the store Durwyn had insisted they carry away with them—provisions he'd inwardly felt guilty for taking from people who he much doubted would be so generous were they aware of their visitors' true identities.

After the meal was done each drank a measure of water from a nearby stream. Then, with covetous eyes Torvyn watched Evain fill a particularly fine, silver-capped drinking horn. And, having not been specifically denied the right, the less than welcome newcomer took up the last position in the small retinue trailing a sorcerer along an unmarked path moving steadily southwest.

The journey continued throughout the afternoon and beyond the span of time during which the setting sun won a minor victory over the day's unrelenting clouds by tingeing them with a rosy hue. Evain was anxious to reach his destination yet knew that after a day's marching, Anya and Keir were worn with fatigue. He suspected the past night's rest had left them only the more aware of a weariness hourly increasing. 'Twas a situation he feared might result in foolish actions endangering his objective. Thus it was that as dusk's shadows intensified, he signaled them to halt by raising one powerful arm. A gust of wind caught his black cloak and carried it out to float like a raven's wing.

When the group was gathered in yet another small glade, once again foodstuffs were distributed. While tired people ate in silence, Anya was amused to see Keir sharing a portion of his food with Noddi. Moreover, the fox pup was plainly as weary as his human companions and remained at the boy's side when, after hunger had been appeased, Keir rolled up in his cloak, rested his head atop his bag of possessions, and dropped off to sleep.

Deeming such an action his wisest course, Claud also pulled his cloak closer, stretched out atop a cushion of thick grass, and closed his eyes. But Evain rose and moved to stand gazing into the formless dark in the direction they had been traveling. Anya watched her beloved sorcerer and knew that he'd still be going onward were it not for the exhaustion of his companions. That fact acknowledged, she thought Evain would be justified in wishing himself unencumbered on his important mission. Lacking such hindrances she'd no doubt but that within the span of time between the quest's beginning and now he could've made the journey, freed Adam and seen them both returned safely to Northumbria.

Along with a courageous spirit unafraid to take chances, Anya possessed an inner strength able to admit her errors unflinching. Thus, she again assumed responsibility for this wrong. In the first instance it was by her willfulness that Evain had been forced to accept her company. And without her tumble from Blossom, Keir was unlikely to have ever stumbled across a sorcerer's path. To add to those mistakes, not only had she lost Blossom but she was responsible for Claud's continuing presence.

A dragging tiredness was defeated by Anya's frustration over the inability to immediately *do* anything to right her wrong by aiding Evain's cause. Nonetheless, she was determined that in the end she would. But how? To consider the matter more carefully she felt a desperate need for leastways a short period alone with the spirits ensouling all nature, free from any possibility of curious eyes. Knowing she would not be challenged for claiming privacy to attend personal needs, Anya rose and quietly slipped into night shadows.

Anya absently moved deeper into the wildwood while improvising a silent chant to unseen powers, entreating their aid in finding some method to ease Evain's difficult path. Soon was heard the restful sound of gently flowing water. The peaceful rippling proved an irresistible lure, drawing her on through the dense woodland's luxuriant foliage. Attuned to the stream's melody, Anya wasted no thought on useless debate of either the wisdom or direction of her course. She wove her way between huge trees and tender saplings until, when the source of the sound seemed within an arm's reach, she faced what appeared to be a solid wall of vegetation. It was formed of amazingly tall rosebushes plainly host to as many thorns as fragrant flowers and thoroughly entangled with abundant ivy.

While Anya stood startled into a moment of immobility, a single tendril of ivy tumbled from a high point on the barrier. Without an instant's hesitation, she took the vine into her hand and gently tugged. The thick shield of fragrant blossoms and shiny leaves parted. She stepped a brief distance beyond the opening and released the vine. It closed behind her. Before Anya flowed a brook that glittered with dancing lights despite the absence of a cloud hidden moon while on its either side nature provided a semicircular wall. Filled with a restoring sense of peace, Anya was certain that this magical haven was nature's answer to her plea. She immediately offered a brief chant of gratitude for having been permitted the privilege of its seclusion—something she knew would be denied any lacking a bond with such powers. And was proof that even if not so strong as her mother or Evain, she did possess such a bond.

Wrapped in nature's embrace and feeling utterly safe from prying eyes, Anya freed plaited hair and ran her fingers through shining tresses. Next she released the seed pearl brooch holding her cloak fastened at the throat. It dropped and fell a safe distance back from the water before she moved to sink down on a moss softened bank.

Anya dipped a portion of her gown's hem in cool water and used its refreshing coolness to cleanse her face and throat. It merely made the rest of her seem uncomfortably warmer. With the faint melody of flowing waters came a powerful urge to submerge herself totally in refreshing liquid. But with an awareness that Evain might well come to seek her out were she gone too long she forestalled the desire. Indeed, even now she'd an odd sense of Evain's nearness . . . likely wishful thinking. And no matter, she could leastways refresh herself with the cool liquid.

By the bond shared between Evain and his elfling, wrong or right, he had been aware the moment she left the campsite. He'd patiently awaited her return until she was dangerously later than ought be permitted. Then, though Evain sensed no danger near to her, he couldn't take the chance that his feelings for her had warped their tune and allowed her to walk into peril. Taking his staff and by a seldom inaccurate sense of where she was to be found he easily traced her course.

Rarely was a sorcerer surprised but Evain was startled to find Anya in the midst of a secret haven in the norm impenetrable to humans lacking the knowledge of a Druid. Watching the dainty figure kneel at the water's edge, he wondered how she'd happened upon it. Was it possible protective forces recognized her as the daughter of a sorceress? Or had she merely chanced upon its beauty? He'd been taught 'twas an impossible feat for those lacking a hereditary bond. But after Keir's amazing appearance in an equally well-shielded cave he'd cause to either question the rule or to fear that the encroachment of Saxons had so weakened natural powers as to permit what once had been denied.

Serious considerations were driven from Evain's mind by the sight of Anya stripping off her deep green kirtle and then fingers returning to her throat to begin unlacing the pale undergown's front closure. The tender maiden seemed intent on stepping nude into the stream. His apprehension of a deed hazardous to his self-control twined with the flaring of a fierce temper. How could she be so naive as to fail in recognizing inherent dangers? As one untrained, she couldn't possibly know of Druidic spells shielding her from the leering eyes of constantly searching foes or of the untrustworthy Claud too disgustingly near. Moreover, by past experience, she ought to have expected the coming of one already proven a threat to her chastity—himself.

"Cast aside any daft notion of again bathing unguarded in the wild."

At the sound of her beloved's dark velvet roar so near, Anya made to leap up. Unfortunately, 'twas not a wise choice. The mossy bank was wet and slippery. She fell back, landing on her derriere . . . hard.

"Oh, poppet—" Evain rushed forward and dropped to his knees, reaching out to sweep the injured maid into his arms. "Have I caused you harm?" The question required no answer. He already knew his temper to be responsible for the pain of this innocent temptress long the center of his dreams. Filled with self-disgust, he sat back with her across his lap and absently began rubbing the portion of her anatomy that had taken the blow.

Despite the endearment most oft given a child, Anya refused to question the source of this gift and snuggled closer to bury her face into the crook between Evain's shoulder and throat. Reveling in a nearness she feared would too soon be taken from her, Anya closed her eyes and purposely sank into the welcome realm of unthinking sensations. Pressing soft lips to the skin of a throat that seemed to take fire beneath the touch, she planted curious little kisses in its curve before giving into temptation and letting her tongue venture out. Anya tasted the flavor of skin vibrating with the groan rumbling from his depths as she slowly moved her mouth down to nuzzle at the lacings holding the neck of his tunic closed.

Under that tantalizing touch flames coursed through Evain's blood. One hand lifted to tangle in the wealth of moonshine hair at the base of Anya's neck and gently urged her head back until he could claim the teasing mouth with his own. He captured her adventurous tongue and taught her anew the stormy depths of the need she'd evoked in them both.

With innocent abandon, Anya twisted to press fully against Evain's strong chest while a tiny, inarticulate sound welled up from her core. But it wasn't enough and inquisitive fingers daringly burrowed beneath the obstruction of his tunic to smooth over the satiny plains of his back, savoring the feel of its heat and iron thews.

Evain went still beneath her touch. He found a dangerous delight in her enticing caress while in the same moment was too deeply aware of the burning temptation of lush curves. It brought potent memories of their last embrace when despite a never removed tunic her tempting flesh had imprinted a seductive brand upon his wide chest. More than anything he wanted to rid them both of clothing and truly experience the pleasure of her body melding with his. . . .

This delicious play, sweet and devastatingly hot, forced upon him an unwelcome awareness of what was happening—all too enjoyable but utterly wrong. Muttering faintly violent words she could nowise understand, his eyes clenched shut against erotic sights dangerous to his control as he unclasped her arms to gently yet relentlessly push her away.

Anya, still in his lap, sensed Evain's tenuous hold on self-restraint. And as he'd said they would reach their destination on the morrow she knew this too certain to be her last opportunity for winning from him all the secret joys she'd no hope of finding with another.

"I love you." Without bothering to struggle against the inflexible grip forcing a cold distance between them, Anya spoke with simple honesty. "I always have and I always will."

Evain's eyes snapped open. He wanted to tell Anya she was still a child and too young to make such a claim but the quiet truth of a love selflessly bestowed prevented him from denying precious words. 'Twas a gift he'd hungered to possess as fiercely as ever the pleasures of her exquisite body. Yet, knowing the impossibility of giving a like commitment, he had hoped leastways to save his sweet elfling from the same anguish of doomed love that his destiny demanded of him.

Anya saw the shadows of unspoken pain turning blue eyes nearly black. Fighting his hold's suddenly lessened restriction, she wrapped comforting arms about him and lay her head on his shoulder.

Evain crushed the dainty form against the broad strength of his own. Burrowing his face into the wealth of fragrant curls on her shoulder, he hoarsely whispered, "My destiny forbids our bond." This was the statement of an aching loss Evain feared himself unable to bear.

"Nay, the bond you fear forbidden is the lifelong bond of our being wed." Though still host to a likely forlorn hope of altering his belief of her unworthiness as wife for a sorcerer, she couldn't let slip from her grasp this chance to seduce him into sharing with her the sweet pleasures only love could provide. "'Tis not that bond which I seek this night."

Her bold statement shocked a half smile from Evain even as she began again to nibble at his throat. "Beware the baiting of a sorcerer with innocent wiles." Strong hands tangled in bright tresses to pull her head back until he could gaze down at her, sparks of blue fire glittering in his eyes. "Once roused, my tempest is not easily tamed."

"Then take me. Give me this one moment out of time to treasure against all the loneliness to come." Quiet desperation filled Anya's words. Closing her mind to the possibility of this "one moment" bearing a fruit unwelcome to him, she joined her mouth to his with the sweetness of love and fire of unrestrained passion.

Evain's warning had not been lightly given and the enticing beauty's untutored, reckless surrender destroyed the last fragments of a sorcerer's restraint. As if they'd a will of their own, his arms swallowed her into a fierce embrace while he returned her kiss with a warm assault that searched within parted lips. And when his mouth trailed liquid flame down her throat to the laces which she'd been working to unfasten when he arrived, Anya sank headlong into a hungry blaze, arching deeper into his hold while tingles of hot pleasure rippled through her.

Deeply aware of Anya's trembling hunger, a rough shudder ran through Evain as well while he laid her back against this magical haven's moss soft carpet. Rational warnings were lost in the smoky haze of desire as he welcomed her justification for taking what he desperately wanted. Though he knew it for a mistake, knew he would rue it later, he would give them both a single hour of despairing love's hottest fires and passions fulfilled.

With an awkward haste uncommon to him, Evain tugged wider her gown's laces, opening its front closure. A masculine satisfaction deepened his potent smile as a ravenous sapphire gaze moved over her luscious bounty. Losing no further moment, with the experience of having rid her of this gown once before, he soon had it stripped away—but this time not with fear of forbidden temptations but with the promise of a sweet satisfaction.

His burning scrutiny swept Anya up in a vortex of blue flames and when Evain's fingertips brushed

down the soft curve of her cheeks and across passion
swollen, half-parted lips, a faint gasp escaped. Slender
arms enticingly lifted in a wordless plea but Evain
held back from this untutored temptress the more
powerful for her unfeigned needs. In the first instance,
he was not by nature a selfish man and now, in this
joining with his precious elfling, he meant to tame his
own fiery hungers. He must if he were to succeed in
seeing that their single experience of mutual love
would be for them both one so memorable, so pleasur-
able they could live on it for a lifetime.

Even while striving to slow the driving beat of his
heart, Evain's hands began an adventure. Palm-flat,
they lightly brushed a slow searing path up her sides
from the first gentle swell of her hips to the sensitive
flesh beneath arms that had settled about his wide
shoulders. Up and then down, smiling through his
own intense excitement, he repeated the action again
and again, moving fractionally closer together until
the heels of his hands imperceptibly brushed against
the sides of her breasts.

When at last Evain's fingers slipped over the velvet
softness of her breasts in a tantalizing, tormentingly
light caress, Anya cried out and instinctively sought to
press them nearer. But Evain once more drew back
and a small whimper escaped Anya's throat until she
realized he meant to strip off his tunic in a single
smooth movement. Curious green eyes watched unblinking but the haste of his actions prevented her
from catching more than a glimpse of his bare chest
and the rippling of powerful muscles. Still, she was
stunned by the male beauty of his form.

Evain immediately lowered himself to lie at Anya's
side and pull her into the hungry cradle of his arms.

She melted against him like wax turned pliant by the heat of the sun. Eyes closed, he savored the reality of so many fantasies—this complete yielding of her supremely soft body to the hard contours of his own. And yet, it wasn't enough. As his mouth trailed the fire of a tender torment over the ripe curves and gentle valleys of her body, breath caught in Anya's throat only to sigh out in little gasps.

Under the shocking delight, Anya's fingers wound tightly into black strands, striving to bring its source even nearer. Evain purposefully drove her deeper into the fire storm's depths, teasing her senses mercilessly until, overwhelmed by blazing sensations, she shifted restlessly against him, wanting to be nearer, wanting something more and certain only her sorcerer could give it to her. Smoothing her hands over the strong muscles of his back, she felt the heavy beat of his heart. Anya clung to him and in the searing heat of their embrace pressed even closer to writhe against him.

A harsh groan escaped Evain's throat and his hands slid down her slender back to pull her tighter. Her enticing, inciting motions pushed him too near the edge of his control. Evain couldn't prevent his body from rocking against Anya's in the magical rhythm as old as time itself, and when she instinctively matched the motion, he knew the inevitable culmination was perilously near.

Abruptly pulling from her arms, Evain fought to see himself rid of the last physical impediment—cross-garters and chaussures. To Anya his withdrawal and the sapphire eyes clenched shut seemed another rejection. She sobbed a protest.

"Don't leave me." Lost in the dark vortex of wicked

sensations, Anya fought to prevent him from deserting her by wrapping her arms about his neck and arching up to brush generous curves across the width of his chest, reveling in the sweet rasp of its wiry curls across sensitive tips. "Please, Evain, don't leave me now."

"I couldn't even if I tried." Evain felt himself drowning in a sea of liquid fire as with trembling gentleness he urged Anya to lie back. Then, sliding one leg between her silken thighs, he shifted to lie full atop her slender length but rested on his forearms to hover above.

Moaning with erotic delight, Anya was aware only of the gentle abrasion of his skin against hers. She tried to draw him closer but in spite of his urgent need to immediately merge their forms completely, Evain fought for a moment's mastery over his desire to see her initiation into passion's sphere a gentle one. He gazed down into eyes darkened to deepest emerald by her wanting of him and watched for the first hint of discomfort as he pressed intimately nearer. . . .

Caught in the tumult of a raging whirlwind summoned by the sorcerer to send her spinning into a myriad of stinging pleasures, Anya gazed into the steady blue flame of his gaze. Hosting a feverish need to be carried deeper into the fiery eye of the tempest, she urged his hips nearer and with a yearning desperation surged upward. Like an abrupt flash of lightning the sudden stab of pain seemed no more than a natural part of the storm's fury. And it was as quickly lost amidst the black thunder of Evain's mastery as with hard, sharp movements he drove them both deeper into a fiery anguish of need. His harsh breathing slid into low growls while he rocked them both beyond sanity and into the deepest abandon where storm and fire meet and crash together, shattering in an explosion of searing sparks and unfathomable ecstasy.

Floating through blissful mists of a sweet contentment never known before, Anya whispered her love. Evain heard the words which, though more precious than any king's golden hoard, were an unintentional condemnation of him. But still he pressed a gentle kiss into her now tangled mass of silk soft hair and held her trembling body close—leastways until she'd descended from the heights of passion's unthinking sphere.

While Anya lingered in the smoke of pleasure's satisfaction, the reality of his unforgivable misdeed washed over Evain with regret. He'd drawn too close to the flame and the all-important barriers built over years had been incinerated. To take what he badly wanted, no matter the cost, he'd accepted a justification he had known was that of a fool. Their storm of passion earned no consoling memory. Rather it worsened the painful, lifelong price he already owed for stealing tempting visions of his beloved. 'Struth, now knowing too well the full measure of a contentment forever denied, those potent memories could only deepen the abyss of despairing loss.

When Anya's breathing steadied into the pattern of untroubled sleep, Evain carefully eased away and began pulling his clothes back on. Then, standing at the beauty's side, he gazed down as she rested in the sweet sleep of innocence and his guilt increased. Although he had enjoyed the intimate company of many females, none had been a threat to his destiny. He'd no more cared for them beyond an evening diversion than they'd sought him for else than an hour's pleasure or the ability to boast of a sorcerer's attentions. Anya was different; Anya he loved. And only gentle Anya held the power to bend a sorcerer's will.

Evain carefully settled Anya's cloak over her too tempting form—the evening would grow ever more chill. Asides, he'd already proven unequal to the task of taming his passion for her. And yet . . . he must, he would prevent a repetition of the honey-sweet folly.

As Evain tucked the cloth tighter around her shoulders, Anya's head tilted to brush a cheek against his strong hand while a sweet smile curved rose pink lips. The hand was snatched away as if her touch seared. Struggling through the warm fog of love and passionate memories, Anya rapidly blinked to gaze up at a lover fully dressed.

"My existence is but one link in a continuous chain—an eternal chain far more important than any of its links." Having moved a pace back and firmly crossed powerful arms over a broad chest as if in defense, he tried to explain. "'Tis a chain I must *not* sunder, for by doing so I fail all that came before and all that are meant to come after."

"I know. . . ." Anya's attempt to assure him that she understood and expected no more of him faded into silence under the forbidding power of eyes gone to blue ice.

"No. How could you possibly know that *you* are the single peril to a commitment demanded of me by my father since near the moment of my birth, a commitment reaffirmed by Glyndor's passing of his stave to me? You, only you have ever . . . could ever . . ." Evain bit the words off. Enough and too much had been clearly stated that ought to have been left in the safe realms of things neither one way nor another.

Evain felt he must go for a time into the darkness, there to seek forgiveness from nature's powers for the deed surely threatening to weaken his link in the chain.

"Wait here in safety until I return."

Without further explanation for his departure, Evain lifted his staff and held it toward the green wall bedecked with roses and thorns. The barrier split open as if parted by the hands of an unseen giant and once he'd stepped through immediately closed.

Anya was again alone in the magical haven but the comfort it had seemed to provide upon her arrival had been diminished by her sorcerer's unpleasant though doubtless true words. She was not upset with Evain for speaking what she'd already known he believed. Anya's despair sprang from her own misdeed. Again she'd allowed selfish wishes to convince her a wrong could be right and had smothered the fact that by giving into her demand Evain would do something he rued. It was no different than when she'd forced him to accept her company on this quest which he could've completed faster and easier without the added burden of her. Nay, there was a difference between the two offenses. Their lovemaking was much more serious and could have a far more lasting effect. The image of a babe with Evain's black hair and blue eyes promptly flashed through her mind. He was unlikely to forgive her for forcing upon him a child bearing even a quarter-strain of Saxon blood. But—her arms instinctively crossed over a flat abdomen—because prayers must be sincere, she couldn't beg God to see no child be born of their union.

Though neither a leaf stirred nor long blade of grass moved, Anya felt as if a cold wind were sweeping over her. She rose and rapidly dressed. To longer stay here in this place where they'd shared the sweet pleasures that would never again be hers was too difficult and would only deepen the pain. She'd safely gotten to this point by herself and could return to their campsite the same way.

Anya stepped to the green wall and again a tendril of ivy fell for her to tug and open the path back into the midnight wildwood. Distracted by bleak thoughts, it was by unconscious memory that she steadily retraced her path through bushes heavy with summer's ripe growth and avoided thick clumps of grass able to tangle her feet. . . .

Thick clumps of grass were able also to cushion Anya's abrupt fall and muffle the sound of the figure hauling away his prize.

Chapter
12

"Take her and make haste." Torvyn motioned toward the limp body bundled inside a homespun blanket and draped over the rear of a massive war-horse. "I will follow on the morrow and lead others into—I have no doubt—welcoming hands."

The gleam of his cohort's vicious grin could barely be seen through the gloom but agreement was made plain enough by the man's nod and the snap of reins urging the destrier into motion.

As the black forms of departing figures disappeared into the wafting tendrils of a hollow's gray haze and blended into the night, Torvyn turned back toward the camp, well pleased with his night's work. It was fortunate that the boy had quickly fallen into a slumber deep enough to permit him to slip away in stealthy pursuit of a sorcerer and the beauty he'd followed.

Torvyn's hunt had not easily won its prey. Indeed, although he carefully searched the area into which the pair had disappeared, they seemed to have vanished into the woodland's night shadows. He'd given up the chase and begun retracing his steps to the camp when the lovely damsel blundered across his path. It had required but a single, sharp tap on a golden head to see her tumble senseless at his feet. The confederate trailing a safe distance behind since first he'd joined the sorcerer's band had been soon summoned to haul the woman away.

Truly, a well-content Torvyn felt he couldn't have planned it better. Their afternoon journey had done him a good service. The abbey at Ecley lay due south and not far distant. His mounted supporter could handily see the lovely maiden delivered to the bishop before dawn broke across the eastern horizon. And on the morrow . . . Torvyn's gloating smile widened.

In the camp still some little distance away, a bulky figure bent over the sleeping form of a boy.

Keir was awakened by the wad of cloth stuffed into his mouth. Choking, he attempted to sit up while at the same time striving to shove the obstruction from his mouth with his tongue. His actions went for naught as a length of cloth was speedily fastened behind his head to hold the muffling gag in place even while his arms were roughly jerked back and tied against his spine.

The rumble of a menacing growl was heard. It was promptly followed by the blur of a wild creature pouncing, then a pained grunt from the brute on the receiving end of Noddi's defensive assault.

Wielding a thick hand possessing the weight of a bludgeon, Rolf smashed the creature which had fastened itself to his wrist. And when the animal thudded to the ground he took pleasure in kicking it aside.

Tightly, painfully bound, Keir's wide blue eyes moved from poor Noddi's limp body to the malicious grin exchanged between the hefty oaf who pulled him to his feet and another who hoisted him up and over a meaty shoulder. Breath knocked from him by the impact, Keir was hastily carried into the forest's gloom.

Evain gazed upon the serene beauty of the rippling stream flowing through the center of a rose and ivy guarded haven . . . and heavily frowned. 'Twas an empty haven. Nary a single sign remained as evidence of what had occurred here—no indication of either the dangerously pleasant misdeed committed here or its unforgettable ecstasy.

Abruptly turning about, Evain's cloak spun around him like a black whirlpool. Anya ought to have listened when he warned her to wait for his return. This close to their goal, the dangers could only have increased. These were hazards whose evidence she'd repeatedly seen.

Blue flames flashed as Evain strode into the forest, hoping Anya had merely returned to their campsite—a deed for which he'd heartily chastise her but which would be a great relief. If she were not there, if harm had befallen his sweet elfling, he'd see that any perpetrator so ill-advised as to assault a sorcerer's own would pay a heavy price.

Moving ever faster toward his goal, Evain's anger grew with each long step. He would summon a storm and call a fierce bolt of lightning down upon such a wretch. . . . He'd . . .

Evain froze midstride. His loss of a Druid's all-important emotional control would prevent him from accomplishing any worthwhile deed. Moreover, to call upon awesome powers in anger could cost a sorcerer dearly. Had rousing a savage storm not cost his mentor, Glyndor, the life of his only son? And once raised, immense calm was required to have any hope of controlling unruly forces and their inherent deadly perils.

Having learned well the lesson that seeking the harsh tempest's fury in anger would too likely end in a ghastly defeat, Evain tempered his justified fury. He would seek retribution in some more controlled and carefully executed manner. He had attained formidable powers by paying homage to their source and by wielding such powers only with deep respect for the spirits that lent them. Any demand made in anger was the betrayal of a Druid's bond with nature, and the raising of a storm's treacherous forces must be invoked for naught save the direst of needs.

Torvyn stared at the view before him with disgust. Save for the small fox lying in an awkward heap, the campsite was empty. Oh, aye, the boy's bag of possessions remained but the boy was gone.

"What ho?" Evain growled just behind the angular man's back. Clearly he'd lost not only his elfling but Keir as well—an ominous fact. One hand clenched about the staff in his hold, the other on the hilt of his sword. This then, Evain acknowledged, was the price that must be paid. The price for leaving Anya's side to claim moments of solitude in hopes of restoring a necessary balanced perspective and reaffirming his commitment to the all-important purpose of a sorcerer's existence.

Beyond the unpleasant shock of his two companions' disappearance, Evain was surprised to see that Claud appeared as shocked and dismayed as he. Nonetheless, he demanded, "What happened here?"

After inwardly cursing the Druid's ability to move without sound, Torvyn fought to revive his composure. "Seeking privacy for personal needs, I slipped into the forest."

Evain said nothing but his impatience was almost tangible and billowed out to greatly intensify Torvyn's discomfort.

Shrugging with mock unconcern, Torvyn slowly turned toward the furious sorcerer. But at the deepening of the man's frown, he hastened to add. "Only for a moment was I gone and I went but a brief distance into the dark. Returning an instant afore you, I found just what you see. Thus, I know nothing able to explain the boy's absence."

No matter the Saxon's role in either disappearance —and Evain suspected he had played one—like most of his race this man was unlikely to openly speak the truth. Therefore, Claud's answer was unimportant and Evain moved past him to crouch beside Anya's wild pet.

By fingers burrowing through fur to lightly press against the little creature's chest Evain learned that Noddi still lived. He reached into his satchel and withdrew his vial of a sense reviving potion. This he held beneath a pointed nose. Noddi jerked, shook his head, and struggled to unsteady feet. The response earned a sorcerer's wry smile.

Torvyn was surprised. Not by the resuscitation of the animal but by the reputedly shrewd man's failure to pursue the clue carefully dropped in his stated denial of information about the boy's absence . . . but not the maid's. Torvyn quelled the acid of his scorn for the Druid's obvious lack of sharp wits to manageable levels before attempting to force the matter. He meant to restate more clearly the clue apparently too oblique. But even as Torvyn opened his mouth Evain abruptly rose to face him while the disconcerting peals of his gleeful laughter echoed through the forest.

Evain was gratified by the effectiveness of his mood shifting trick upon this man he suspected puffed with self-importance beneath the facade of clumsiness. Schooling his expression into a sardonic delight, Evain demanded, "So, tell me what you will of Anya's taking."

Torvyn shifted uncomfortably beneath this man host to startling and wildly inappropriate mood swings. Was he crazed? Torvyn fell two paces back. Was he violent and would his madness lend extraordinary strength?

"What do you know of her abduction?" Eyes gone in an instant to dangerous blue ice, Evain took one long stride forward and stood less than a handsbreadth before the quivering Saxon.

Torvyn backed up until his shoulders were blocked by a sturdy limb.

Evain deemed the man's actions verification of his belief that the reality of this man bore little resemblance to the weak and bumbling person he pretended to be. "Who took Anya and where is she now?"

Torvyn was furious with himself for the fact that the

quaking of his knees was *not* feigned. It was this self-disgust which enabled him to resume his disguise and answer with a suitable appearance of alarm.

"Whilst I was about my business, I heard two strange men speaking in whispers," Torvyn said, then straightened and even leaned a brief distance forward and lowered his voice to say, "Peered I out from the bushes to see your lady laying on the ground as senseless as recently was that little fox."

Under this news of harm to his elfling the flames of Evain's anger once again threatened to consume wise restraints. "Did you *see* what they did with her?" The power exercised to maintain his calm flattened every trace of emotion from the words questioning the honesty of Claud's claim.

"Rolled her in a blanket, hoisted her atop a huge horse, and rode away." Beginning with a roll of his hands Torvyn purposefully made a foolish display of pantomiming the actions.

"Did these strangers say where they were taking her?" Evain had no need for the Saxon's aid to answer this question. Only man-hewed stone and a precious few other impediments could prevent a sorcerer from learning the position of any human. In truth, for wrong or for right, Evain's bond with his elfling would likely direct his path to her side without resort to a complicated spell elsewise required. Thusly, Evain asked this question of Claud not to learn Anya's location but rather for the sake of clues able to reveal the Saxon's part in the scheme. By seeking such knowledge before attempting the rescue of those stolen away Evain would be in a better position to stand prepared against possible treachery.

"Aye." Torvyn fervently nodded his head. "Aye, they did that. They mean to see her locked away in a small abbey just over the border into Wessex."

Despite the pause wordlessly demanding that he speak, Evain said nothing but patiently waited for what he felt certain would follow.

"On the morrow, I'll take you there." Vexed that the sorcerer had failed to make the expected plea for aid, Torvyn smiled but spoke through gritted teeth to offer what had not been requested. "I know a direct path which will shorten the journey."

"How is it that a ceorl from the border of Northumbria knows this *small abbey* so well?" With the unpleasant image of Anya again lying unconscious as she had after falling from Blossom—this time by another's violent act—Evain wanted to see the man squirm. 'Twould be a small foretaste of the punishment to come.

"My grandmother took the veil and retreated when I was yet a child." Torvyn instantly gave a response that contained the ring of truth because 'twas a fact. "So, you ken why I will be able to lead you there first thing on the morrow."

Evain met the explanation with a bland smile. Yet in his view the speed and patent honesty of the man's response were as much a betrayal as stumbling hesitation would've been. The latter would be proof of an ill-thought scheme but the former even more clearly revealed the man's tie with this area so far distant from his supposed home. For a simple ceorl, such as Claud claimed himself to be, so remote a link was improbable. Aye, retreating to a nunnery would be a common haven for the aging grandmother of a man well-born, but for a ceorl? Never.

With bruising force Evain's eyes blindly narrowed on a hapless flower daring to peek from the shadows. In the Saxon's unspoken words Evain clearly saw a trap. His suspicions had earlier been roused by the fact that in near all previous encounters no foe had willingly engaged him in combat. Evain absently drove the bottom end of his staff into the damp ground below. Aye, 'twas plain he was being herded into a trap. Were Anya and Keir merely the bait intended to lure him into their foes' cage?

No matter, Evain acknowledged, the two innocents must be freed before he could return his attention and talents to fulfilling the rescue which lay at the very heart of his quest. But still he refused to waste time ruing the company of the pair who had again slowed the pace. They were here and his responsibility, one he would no more shirk than any other.

"On the morrow? Why not *now?*" Evain's piercing glare shifted to the man, who instantly realized he'd been wrong to think the rough stretch of his difficult path successfully navigated.

"Because, my friend . . ." Not even the cloying syrup in Torvyn's voice could smother every drop of its acidic sarcasm. "I lack the skills of a sorcerer and needs must have light to find the landmarks that will point my way."

Annoyed by the fool's skepticism, Evain's eyes became narrow bands of blue ice as he stepped back. Evain thrust his staff upward toward the night sky's black dome while a low chant rumbled from his chest.

Before the eyes of a Saxon who wanted not to believe, unknown words of mysterious power seemed to drive the forest into silence. Torvyn found himself so completely frozen in place that he could neither lift his arms nor shift his feet. More intimidating still, as the eerie tune expanded and dropped deeper into shivering depths, the claw held crystal atop an extended staff began to glow with an unnatural white illumination brighter than any full moon.

"Now you have light." Evain turned his intimidating gaze upon a man who nearly trembled. "Take Keir's bag and lead the way."

The command brooked no argument, and despite a deep resentment, Torvyn immediately obeyed. No matter, he comforted himself. He could guide the other over a circuitous route which would ensure they not arrive before the time appointed for a sorcerer's capture.

Chapter
13

Vastly pleased by a sudden increase in the pace of his scheme, Wilfrid's ever ruddy countenance shown brighter than usual even amidst humble surroundings poorly lit by a single malodorous oil lamp perched on an upended box. Standing in the shadows of this small stable temporarily converted to a prison, he watched as rough hands deposited a tightly bound, unconscious lad in a cage crudely formed of saplings stripped of limbs and woven into a pattern of crossed bars. Inside the odd structure secured by an inordinate number of locks, the youngster lay next to the slender, equally motionless form of the bishop's first Ecley captive.

"Rolf, seems your glittering accomplishment of fulfilling Torvyn's promise afore he could has cast the thegn into shade." The bishop privately admitted surprise that this less than needle-witted oaf had accomplished the feat yet was pleased that he had. "'Tis a deed for which you've more than earned this token of my gratitude."

The gleam in Wilfrid's eyes proved he meant precisely what he implied. This payment was given as much in appreciation for outmaneuvering the arrogant thegn as for the delivery of a youngster fervently sought.

When a small bag dropped into an open hand, the sound of coins chinking together earned Rolf's smile and deepened his pride in having bested the condescending Torvyn on leastways this one point.

"I trust you will see your cohort receives his half of this reward?" In truth Wilfrid believed no such honorable thing was apt to be done by this man, but his asking of the question preserved the fair-handed image expected of a bishop.

"And a like amount will be yours should you do as earlier I requested." Folding plump hands atop the shelf of his large belly, Wilfrid obliquely restated wishes previously listed in unmistakable detail. "Meet your erstwhile ally as planned . . . but see a surprise delivered to ensure success in acquiring for me the most critical implement needful to reap an overripe harvest of vengeance."

Wilfrid's jowls quivered with his bark of cold laughter. That cruel pleasure was returned in full by the nodding guardsman's spiteful grin.

Yet Rolf had learned to fear the bishop escorting him to the barn's oversize door. To be certain he missed nothing likely to later rouse the man's ire, he anxiously listened to each word spoken though it proved to be merely a crow of anticipation.

"Now I need wait only for the coming dawn to see my collection complete."

Anya had watched from beneath thick lashes lifted a mere fraction since near the instant Keir landed beside her. Despite an aching head and body that felt bruised all over, she saw the man garbed in a bishop's robes swing shut the heavy door of planks amazingly sturdy for a structure so humble. Moreover, the door's paler hue proved its wood considerably newer and its construction more recent than that of the stable's walls.

Shaking a cloud of unbound hair to disperse useless thoughts under the motion's discomfort, Anya's gaze narrowed on the portal closed behind a departing man she remembered from his sword fight with Evain. Anya had no doubt that the man who remained was Bishop Wilfrid, the object of Durwyn's disgust and the figure looming so large in much told tales of a bishop's greed vanquished by Saxon might—and Druidic powers. Aye, the feat had been wrought by the joined efforts of two Saxon ealdormen, one her father; and the spells of sorcery spun by her great-grandfather, Glyndor, and Evain along with his sister, Llys.

Having observed the bishop's odd exchange with the bulky guardsman, her attention centered on deciphering the meaning behind the bishop's ominous words—a task she feared all too easily done. Plainly he meant to complete his collection by seeing Evain join her and Keir in captivity. And equally clear was his intent to use them, in doubtless the same manner as Llys's Adam was being used, to wreak the vengeance he—

"So you are awake, hmmm?" Wilfrid made no attempt to shield his delight in seeing the dainty maiden caged. She was, after all, the direct descendant of a fearsome mage and thus deserving of punishment.

Ponderings rudely sundered, Anya's green eyes changed from gentle silvery mists to glittering emeralds as they focused on the speaker.

"Now that you've revived, mayhap I can convince you to tell me what uses are possessed—" His emphasis of the word *convince* made it certain that were she to hesitate in complying he had no compunction against forcing her answer.

Anya was initially host to a dread filled curiosity as to what this strange man would demand of her and then amazed when amidst shadows on one side of the door he reached into an object hanging unnoticed from a beam. He pulled an item from her missing satchel. Turning, he approached Anya while from his fingers dangled the small pouch absent since the theft of Blossom and the goods once carried upon her back.

"Tell me what uses there are for these implements of pagan rites."

Green eyes met his unblinking and a measure of Wilfrid's initial pleasure faded beneath their steadiness to be replaced by the discomfort of annoyance. Muttering under his breath, he reached through crossed bars to carelessly shake the upended bag until its contents softly thudded to a floor padded with musty straw. Meaty fingers scrunched the bag itself into a ball before tossing it into one corner of her peculiar cage.

Aware that the reason behind these deeds was almost certainly a desire to see her bowed at his feet,

Anya fought the powerful urge to sink down and scoop precious possessions into welcoming hands.

Wilfrid's temper began to simmer in earnest. "Pick them up!"

With a serene nod, Anya gracefully dipped down and slowly gathered the vials, flint, and crystal. But when she moved to the corner, recovered the thrown pouch, and made to restore the items to its protection, her action earned an even more vehement command.

"Nay! *Tell* me the purpose of each."

Delicate brows rose in mock amazement yet she carefully lifted the first item between thumb and forefinger. "This is flint with which to strike flame to a campfire."

The bishop growled but Anya lent the man's growing ire no attention as she calmly continued, holding up one vial and then the next. "This is a tisane to ease sleep, and this an elixir to slow the overabundant flow of lifeblood from any wound thus rendered dangerous."

Wilfrid's eyes glittered with renewed excitement. Here was verification of all his worst but most carefully nurtured suspicions. Here were wicked potions created to alter God's will. Man's ailments were sent by the Almighty and any human's interference in His wishes was surely a mortal sin.

Anya went still. The bishop's abrupt change of mood was near worthy of a sorcerer. And though Anya would've expected it of a Druid, she was unprepared to see it in her captor.

Repeatedly rocking from heel to toe and back, the bishop beamed. After years of seeking, of a sudden he had in his possession proof able to justify his relentless pursuit of the unholy pagans responsible for such sacrileges. Aye, pursuit and extermination of all Druids as well as their followers and friends. He had proof and yet there was more—another item which his own experience had shown to be of the greatest import.

"What of the white quartz?"

Anya permitted a shy smile as she pressed the crystal to her cheek. "'Twas a gift from someone I love and for that reason precious to me." It was the truth, though not all. And never would she admit anything more after seeing the unholy gleam in the eyes of this man who, as a Christian herself, she was shamed to name bishop.

Practicing both well-learned patience and serenity, with leisurely movements Anya restored each item to her pouch. This she then tied to its long-empty place on her belt of plaited reeds.

Knowing the girl to be of half-Saxon blood and having been assured by Mathru, Cymry prince of Gwyll, that mixed heritage barred anyone from practicing Druid powers, Wilfrid felt safe leaving Anya in temporary possession of her trinkets.

"The poisonous influence of Druids and their supporters," the bishop unwittingly spoke self-righteous, bitter thoughts aloud, "will be eradicated soon enough."

Startled by this blunt statement of his vicious intent even though 'twas a goal already deduced, Anya immediately defended a heritage as surely hers as it was Evain's. "You are only frightened by what you don't understand."

"Hah!" Incensed by this tender maid's slighting of his intelligence, the hands ever resting atop the shelf of Wilfrid's belly clenched.

Anya heard his anger but stood her ground. "Truly, it can only be by unfounded fear of the unknown that you would seek to destroy it." When she shook her head the oil lamp's limited light glowed so brightly on pale hair as to near illuminate the stable's farthermost corners. "'Tis as useless, nay, lamentable an action as standing in the midst of a dungeon's gloom and snuffing the sole candle in fear either of possible revelations or the heat of its flame."

"I have neither need nor wish for the knowledge of wicked pagans," Wilfrid sternly announced. "No Christian has need of such abominations."

"You are wrong. There is a vast ocean of difference between the many gods of Saxon pagans and a Druid's bond with natural forces," Anya earnestly argued. "I am a fellow Christian yet I know that Druids draw their powers from the same source which provides answers to heartfelt prayers. One need not destroy the other."

"Nay, 'tis you who are *wrong!*" Wilfrid turned near purple and puffed with his rage. "Druids are a plague threatening to spread illness through the church. 'Tis a plague which must be utterly destroyed to prevent its sickness from weakening the whole!"

With a mournful grimace, Anya calmly responded. "You purposefully confuse a bishop's proper goal of the church's good care with your hatred of Druids for frustrating a scheme to feed personal greed." She saw the bishop's anger burn brighter but still did not hesitate to speak plain truths. "In your malicious determination to exterminate man's last links to natural powers you are unable to comprehend, you would misuse your religious position to lead a holy war and wreak a deadly vengeance."

No verbal answer was required. The fire in the bishop's eyes made his confession of these facts as clear as if the words had been shouted.

"'Tis plain that to satisfy your monstrous needs you'll see an end to the lives of both I and Keir. Yet, how else when your deadly habits were early revealed by the murder of an innocent youth—a monk. Well-known is the fact that a decade gone by 'twas at your behest that Adam's brother was killed!"

With a past misdeed quietly raised to stand before him like an otherworldly spirit, the acid of Wilfrid's animosity burned the cords of wise restraint and bubbled forth in venomous words.

"Kill you? Aye! Eventually you and all your kin!" The bishop could nowise staunch the flow of words which for the sake of his wider plan were far better left unsaid. "The legions of longtime foes soon will begin marching upon Throckenholt, where again there will be a great battle. But this time 'tis I who will win!" He near chortled his exultation in a certain victory. "And your family, along with others dwelling within the shire's boundaries, will be destroyed."

It required every shred of Anya's emotional control to prevent the pain in her chest from escaping in a moan at the prospect of family and home in the path of sinister forces.

"Then the horde will move onward, crushing all in their path until, with you and your companions dangled as bait, the Northumbrian fyrd will be lured to meet their doom in a final conflagration. Even that fool, the ineffectual, peace-loving Aldfrith will be consumed."

As the final word faded away like a death knell

tolling doom, Wilfrid had quit of the stable and the wretched female captive it contained.

Anya tempered fear for Evain's immediate danger and dread of the foretold assault upon her home with the knowledge that only serenity could keep her calm enough to find some method to alter the bishop's vile predictions. Leastways the bishop had made one foolish mistake. He'd left the pouch in her hands and for that Anya was thankful. Diving into it again, she pulled out and unstoppered the vial containing the blood-staunching elixir which also held a second, less potent usage. Keir lay on his side in what must be an uncomfortable heap, and Anya sank to her knees beside him, skirts billowing out in a pool of green that seemed the darker for its background of tawny straw.

Hoping Keir not too deeply lost in unnatural slumber for this simple remedy to revive him, Anya carefully waved the vial beneath Keir's nose. Head twisting away, he struggled to open his eyes. When at last he succeeded, blond brows furrowed above eyes studying unfamiliar surroundings before a head of flaxen hair twisted about until he could look over his shoulder and up at his companion.

"Do you know how you came to be here?" Anya gently asked as she began tugging at the cords binding wrists at his back.

"Tcht . . . I remember the filthy toad who fell upon me as I slept and stuffed my mouth with a gag whilst another fastened my hands afore throwing me over his shoulder. And I remember their irritation with my struggles to win free . . . guess they stopped me with a blow."

"Our foes appear most talented at such defenses. I,

too, was struck senseless, doubtless to lend ease in quietly carrying me away."

Anya gave him a reassuring smile. "No matter, I'll have your restraint undone in a trice and then we'll find the way from our prison." Finding the knots too tightly drawn, she put her flint's sharp edge to the task of slicing through them. But she feared the necessary results too gradually won and worked the harder to quicken the pace.

"But where is here?" Pale blue eyes again narrowed on dingy surroundings. "And how do we get free?"

"I have a plan," Anya announced, determination infusing the words with a hope she wished were more honestly felt. She'd achieved success with but one spell, yet it might—nay, it *must*—be adequate to meet their present desperate need. "'Tis one in which a would-be sorcerer's apprentice can play a valuable part."

A mixture of surprised curiosity and doubt haunted blue-gray eyes, yet Keir lost no moment in nodding his willingness to try.

While with slow but steady progress Keir's bonds were shredded, Anya recounted the bishop's threats. Once the boy was free and rubbing aching wrists, she replaced the flint and vial used in her pouch. Then, taking out her crystal, she began to roll it between her palms.

Seeing Keir intently watching, Anya smiled upon this one plainly as anxious as she'd always been to learn profound mysteries whose lessons only a chosen few were deemed worthy to know. Anya's heritage, and indeed her small successes, lent reason to hope she might be permitted to join their number. But Keir? On the face of it, 'twas a dubious possibility even though his blood, too, was half Cymry. But then, Anya reminded herself, her assumption might be as misguided as was Evain's in wrongly believing her barred by that same fact. Keir ought be given an opportunity to try—and there could be no more propitious time than this moment of critical necessity.

"Thus may nature's spirits be sought," Anya explained her purpose for rolling the rough white quartz.

Keir went motionless as he softly announced, "My mother's father was a Druid sorcerer."

Anya blinked and her hands stopped moving, yet having been overblessed with surprises in recent days, she wasn't truly shocked. Biting her lower lip, she urged Keir to continue with a brief nod.

"I never knew him." Regret tinged the boy's words. "Afore I was born he and my grandmother were killed by people frightened of his wizard's ways."

With a rueful smile Anya said, "'Tis a sorry fact that so many are fearful of inexplicable talents they can't understand." The statement echoed her unpleasant argument with the bishop, but it was a fact earlier learned. "The vile practice is one common enough to make all of Druid descent justly wary. 'Struth, as you heard from Evain, an end much the same came to his parents. And your mother was fortunate to escape the fury of those who assaulted her parents."

"Already was she wed and had long been gone from their home. But I think fear of such a deed lay behind my father's dread of anyone discovering her heritage. And 'tis certain sure why—though she told me 'twas so—Mother demanded my oath never to speak of it with any save those trained in such matters. I've kept my oath . . ." He paused and solemnly gazed into green eyes for a long moment before earnestly adding, "But I do *want* to learn all the mysteries that Grandfather knew. And from deep inside I feel that I *must!*"

Anya's quiet smile deepened. She understood precisely how Keir felt, having long experience of such powerful lures and wordless summons. Learning that this was an experience shared explained her empathy with the half-Cymry boy and convinced her of the rightness in easing the rule of Druidic secrecy to seek his help by sharing the necessary first steps.

"A desire for Druidic knowledge is something we have in common. Yet, from Evain's statement that anyone of less than pure Cymry blood cannot attain the bond which allows mortal man to commune with the spirits of nature, you must realize he no more believes me capable of sorcery than you."

In Anya's instant of hesitation, Keir caught a glimpse of her forlorn dreams but they were washed away by determination.

"What Evain doesn't realize is that I *have* achieved such small feats as would suggest he might be wrong." Anya's claim reverberated with hope. To cover any possible betrayal of deeper emotions, she hastily shifted attention back to their plight and the plan for escape.

"'Tis an absolute certainty that the basic requirement of Druidic training—without which there is no hope of wielding its powers—is serene patience. To win our freedom, this you *must* strive to maintain. Then, although any spell can better be chanted in a site lacking the obstruction of man-made walls betwixt a supplicant and the sources from which such power is sought, we've no choice. We can but pray our earnest need will overbalance that barrier."

On the whole Keir was pleased with these explanations for his mother's indefinite hints.

"I am not so confident of my knowledge as to risk misteaching you the words of sorcery." By the glitter in sky blue eyes, Anya recognized Keir's excitement and worried his unsteady emotions might weaken the chanted threads of her plea's already gossamer thin cloth. Thus, she took another tack to see his vibrant emotions work to good effect. If he could not be calm, then mayhap he could focus all his energies into a positive force. "I must have your trust, elsewise we've no hope for success."

Keir nodded fervently, and his face was so solemn that Anya was reassured. She closed her eyes and concentrated. Anya resumed rolling the white stone, rubbing it ever faster between her palms. As it warmed she began an eerily beautiful litany of thrice repeated phrases. On the last word her hands opened to reveal the rough-edged quartz still cupped within but now brightly glowing.

Having but a faint inkling of what to expect, Keir's jaw dropped and eyes widened in awe. That the gentle radiance of moonbeams shone from so humble an object and that this magic had been worked by Anya made this feat more amazing even than the brilliance which Evain had drawn from the claw held globe atop his staff.

"You must believe, earnestly believe that what I tell you will happen, will in truth occur," Anya whispered, staring steadily at the bright crystal, willing it not to fade while she added to the vital plea an explanation of her chant's purpose and simple directions.

"Doubts weaken this spell able to ensure our departure goes unnoticed, thus, we cannot let it fade afore someone comes to open our cage." Inwardly she prayed 'twould be soon, else her inexperienced spell might wane. "The moment its portal stands unblocked, slip quickly out. Then, if necessary, open the outer door. I mean to follow close behind and together we'll escape."

Suddenly overwhelmed with an urge to immediately intensify her call, green eyes closed while Anya's lips moved, concentrating on the words in her silently chanted spell of shielding . . . and just in time.

"Saint's tears!" The bishop stood aghast, framed in an empty stable's open doorway while his rage demanded explanation from mute walls. "What wickedness is this? What wretch is responsible?"

Flushed so brilliant a red that it gave reason to fear an imminent explosion, Wilfrid rushed forward and fumbled to release each of the cage's many locks. As the last sprung open and dropped to the floor he glared at this physical evidence that all had indeed been securely fastened.

He stepped inside and, standing in the middle and with hands on hips, slowly turned full about. There were no visible signs of any possible escape route . . . not for humans lacking uncanny abilities. The pair's disappearance was infuriating! But if ever he'd needed proof of the godless powers he meant to exterminate, this was it.

Keir obeyed Anya's command, more than glad to slip past the portly bishop as soon as the cage was unlocked. There was no need to open the outer door. The irate bishop had left it ajar, and both captives escaped unseen into the gray haze of predawn.

* * *

While moving through the wildwood's green shadows with staff in hand and Noddi trailing some distance behind, Evain was well aware of dangers pressing near. And, too, he knew that dark sensation's slime oozed from more than merely the bony figure ahead. He had expected precisely this when he'd agreed to follow Claud into what was almost certain to be a trap. Concerned for Anya's treatment at the hands of vile toads who once already had roughly mistreated her and confident of his own abilities, he deemed the rescue of his elfling—the boy as well—worth any risk of unseen threats.

Alert to every movement within a wide radius, Evain calmed annoyance with the need to restrain his strides and remain behind Claud's unnaturally slow pace in awkwardly picking his way through thick-leafed foliage and over fallen trees. In short, by choosing the most preposterous and difficult path Claud delayed their journey to match his own schedule. Doubtless, Evain acknowledged, when the planned moment arrived, he would find himself surrounded. . . . But once these faceless foes dared step full into his path, they would learn that a sorcerer was prey not so easily snared.

Moving from the dense forest's heavy cover, Evain's ungainly leader led the way into a small clearing. There the faint gray light which precedes the start of day found and caressed the gentle beauty of flowers nodding their heads above scattered ground mists. Distracted by the sight for but a moment, Evain failed to hear the whistle of a missile launched and stood utterly unprepared for the rock that struck the back of his ebony head.

But Torvyn was host to the greatest shock when the man about to be formally claimed his prisoner fell to the ground senseless. When Rolf stepped from behind a shield of leafy vegetation and green shadows with a sling dangling from his fingers, Torvyn was enraged. Not only had the clumsy fool needlessly assaulted a man already in custody but he'd used a weapon more suited to a child than a warrior.

"You dolt! What maggot found its way into your simple brain that you'd do such a witless deed?"

"Hah! After the time you've spent in the sorcerer's company you ought be aware he possesses frightful magic which warns him when a foe draws near and by that talent can never be caught unprepared for battle man-to-man."

Torvyn's eyes narrowed on the speaker he knew was not bright enough to have figured this out on his own. "What sly soul created your scheme?" Shaking dirty-thatch hair, he negated the words. "Consider the question unasked. I can plainly see the marks of our pious bishop's work."

Irritated by Torvyn's immediate dismissal of even the possibility that the scheme was his—even though it wasn't—a heated Rolf added an indisputable fact. "To defeat his strange ability, I remembered the childhood games you scorn. And it was *my* thought to employ this sling as a weapon able to forestall the sorcerer's powers by making an assailant's approach unnecessary."

"And of talent with a child's sling you boast?" Torvyn's scorn further rasped a mutual dislike.

Rolf allowed no sign of having heard resented words as with a sneer of his own he continued his condescending argument certain to anger the thegn.

"Asides, how better to ensure that 'twill be I who hauls the sorcerer off into his enemy's hands? And I who claims the reward."

"That reward you will not claim!" Torvyn drew himself up to a height considerably taller than Rolf and growled his denial. "Already the sorcerer was in *my* control when you needlessly rendered him a lifeless lump, succeeding only in making more difficult the task of hauling him into Ecley!"

"Mayhap once—" Never would Rolf willingly accept defeat in this matter nor would he allow the thegn to do a deed he'd sworn to perform—not again. "But you've lost control of the prize who now is *mine*. And I am strong enough to carry him into Ecley on my own back."

Torvyn took a threatening step toward his antagonist and snarled, "Not while I draw breath!"

"Fine words from an arrogant toad—and a challenge I gladly accept." Rolf dropped the sling at forest edge, drew his sword, and advanced to confront his adversary.

The zing of another blade's unsheathing proved 'twas an action instantly met. With no care for the body lying betwixt, they joined in an earnest battle intensified by a long-simmering animosity bubbling over into open hatred.

Chapter
14

Once beyond the stable door, Anya glanced up and as if a beacon summoned her attention saw another thing long missing. A placid Blossom stood in a small stone fenced enclosure contentedly munching hay. The mare might slow them down and leave an easily tracked trail but an insistent inner voice urged Anya to tuck her crystal away, unbar the gate, and take back the fat little horse. She obeyed the wordless command.

Having neither time to waste nor care for the immodesty of her desperate action, Anya scrambled up on the fence's unsteadily piled rocks. Then, despite both encumbering skirts and the lack of a saddle, she launched herself atop Blossom's broad back.

At Anya's behest, Keir promptly jumped on behind her. Together the pair rode into the shadows of the nearest line of trees with as much haste as Anya could coax from the plodding mare.

Anya was thoroughly aware of pursuers who, if they had not already begun, would soon swarm after escaped captives. Of more import, she remembered the bishop's threat of fearsome peril looming over Evain. To defeat these dangers she put her faith in the single source of all powers. Anya silently offered up an earnest prayer and ended it by surrendering herself to the natural currents she sensed strongly flowing above, beneath, and around her.

Delving into her pouch, Anya retrieved the crystal and in cupped palms lifted it toward the bright hues of a clear day's breaking dawn. Dawn—a mystical, magical time of in-between and the source of her mother's greatest strength. Heartened by these facts, Anya maintained her serenity even when began inexplicable deeds beyond her control.

While the white stone shimmered with light, rose lips formed words in a chant whose lyrical beauty was matched by the ethereal delicacy of its melody. These were qualities Anya had long rued her inability to create. Where they came from now she didn't know. Yet, rather than questioning their source, she accepted them for the precious gifts they assuredly were.

Caught in the wonder of these events, neither Anya nor Keir lent any attention to the direction in which Blossom moved. Thus they were unprepared when their mount breached the forest wall to halt at the edge of a green clearing wherein a terrifying scene was being enacted.

Evain lay motionless, cloak fallen in a black arc across his body, while the clash of blade striking blade filled the air. Claud and Rolf heedlessly trod upon dark cloth as glittering swords met in vicious battle above the prone sorcerer. At the sight Anya felt as if an ogre were mercilessly squeezing her heart as tightly as she gripped the crystal gone cold. At the back of her thoughts was a question. How had anyone hosting such a wicked intent gotten close enough to a sorcerer to commit so dastardly a deed?

Though Claud had last been met as friend, some mysterious force restrained the two ahorse from intervening on his behalf. Indeed, the only blessing Anya found in this view was that neither Mercian warrior, erstwhile allies now combatants lost in the heat of battle, was aware of being watched. 'Twas a fact gifting her with a needful moment to wend her way through the maze of hazards abruptly raised and questions of what action to take.

Scrutinizing the two moving through a deadly dance, Anya realized that one of them had made her the fool by enacting a near perfect charade. Since the day she'd launched herself at Claud and knocked his arrow askew before straddling his back to prevent the success of his lethal intent, he'd pretended to be what in this moment she saw he was not. She'd believed his pose as an awkward ceorl driven from his lands and inept at his stated desire to survive on the questionable fruits of a forest bandit. In reality the man moved with considerable grace and wielded his weapon with great skill. She wondered what further hidden realities lurked behind his facade.

Keir, too, was struck by the revelation of a person who was not what at first he'd seemed and felt shame for having been gulled.

Both wondered how to interpret this fight. Did Claud merely defend a fallen friend? Though a logical assumption, Anya sensed a fault at its core. Keir started to question the same of Anya but before words could be spoken, the two swordsmen unknowingly provided answer.

Beneath a fierce assault, the man who had stuffed a gag into Keir's mouth dropped to one knee. His opponent held a sharp blade poised above his head but held back long enough to sneer, "The sorcerer will remain my prisoner."

The scornful claim seemed to reinvigorate Rolf. His flashing sword deflected the threatening blade and continued with a barrage of strikes, allowing him to regain his feet. "Nay, both he and the reward will be *mine!*"

While the battle continued, Keir leaned closer to the woman in front. With faint hope and in a whisper barely more audible than an indrawn breath, he asked, "Have you magic to quell these foes, too?"

This proof of an enemy where she'd thought was a friend spun another thread of complication for the tangled web of difficulties to be overcome and in whose center lay trapped the sorcerer struck down. First she must solve the spider's riddle of how a boy and young woman might defeat two healthy, armed, and clearly able warriors. And once that was done, another puzzle awaited. How could they transport the unconscious and thus unusually heavy sorcerer? Only after these mysteries were solved would she attempt the question of how to locate a secure haven.

Anya was grateful for the compelling urge which had motivated her to bring Blossom away from the abbey. The source of that unspoken prompting she'd suspected even then and now its reasoning was clear. They could use the mare to carry Evain into safety . . . although how to heave an unconscious sorcerer across a horse's broad back posed a challenge. She dismissed the possibility of reviving him with her potion. Evain had yet to move and that fact indicated an unnatural slumber too deep for him to be so easily revived. She refused to consider the only other reason for his immobility—death.

Shaking a mass of bright hair, Anya sought to disperse questions that could wait until they'd rid themselves of the two men offering immediate danger. Toward that end she began rolling the crystal still in her hands while silently offering pleas both for renewed shielding from their foes' view and for aid in directing her actions to save a sorcerer.

As a glow began to build in the stone her eyes fell upon an odd item out of place amidst the green of a forest floor. 'Twas a child's toy and an answer to more than a single question. Clearly this was the method by which a sorcerer had been struck by someone a safe distance behind. It also provided a method for dealing with their foes. Leastways in part.

Anya calmly asked Keir, "Have you skill with a sling?"

"Aye." Keir thought this a strange question to ask when serious problems threatened but instantly responded. "I used such a means to drive birds away from my father's new-sewn fields."

"One lies at the forest edge." She motioned toward where the object lay, pale outline sharply defined against a verdant background. "'Tis likely what brought Evain down."

Keir's hands, which had lightly clasped the waist of the maid in front, abruptly curled into fists. He was filled with anger at the wrongdoer and regret for his moment's doubt of Anya's right reasoning.

"As was true in the abbey, we can be neither seen

nor heard so long as we remain within the crystal's circle of light." Anya quickly set out to explain her intent, unwilling to lose possibly precious moments while the two swordsmen began to weary and their battle to slow.

Keir nodded his comprehension of this proven fact and his understanding of what he suspected Anya meant him to do.

Anya prodded the mare to skirt the clearing and move toward the sling. "Use the weapon to bring down Claud's opponent."

Again a head of sun gilded hair nodded.

"Once the man unaccountably falls, doubtless Claud will thrash about looking for the cause. And when his effort fails, he'll worry that further dangers hover near and be torn between fleeing to ensure his own safety and devising some method to see his captive delivered to the abbey."

Her reasoning made perfect sense to Keir, who slid to the ground beside the abandoned sling. While he lifted it, Anya shared what she intended to do.

"I mean to send Blossom out to Claud." As Anya, too, slipped from the horse, carefully holding the glowing crystal, she explained her decision. "I hope that despite this mare's unexpected appearance, he'll welcome the aid and with all good haste load Evain upon her back—saving us from a chore difficult if not impossible to achieve."

Having heard Anya repeatedly call the horse by name, Keir realized the mare must be known to her. However, he made the choice not to ask how that could be until difficult tasks were done even before she added another direction which drove the thought from his mind.

"Once Claud's done that, you can lay him low as well."

Keir went motionless. A sling's accurate usage was nowhere near as easily done as it might appear when in the hands of someone skilled. Once would be difficult for him. Twice would be nothing less than a miracle. Eyes gone cloudy clenched shut for a moment while Keir gathered courage, yet he nodded a willingness leastways to try.

"Take heart . . . and trust the forces you would seek to know." Anya gave quiet reassurance.

From the pile of smooth round stones plainly left at the ready by the weapon's previous wielder, Keir fitted one into the sling. He whirled it round and round. The whoosh of the motion ended in a sharp snap as the missile was loosed.

Its target was as suddenly felled as if struck by a bolt of lightning.

Startled, Torvyn jumped back. He was no less shocked by this event than when the sorcerer had dropped at his heels. With sword at the ready he marched to the forest's edge, thrust his blade into bushes, knocking them aside to glare into the empty stillness beyond. He repeated the action all the way around the small clearing to no better effect. His only discovery was not something found but something missing. The sling was gone, completely gone.

Returning to stare down at the motionless sorcerer, with disgust Torvyn acknowledged the difficulty of hauling a deadweight so far as the abbey. He weighed his options—all unpleasant. It was possible to go and return with a conveyance of some sort, but Torvyn feared that while he was gone the man would awaken and depart. At best, others would insist on returning with him . . . and insist also on sharing in the reward.

While Torvyn stood in frowning consideration of the matter, a noise interrupted. He whirled, again prepared to fight, and found only a horse plodding toward him.

A horse? Torvyn's eyes narrowed on the plump beast. It was indisputably a horse but one which most definitely had not been there moments past. How could it have come from nowhere? No matter, he wasn't fool enough to question a gift of fate.

Though the task was not a simple one, under the motivating lash of looming danger, Torvyn soon had Evain lying over the horse's back. Grabbing a handful of mane with the intent to thus direct its path to the abbey, he turned in the direction they must travel.

Keir's second target was as neatly felled as the first. Yet, as he stared into the green clearing where two men were sprawled and a third lay draped over a mare's broad back, he was certain each missile had been aided to its goal by more than his less than expert skill. He turned to the woman still cradling a glowing stone in one palm.

"What step next do we follow?"

Green eyes gazed into the luminescent crystal. "We find a safe haven." Anya would trust the spirits of nature to lead her into another shelter just as they'd opened the way into the rose and ivy glade the night past. As if in confirmation of her reasoning, a streak of auburn fur appeared. She dipped to scoop Noddi up with one welcoming arm.

"How?" Keir's question was not lightly asked. It was meant to request guidance for seeking aid of powers able to answer . . . but held a shadow of doubt for worthiness to be taught secret ways.

"We've been brought this far and permitted to see a sorcerer saved." Anya applied logic to defeat Keir's apprehensions. "Half-Saxon blood or no, we'll not be abandoned now."

"Not now." An unfamiliar voice from behind spoke a soft reassurance. "Not ever."

The sound of another so near caught Anya and Keir as thoroughly unprepared as sling propelled stones had found the two men they'd rendered unconscious. Moreover, these words momentarily left the pair as motionless as were the men robbed of their senses. Yet even Keir knew that the spirits of nature communicated through the heart and mind—not with human voices, no matter how sweet.

"Mayhap I can provide what you seek." The speaker continued with an offer of the gift they had thought to beseech of silent forces. "I give you an oath—on the power of your glowing crystal—that until Evain recovers, my home will provide safe haven for him and for you."

Upon hearing the oath only a Druid would know, Anya's fine brows furrowed as she whirled to face the one who swore it. What Anya found drove the confusion of that trespass from her thoughts.

Green eyes darkened with a bewilderment of apprehension and faint recognition. Save for a broad band of white running through black hair, the speaker was an eerie replica of Evain's sister, Llys. She was the same height, had the same slender form, and possessed the same sweet smile.

Though delayed by confusion, of a sudden the woman's words flashed through Anya's daze with a realization bearing the force of rolling thunder. The woman had spoken Evain's name as if the sorcerer were well-known to her.

"I am Elesa."

Anya gasped. Of course, the explanation was obvious enough she ought to have known it the moment she saw the similarities. 'Twas a name she knew. She knew, too, the tale behind the few meetings between Evain and this woman, this once mislead and never known sister. It was a less than encouraging invitation to trust.

"Evain accepted a risk in permitting me freedom when last we met. He gave me an opportunity few would have permitted, and I have been sent to return the gift in kind." Elesa paused while eyes as deep a blue as her brother's gazed into the younger maid's delicate face. "And I beg that you will give me that chance."

Anya wanted to know who had *sent* the one speaking in riddles but thought better than to flatly ask. In the next moment she knew the answer. This woman was the answer besought in human form. That her ever-protective fox had remained quiet at Elesa's approach lent additional faith in the rightness of giving trust.

Elesa could near see unspoken questions and concerns in clear green eyes. She felt the boy's unshielded curiosity as well. But she did not respond. Any honest explanation would be too difficult and require more time than good sense would permit to be wasted amidst surroundings already shown dangerous.

"Come, I'll lead the way." Elesa stepped through a seemingly impassable tangle of bushes. Anya saw the fact that Blossom, without prodding, immediately followed the stranger as further proof of the correctness in accepting what was plainly meant to be. She took up Evain's satchel and Keir retrieved his bag of treasures, dropped at the sword fight's scene, before trailing behind the stranger with Noddi at their heels.

"You lost the sorcerer?" Bishop Wilfrid's condemnation filled the small chamber in Ecley Abbey where he met with two bruised and ragged guardsmen.

"Nay, I had him in my hands until this witless fool interceded and fouled the whole!" Torvyn snarled. "'Twas a deed done, I believe, at your command." Slowly turning his head until tangled, dirt brown hair slipped over a shoulder, he focused his disgust upon the impious bishop. "Thus I demand payment of the reward your deed is responsible for costing me."

"Fouled the whole? Hah!" Rolf drew his hulking form up to its full daunting size. "I did precisely what I promised, and 'tis I who ought be paid!" While vehemently denying Torvyn's claim and declaring his own, he took a step nearer to the one he asserted must pay.

"But neither of you produced the prize." Wilfrid's voice was so soft the other two had perforce to go quiet and strain to hear. It was a tactic the bishop found most useful. Particularly when dealing with loud and quarrelsome warriors. "Without the sorcerer in my hands, my gold I keep."

"You blame us for the man's disappearance?" Rolf loudly complained. "It was not I who stole him from you. Indeed, I paid for that theft with a lump on my head. And in gratitude for that deed, if naught else, I ought be recompensed."

"And if we are to blame for the sorcerer's loss, what

of the pair you had locked in a cage and yet still managed to lose?" To fight a common foe, Torvyn joined his protest to the warrior earlier his rival. "Are we to be blamed for that wrong as well?"

"Find me any single one of those lost and I will pay." Wilfrid was tired of their petty grievances and made a promise likely to divert them from thought of past wrong with visions of future wealth. "Deliver all three into my hands and thrice as dearly will I pay."

It was a goal fervently sought, although 'twould be too late to aid the bishop now when two kings would soon descend upon him for a meeting in which he had deals to strike and a scheme to sell.

Chapter
15

Forcing lashes that felt lead weighted to rise, Evain silently studied an unfamiliar view. The only light in an elsewise dark chamber came from the glimmering coals of a fire plainly banked for night but burning beside where he lay on a simple grass-filled pallet. Barely visible through the darkness were natural walls of dirt and stone, a match for the slightly uneven surface of the floor beneath. Without turning a mercilessly thumping head, he could make out the silhouette of a table whose one end was cluttered with an array of vials and jars while behind hung plants suspended above a loom awaiting its user's return.

Even with a scope limited by gloom and the restriction of an aching head, Evain saw enough to convince him that this abode was a cavern deep in the ground—a Druid's secret sanctuary. But how had he come to be here? Assuredly not by his own strength

when the last thing he remembered was a trip undertaken to rescue his elfling and the missing boy. But
then that effort had entailed his agreement to knowingly follow a Saxon into a trap.

Black brows snapped together in a fierce frown.
Seemed the Saxon had won. . . . Evain's hands
clenched into mighty fists anxious to do battle with his
wretched foe. The next instant he realized no Saxon
trickery could explain how he'd come to rest in the
shelter of a Druid.

Stretched out on a makeshift bed at her patient's
head, Anya lightly dozed until the long awaited rustling sound of his awakening nudged her also into
wakefulness. She immediately sat up and leaned forward to gaze upon the countenance below, one even a
deep scowl could not rob of stunning good looks.

Sapphire eyes narrowed on the sudden appearance
of a tender beauty hovering above while on one side
unbound hair drifted down in a shimmering curtain.
Feeling enveloped by her nearness yet too oft host to
such dreams, Evain reached up to touch and test the
fantasy. The satin-warmth of her cheek was more than
proof of her reality. It was an enticement. His fingers
spread to slide into flowing tresses and draw her down
to meet the mouth he lifted to hers, despite the
action's price in pain.

Heart pounding with unexpected delight, Anya
gladly gave him the kiss but, knowing his recovery
depended upon quiet rest, reluctantly drew back.

"I have prayed for your recovery, beseeched the
spirits of nature to restore their sorcerer," Anya
whispered with a smile of aching sweetness. "And I
am grateful my pleas have been answered."

Evain's eyes warmed to caress the petite woman-child who ever insisted on tightly intertwining the two doctrines of belief. As it seemed Anya had won what she sought was it possible this half-Saxon maid knew something a Druid's training to wariness prevented him from considering? The mere fact that she was free and here with him in a haven open solely to those familiar with the ways of sorcery was sufficient to unseal a well of questions without clear answers. 'Struth, the only certainty was that strange events had taken place of which he had no knowledge . . . an uncomfortable reality for a sorcerer.

Having once dared the pain and survived, Evain turned his head to visually delve into the gloom on his left. His action was rewarded by a glimpse of Keir lost in untroubled slumbers whose peace had apparently been restored. Snuggling near to the boy was the fox pup Evain had last seen trailing behind him while he, in turn, followed the treacherous Claud.

Before Evain could ask Anya how all of this had come to be, another voice was heard from the farthermost shadows. Defying the discomfort it caused, he shifted to the right and watched the approach of a memory come to life. He immediately assumed that this woman embodied the answer to each of his multitude of questions.

"Thank you." His two sincerely meant words encompassed the entire list of deeds he mistakenly believed performed by a sister near unknown.

Elesa brushed her brother's words aside. She'd a message of more import to communicate—the purpose behind her initial search for him.

"I've been shown a vision which you must hear."

Evain's frown returned but it was faint, merely a

mixture of gentle questioning and wry amusement. "A vision? What strange matter is this?"

"A matter most serious, and the reason I was sent to find you." Elesa could see Evain had trouble accepting the gravity of her words—plainly an example of a sorcerer finding it as difficult to believe in another's skills as it was for any human untaught to understand the powers of a Druid. She gazed at him steadily, striving to wordlessly convey the urgency of her message even before it was stated.

Evain no more thought to ask who the sender was than Elesa thought to state a fact plain to each. But still, personal knowledge of Elesa's history joined to the lingering fog left by the injury that had laid him low blocked Evain from sensing either the pressing nature or importance of her mission. Rather, to his mind came remembered rumors of another sort. And as clearly as if revealed by the crystal atop his stave he saw that before him stood their source.

"You are the witch of Illsdene Wood of whom so many speak with fearful awe?"

Vexed with this further distraction from her goal, Elesa shrugged. "I did not choose the term but neither can I reject it. What alternative could I suggest?" One pair of piercing sapphire eyes directly met another. "Since the day my crystal was shattered, never could I again claim to be a Druid sorceress."

Unnoticed by others, Keir had been awakened by the drone of somber words and at the mention of Illsdene Wood's seeress his eyes went wide. Here another of the tales told by his mother had come to life.

Anya, too, was amazed to learn that this dimly

remembered character from a past confrontation had become a near mythical figure. And, considering the woman's rescue it seemed she'd secured a role in yet another clash involving the greedy bishop so central to the first.

"As you no longer claim a Druid's skills how do you explain these visions?" Evain solemnly asked, despite his doubts opening his mind to the possibility that Elesa spoke true.

Again Elesa irritably shrugged, taking up a flame darkened stick to jab the coals beneath a suspended pot to renewed life. "I said that I can no longer claim to be a sorceress—nor can anyone unable to either converse with natural spirits or invoke their powers. But I did not say they were unable to speak to me. And through dreams and portents that they do."

Evain nodded though his aching head made it a slight motion. This was within the realms of possibility. Natural elements could be capricious. Only see how oft warm summer days ended in violent storm. And on many occasions he'd seen where when nature took with one hand, it gave with the other—much the same as with winter snows that froze the ground but in thawing prepared it for new growth.

Placing the stick done with its task carefully aside to await its next need, Elesa saw that her brother had leastways come to honestly consider her gift and lost no moment more to press the point. "You must listen to what they've revealed, listen to news I've been commanded to tell you."

Evain lay perfectly still, composed to hear whatever she had to say. Seemed certain to be unpleasant, but he was prepared, although he first offered one caution. "If you mean to warn us about dangers lurking on every side, 'tis too late. We've already endured days filled in great measure with all manner of peril."

"That's plain enough." Elesa nodded, faintly smiling at a sorcerer laid low. "Unfortunately, my message involves a scene for which I have no explanation. I know nothing about it save that 'tis of great import." Though many of her dreams were jarringly distasteful, their meaning was clear. It was difficult to accept that only in this instance which touched a person whose health was of personal concern did its significance remain lost in an uncertain haze. *"You* are not a part of the vision at all. And yet there is no doubt but that 'tis you who must be told."

Evain's interest was piqued by the mystery she plainly found in her own message—a fact which conversely lent it validity.

"I have repeatedly seen a boat embarking from the wharf jutting out from a massive building of man-cut stone. In its prow sits our sister's husband with a toddling in his lap. 'Tis a little girl whom he shelters with his strength." Elesa gazed intently at Evain, searching for some flicker of recognition in his eyes, some sign of understanding on his face.

But Evain looked as cold and emotionless as if struck to stone. Anya was as frustrated by that fact as Elesa. Nay, more so since she instantly recognized the message's meaning. Adam was no longer at Isca. The trials of their journey had all gone for naught. While the two women's attention centered on the sorcerer's reaction, the boy heard a spark of hope in the seeress's talk of a little girl—his missing sister, Sian?

The pain of the blow he'd sustained muddled Evain's thoughts and yet he also recognized the futility of actions taken in this quest. However, added to that disheartening realization was the confirmation found in these words of another suspicion. Their each encounter with foes had been intended to drive them further into a waiting trap. Evain pressed fingers to an aching brow before running them absently into thick black hair. He recognized the new challenge looming over all, one more desperate than the first. It was imperative that he banish the mists of confusion and discover where his brother-in-law had been taken. The task would be difficult without some physical item from the new location and the aid of Brynna and Llys to again form the eternal triad of balanced power to aid in the search.

Elesa broke through his painstakingly restored concentration and while repeating what she'd earlier said added one thing more—a tantalizing hint of the answer he anxiously sought.

"I saw the boat's departure from a stone fortress built by the ancients . . . and next their journey's end at another dock."

"Where?" Evain abruptly sat up, heedless to the intense discomfort the action caused. Leaning forward, he voiced the same demand burning on Anya's tongue. "Where are they now? Did they sail north or south?"

Firelight gleamed on the white bands in Elesa's hair as slowly she nodded her head. "'Struth, they sailed either north or south." She smiled at the brother clenching his fists and quietly said, "But if I tell you their destination now, you'll put your health in jeopardy by immediately rushing after them." Her eyes narrowed against the explosion certain to follow.

Evain said nothing but by rights the blue flame

bursting from his eyes ought to have incinerated
Elesa. Confident in the wisdom of her decision, she
remained untouched.

"You need a full day and night's rest to restore the
health and therefore the powers that may be necessary
for what you face." Though she'd no knowledge of his
precise intent, she knew enough to be aware that any
objective he deemed worthy of undertaking would
require the wielding of his impressive powers. "Thus
I'll not tell you the site until the morn after the one
breaking across the eastern horizon as we speak."

Frustration building to dangerous heights, Evain
coldly responded, "I will go and without your aid will
find what I seek."

"Then by your folly will you go forth lacking the
strength to work the spells required," Elesa calmly
answered. "Already it seems you've tarnished a
Druid's first shining rule by surrendering your serenity to the burning winds of emotions. Only think what
harm might befall you and yours while you lack that
necessary control."

Anya silently gasped and Keir's eyes widened but
neither dared interrupt the heated exchange between
two possessors of mystical abilities.

The rarely thwarted sorcerer fairly steamed with
dangerous irritation, yet he couldn't deny his sister's
reasoning. It was true that a welter of emotions had
been loosed by the pain in his head and that they
shook his serenity. Equally true was the fact that such
a loss could endanger himself and those dependent
upon him. But these truths did nothing to calm his
lingering temper over Elesa's tactics. Moreover, he
suspected she pleasured in having forced him to face

them . . . a pleasure born of the kind of perverse desire to see him fail which her training to dark ways had taught. That logic was stymied by what next she said.

"Stay and I'll teach you a way to reach your destination with such speed that you'll arrive in half the time your feet could carry you . . . and days before you elsewise could do the deed, even had you departed the very moment my haven welcomed you." With a satisfied smile that revealed nothing more, Elesa turned away and moved back into gloom.

Evain again plowed his fingers through black hair. He received no impression of either dishonesty or ill-will from Elesa but feared to trust senses thoroughly disordered by the blow that had robbed him of conscious thought. The latter was a fact which merely reinforced Elesa's assertion of the folly in attempting to go onward before his stamina was revived and control restored. It was not one to restore his calm.

"What use to rush into danger unprepared and unarmed?" Anya picked up the argument dropped by the woman who'd slipped into shadows to rummage amongst containers clustered atop her table. Anya's first goal was to see her love's health restored, but not for a moment had she forgotten the bishop's ominous plans. Even without knowing what magical form of transport Elesa possessed, she would welcome it. 'Twas true they'd a horse recovered unbeknownst to the recently unconscious sorcerer. However, Blossom could only be more hindrance than help on a journey that must be done in great haste and would be better left with their hostess.

Evain heard Anya's words but annoyance with his

sister continued to simmer. How could a woman who admitted herself no longer a sorceress think to teach a sorcerer the ways in which a deed might be done more swiftly than already he could do it?

"Evain, please . . ." Anya caressed his anger firmed jaw until its tension eased. "For my sake, if not for your own, strive to relax and rest, the better to rebuild your full strength."

Evain gazed into the gentle concern of his elfling's mist green eyes and forced a reassuring smile that warmed to honest pleasure when petal soft lips curved in answer. He could almost taste their honeyed sweetness and fervently wished that he could dip his head and seek that surely most potent cure for all his ills.

While Anya calmed a sorcerer, Elesa found what she sought. She returned to the pair, holding a crockery mug into which she ladled bubbling water from a pot suspended over the banked fire.

"Drink this."

Evain looked skeptically at the steaming mug's murky contents. Did Elesa intend to undo the good she'd done in saving his life? Whether by a sorcerer's instinct for mercurial moods or his elfling's comfort not even Evain knew, but he found himself sufficiently restored to tease and sent Elesa a glance of mock terror.

Elesa returned it with a grimace of stern demand, warmed by this first experience of a natural teasing between two siblings. "'Tis merely a tisane, one able to lessen the pain of your head and ease you into the gentle rest you greatly need if you hope to soon recover and resume your quest."

Reluctantly Evain took a sip only to find its taste so

pleasant that he soon finished the whole. Then, at Anya's gentle prodding, he lay back and with her small fingers firmly clasped in his own drifted into healing sleep.

"Then we are all agreed?" Bishop Wilfrid complacently folded his hands atop the shelf of his belly. "Each will gather his troops. Cadwalla's forces have been guaranteed unchallenged passage through Gwyll to shorten their march to meet Ethelred and his army. Then in three days' time all will join in the assault upon Throckenholt, aye?"

Wilfrid allowed no hint of uncertainty to show despite the ominous silence with which his culminating speech was met. Although Prince Mathru's presence at this meeting was unnecessary as his contribution to the scheme included the commitment of no warriors, Wilfrid unexpectedly found himself ruing the aging man's absence. It was Mathru who most shared Wilfrid's personal goals, and in this tense moment the prince's support would've been welcome.

"I am not convinced of your plan's wisdom." At last a red-haired giant of a man spoke. His deliberate words were in answer to the bishop but he stared belligerently at another strong warrior-king. "Your last assault upon the shire ended in a debacle the sort of which I've never been a part . . . nor have I any wish to be."

"Not even to share in the spoils of a vast kingdom?" Ethelred mocked, gray fringe brushing his shoulders as he tilted a bald pate to one side while with difficulty preventing the depth of his contempt for the man he sought as an ally to show too clearly.

"It can't repeat itself." Wilfrid quickly broke the silent visual duel between two physically strong and politically powerful men oft on the verge of outright warfare.

"And how is it you think to ensure that claim?" King Cadwalla of Wessex demanded of the cleric he'd befriended after a now dead Northumbrian monarch sent him into exile for the very deed under discussion.

"We have Adam, Ealdorman of Oaklea, and the Northumbrians will do nothing to endanger his life." Wilfrid immediately realized his error when both kings looked upon him with equal skepticism. Neither of them were likely to permit the loss of a single supporter's life to alter their path. "Leastways King Aldfrith, the lover of peace, will permit the threat of such a deed to go unchallenged."

Wilfrid was relieved to see that the two men accepted this accurate description. He needed the patronage of both in his struggle to win from the pope a restoration of the full extent and power of his see and, in this moment more importantly, to wreak vengeance upon those who had seen it reduced.

"Aye, we have Oaklea." Cadwalla's cool voice seemed at odds with his fiery hair. "But you've lost the sorcerer and the ealdorman of Throckenholt's daughter." He'd done much to aid the bishop. Even, for the sake of his soul, had he given Bishop Wilfrid a quarter of the conquered Isle of Wight and of the booty taken from it. But he could not be so easily drawn into this alliance that the bishop proposed he form with a king who had already been his foe.

"Lost the sorcerer? The man you most wanted to take captive?" Ethelred feigned surprise at news he'd learned almost as soon as it happened, but he made no attempt to hide scorn for the bishop's obsession with Druids.

Wilfrid's ruddy complexion deepened to a fiery shade. He needed no reminder of his hideous losses but neither would he allow them to prevent the taking of vengeance.

"Ah, but when we've seized the Lady of Throckenholt with her sons and carried them off to join Adam of Oaklea in captivity at the site carefully chosen on King Aldfrith's own lands—" Wilfrid spread his hands wide, palms up in a beseeching gesture that belied the depth of his determination. "By holding one ealdorman, another's wife and sons and part of a kingdom in our hands, we'll possess the bait to lure *all* the others into our snare . . . even the king you both seek to dethrone."

"Is that not what you promised would happen once you had the sorcerer who slipped through your hands?" Ethelred asked with a frightening gentleness.

Wilfrid's hands again rested atop his belly but the knuckles were white as the deep lines on either side of his tight-clenched mouth.

"I fear no victory will be won by this tactic. Nor can I see any justification for sending an entire army on so minor a mission." Cadwalla deemed the proposed scheme a waste of effort. Yet, to hedge a decision offering the slight prospect of a great gain, he added, "Nonetheless, I will send a contingent of men to back your efforts. If you secure the prizes you seek and an honest battle looms, I'll lead the rest to join you at Venda."

"A fine compromise," Ethelred sincerely complimented the other king. He had seen enough of the bishop's plans go awry to expect overmuch of this scheme. And even if it succeeded, after he'd summoned his full army for the taking of a single keep whose warriors had been summoned to duties in their fyrd, was it not likely to make them all look witless fools—like hunters slaughtering tame beasts and naming them trophies of the chase? He'd a fierce reputation for invincibility that he chose not to see thus tarnished.

Ethelred had been willing to try the odd plan born of others' burning desire for vengeance and proposed by the bishop and Prince Mathru. But if it did not soon show signs of an ability to aid the greater triumph, he would abandon it in favor of the simple, proven tactics of superior force. Nothing must be allowed to impede his march toward the conquest of Northumbria, a march begun months past. However, for the sake of personal pride Ethelred offered the same as Cadwalla and one thing more.

"I, too, commit but a portion of my army to your plan—one-third—whom I myself will lead."

"If you are willing—" Cadwalla's smile was mirthless. "Then I, too, will join with my warriors in the fray."

Even with the participation of both kings, Wilfrid was shocked by this ghastly reversal of the promises earlier given by one and the expected support of the other. Here he found himself again, as too oft in the past decade, lacking the position of power which would enable him to argue the decision. This fault, also, could be placed upon the Druids and their ilk. It intensified his determination to prove the right of his plan. He must and, he self-righteously told himself, with God's aid he *would* see not only the sorceress at

Throckenholt but all of Druid heritage destroyed. The mental image of fire from heaven consuming them was sweet. With its inspiration, he drew a deep, calming breath and agreed to less than he'd expected would be forthcoming.

When next Evain awoke it was to find Elesa sitting at his side working a spindle-whorl, twisting threads of the cleaned and carded wool in one hand with the fingers of the other. And all the while steadily watching him.

"How long have I wasted lingering abed?" Evain abruptly sat up. With the action he made a pleasant discovery. The pounding of his head had subsided to a minor thudding which even Elesa would have to agree permitted the quick resumption of his drastically altered quest.

"You've slept through another day." Elesa gave an unwarranted attention to a task she could nearly perform in her sleep.

Evain was disgusted by the news. He'd thought to begin the new journey at dawn but dusk would do as well. After all, during the past sennight they had more than once traveled steadily throughout both a night and day. Now, considering the need to make up time lost in journeying to the wrong destination, they could again. Piercing blue eyes probed shadows and peered into gloomy corners seeking Anya and Keir. They were not present.

"Where are my friends?" His less than complete trust in Elesa spawned unfortunate suspicions.

Elesa's answering smile was an unknowing echo of the cynical half smile so common to Evain's lips. "I requested them to step beyond my abode's limited confines and gather kindling to stoke flames beginning to fade afore nightfall." She nodded toward a fire growing weak.

"Then I will go and call them back." With thoughts of foes and recent captures, his sister's calm dispatch of two companions into the forest alone roused in Evain a most unwelcome prospect. But he gave his concern a just excuse. "We must prepare for an immediate departure."

"Calm yourself. They are safe." Elesa recognized her brother's concern and instantly sought to smooth its ragged tenor while ignoring his stated intent. "Truly, without my call or permission, no one dares come near Illsdene Wood. Humankind fears this Vale of Doom—so ordained by Gytha after we were driven from it by fire a decade past. Even my erstwhile master, Bishop Wilfrid, and the pursuers he commands would hesitate to enter the scorched woodland surrounding my home."

Evain made to rise but Elesa thrust out a hand to hold him back. "I sent them outside to leave us in privacy for an important purpose." As her brother remained tensed to pull away she added, "And I think you've forgot that I am the one who knows what destination you seek."

Her inference that a sorcerer had need of a *witch's* advice rankled enough that it threatened his all-important calm. Despite the tightening cords of his restraints a sharp denial escaped. "My powers are restored and I am quite capable of locating Adam myself."

"But not so quickly as I can tell you." Laughter

sparkled in Elesa's eyes and she absently put the spindle-whorl back into motion. "Nor can you reach the site with the haste my secret method can provide."

Evain scowled and Elesa grinned. Knowing she'd won this minor skirmish, she softened the tone to add, "I plead with you to stay and hear something more you truly ought to know afore you leave my company."

Reluctantly, Evain again settled atop the straw filled pallet dented by his sleeping form.

Elesa quietly began. "I arranged for us to be alone as I much doubt you'd appreciate having this warning shared with Anya and Keir."

A mask of wariness closed over Evain's face.

"Aye." Elesa nodded. "It concerns your companions and although you are unlikely to believe the truth of my words, I must speak them."

All save the blue flame of Evain's eyes seemed to freeze into pure ice. "Did this, too, come as a dream?"

Elesa ignored his sarcasm. "Nay, a waking vision."

Evain waited, striving to stifle tension threatening to break his control while Elesa put aside her spindle-whorl to join her hands tightly together before beginning.

"You are wrong to ignore the maid's talent for sorcery. In truth you must encourage and guide her attempts—timid thus far—to build strong links with nature's powers."

"What?" Evain's immediate gasp of incredulity was an echo of long training in Druidic ways. "Anya is of but half-Cymry blood and for that reason can have no bond."

"For a sorcerer of your undisputed powers, you are

amazingly wrong. The maid was born in possession of the bond. 'Tis rare, I agree, for one of her mixed blood, but possess it she does and in good measure."

Although Evain had on occasion wondered if such a thing could be, this statement accusing him of complete wrongheadedness was more than he could easily swallow.

Two pairs of deep blue eyes clashed and neither won—proving only that both were stubborn.

Evain broke the lengthening silence to scoff, "That is your *warning?*"

"Nay. That is fact." Elesa's smile was grim. "Listen and I'll speak the warning plain: If left without the rightful training you can provide, she'll be lured into slipping sidelong into the much easier routes taken by our aunt Gytha. The terrible end to which you know."

Evain fervently shook an ebony mane against the prospect of his bright elfling falling under the sway of dark powers. Not those same nasty forces that had near killed her as a child.

Elesa paused a brief instant to allow the danger of her meaning to be seen with the clarity of a Druid's crystal. "While I neither want nor am able to commune with the dark powers that filled my past, I feel them awakening and reaching out for Anya. If you would prevent them from snaring her, you *must* block their call."

As her brother looked either unable or unwilling to face the grave danger, Elesa's spindle-whorl fell completely from her lap as she tightly clasped his arm to anxiously plead. "'Tis a path whose seductive nature I know too well. And I beg you to please, please take heed."

Evain put his hand over the pair desperately holding him and in her eyes read the earnest truth of the words continuing to flow like a river in flood.

"The dark powers entice with such simple joys as sweet fragrances and flavorsome spices. Then they offer as gift the ultimate pleasure to be had in wielding mighty forces to attain every whim." Elesa's mouth twisted with a bitter smile. "'Tis an addictive delight . . . until one realizes what ghastly price must be paid for its use. And that not until 'tis too late to sunder the bond."

"You did." Evain sought to comfort the sister clearly in pain. "I saw you."

"Aye," Elesa stiffly agreed. "But for that deed the price is dearer still. Forever will I be alone. A loneliness of far more than lack of companionship, 'tis an emptiness of feeling." Searching for precise words, she gave her head a sharp shake. *"Not* empty, for I have felt and know what I cannot have. Rather, to fill that void I am given merely insubstantial visions of other lives, of happiness and sorrow—and warnings of peril. On occasion even do I see scenes of what for me might have been but now can never be."

"I could train *you* to positive powers." Evain was not certain the deed was possible once a Druid had broken her crystal and sundered the bond with natural powers but he would try if it could help heal his misled sister's injury.

"Nay, what you haven't understood though I've tried to explain is that should I somehow succeed in regaining my bond with nature, I would almost certainly fall again to the dark powers' addiction. I choose never to take that risk."

Evain started to probe further for some method to

free her of an unhappy present and melancholy future but Elesa cut off the first sound with a seemingly foolish statement, one worthy of the sorcerer's mood shifts.

"We have a sister—leastways, we did. . . ."

Evain scowled. Of course they'd a sister. He'd undertaken this quest at Llys's behest. Did Elesa's words suggest some ill had taken Llys from them?

Correctly reading his thoughts, Elesa's lips pressed together in a tight smile. "'Tis not of Llys I speak."

Evain's chin lifted against the implication. A decade past he'd come face-to-face with an unknown sister—Elesa. But surely there couldn't be another!

"Our father had a first wife who died giving him a baby daughter. That child reached maturity by the time he wed our mother."

Evain found it impossible to believe and flatly said as much to Elesa. "Were that true, Llys and I would assuredly have known her."

"Father didn't tell you of my existence." Elesa quietly reasoned with her brother. "So why do you find it so difficult to believe he failed to speak of another?"

"He had a reason for not speaking of you—the goal of safety for us all." A soft growl of disgust rumbled from Evain's chest. "You must admit the same cannot explain why an older child was kept secret."

Evain knew that Elesa was as well acquainted as he with the reason her existence had been kept secret. As any mother who bore more than one child in single birthing was viewed with suspicion, when to the wife of a Druid—to whom all knew the number three was sacred—presented him with triplets it had presented an ominous danger to the babies' lives. For the sake of all three their father had sent Elesa off to be raised by his sister, Gytha.

"The secret behind our older sister is much simpler." Elesa stared down at tight-entwined fingers. "Our *Druid* father disowned her for joining in *Christian* marriage with a simple Saxon farmer."

'Struth, the secret was so simple Evain accepted it without further argument. Easily could he envision such an action taken by the man he remembered their father to have been.

Dwindling firelight picked out the bands of white in Elesa's hair as she nodded, content to see her brother's acceptance of this fact. And yet it was only a part of the whole she'd still to share. "To her farmer our sister gave both a son and a daughter before perishing in a blazing inferno . . . wrapped in her husband's arms." The last words ached with Elesa's wistful longing for a kind of love that would never be hers.

"So, why tell me of her now if she is gone?" Evain had a strong suspicion but with the power of his steady gaze demanded the words.

"Her children live." Elesa wryly bowed to his demand. "One is in the company of the man you seek to free."

Evain's eyes blindly narrowed on the scene she'd earlier painted in his mind—a girl-child in the prow of a boat, sheltered in Adam's arms. But the other? Though he'd demanded it moments past, he hesitated now to see this last suspicion confirmed.

Elesa couldn't allow it to remain unsaid. "Our nephew already is in your care."

"Keir?" Though phrased as a question it wasn't sincerely asked, and Elesa saw no reason to restate an obvious fact. Moreover, she must add a final, important fact to complete the whole. "The boy, too, shares a bond with nature and needs your aid to see it develop in right paths."

Having grown fond of the boy, Evain could accept Keir as his nephew. In truth, he remembered how when speaking with the ceorl, Durwyn, he'd explained the lad as his dead sister's son. Seemed it had been a portent. And yet the suggestion that not only Anya but Keir possessed abilities rare for any half-Saxon was too difficult to instantly accept. In the back of Evain's thoughts, he wondered if Elesa's dark past had reasserted itself and directed her, mayhap unknowingly, to mislead him into sundering his own all-important ties by taking actions unacceptable to natural powers.

"I had to speak and now I have." Elesa saw the skepticism and even the suspicion in Evain's eyes and shrugged. "Believe my warnings or not as you choose."

Scooping up her spindle-whorl, she rose to her feet but looked down to say one thing more. "Ask them how they won free of the bishop's hold."

Black brows rose. "Was it not you who rescued them?"

"They were caring for you when I arrived." Elesa's smile was strained. "I merely led the way to safety here."

"Then who stopped the attack on me?" Someone had struck him from behind, and it couldn't have been the Saxon foe who led the way. Mind recovered from the ill-effects of that nasty deed, Evain clearly saw that he'd lain vulnerable to leastways two enemies . . . danger ended by an unknown force. But whose?

"Who, indeed?" In faint mockery, Elesa's equally dark brows rose as high as ever had her brother's.

"Where's Anya?"

The shock of a third voice sliced through the thick tension between siblings. At Keir's sudden question both instantly turned to the boy standing in the doorway opening onto the tunnel beyond.

Evain's frown deepened. "Was Anya not with you gathering wood for the fire?"

"She was but told me to gather at the bottom of the hill while she climbed to the top. We were to meet here when we'd each gathered a full bundle. I did." Keir lifted a load of fallen branches tied together with the cord of twisted reeds Elesa had provided.

Feeling pierced by two pairs of glittering sapphire eyes, the boy gave a diffident shrug and justified his arrival alone. "'Tis only I expected Anya would finish first. Her bundle was almost full afore she began the climb."

His explanation hadn't softened the sorcerer's scrutiny, and Keir quickly dropped his bundle beside the low hearth and turned back toward the door. "I'll go and find Anya."

"Nay." In one quick, graceful movement Evain leaped to his feet. "I'll find the maid." He disappeared through the doorway before the other two could speak.

Chapter
16

Having left Keir with instructions to return to the cavern without her, Anya felt safe in seeking a few private moments of peace walking through the gentle ground mists rising at end of day. Thankfully Evain was resting in healing slumbers and the other two could surely spare her aid in preparations for the coming night.

Anya's path was simple. With only the vaguest of destinations, she merely wended her way upward through a lush tangle of bushes. The sound of Noddi romping somewhere near, playfully stalking some small creature hustling through the undergrowth, had receded by the time she reached the top of a fair-size rise. Idly walking with no certain goal, she was surprised to find her path blocked by a deep green wall of shiny, thorned leaves. The dense holly barricade reminded Anya of the rippling stream and forest glade protected by another thorny wall, though of twined roses and ivy . . . and sweet memories of delight-filled time spent within put a wistful smile on soft lips.

Fading sunlight caressed the pale gold braids atop a head tilted in quiet contemplation. After a moment Anya burrowed into the pouch attached to the belt riding her hips and withdrew her precious crystal. Rubbing the stone between her palms until it glowed—a feat more quickly accomplished with each attempt—Anya chanted an earnest plea. Before it had been thrice repeated, entrance was granted as a beam from her white quartz pointed a safe passage through the prickly wall.

Stepping through, Anya found herself at the edge of a natural garden of peaceful loveliness which surrounded a gentle spring. Abundant flowers in a profusion of hues sprang up between blades of thick grass that beckoned the weary maid to rest. Taller blossoms grew in banks against the high-grown, prickly walls of shiny green. She felt welcomed and safe from prying eyes. Facts providing the opportunity to perform two longed for deeds.

Anya quickly removed kirtle and undergown. Both garments were in sore need of washing—a problem worsened by the fact that she had no alternate garb. A woe for which she must share part of the blame. Although the initial wrong belonged to the thief who'd stolen the satchel containing her garb, she'd seen it hanging in a shadowed corner of the barn at Ecley Abbey, but in the haste to escape had foolishly failed to reclaim the satchel.

At the point where the spring's waters flowed out in a quickly flowing stream Anya knelt and thoroughly rinsed her clothing. Once they were clean, she spread them amongst limbs of holly, trusting thorny leaves to hold her garments upright while the warmth of a gentle wind dried them.

With that chore done, Anya stood unclothed and welcomed the excuse to indulge herself in a refreshing bath. Ablutions hastily performed during the desperate journey had been appreciated but barely adequate. She began unbraiding glowing tresses which were playfully teased by the same slight breeze drying wet cloth and wafting delicate fragrances through the air. Slender fingers combed through and loosened long-restrained hair as she lowered herself into the pleasant chill of clear waters.

Taught by virtue of both her Christian and Druid backgrounds to offer thanks for blessings given, Anya stood amidst bubbling waters and lifted her face to the first bright streaks of sunset. During this sacred time of in-between she meant to chant her gratitude for health restored and offer prayers of appreciation for freedom regained.

Elesa had termed her cavern's surroundings a "scorched woodland." But despite glimpses of blackened scars, in Evain's first sight of Illsdene Wood he found more evidence of nature's rebirth. Charred trunks were densely covered with healthy vines. Thick bushes vied for position with saplings of many varieties and the forest floor was carpeted by a wealth of vegetation.

The vision of a wildwood rejuvenated joined with a sense of peace to assure Evain no peril stalked his elfling . . . leastways not beyond the danger he presented, and more so now than before he and Elesa had talked. Anya's dainty feet had left a clear path ascending the hillside. Without a moment's hesitation or an instant's guilt, he tracked delicious prey, glad for Keir's unwitting gift of privacy.

At the hill's brow the physical path disappeared but Evain smiled, certain it was a further gift from the source of his powers and meant to greater ensure solitude. He'd no need of a visible trail to follow. The elusive notes of a tantalizing tune beckoned him onward. Making his way through the gray mists of waning day, he followed its call. The closer he drew the stronger the enchanting song became until he stepped through another natural wall assuredly closed to those lacking Druidic bonds. But this time he'd no reason to question how Anya had managed that feat. Her bond with nature was real, as real as his love for the maid. And as the first evaporated the bar to the other his heart soared.

In the dappled shadows a black-clad Evain stood upon a carpet of lush grasses while the sweet scent of many flowers filled the air. Feeling as if a precious memory were being repeated, he saw again the vision of his sweet neophyte sorceress. It was as if the spirit of the spring were rising in human shape from its gently churning waters. 'Struth, Anya was a figure of unearthly beauty, standing hip-deep in liquid crystal, back to him and silhouetted against a horizon emblazoned with hues from palest blue to gold and vivid rose. Clearly lost in the power of this mystical time of in-between, her delicate face and outspread arms were raised toward the glory of a setting sun. In a voice of haunting purity she chanted a song of praise and thanksgiving. Though the simplicity of the secret words she used revealed a need for training, that small lack had ample recompense in sweet sincerity.

When Anya's arms returned to her sides, her head bent forward, plainly in a moment's prayer. Evain waited until she'd done before speaking with appropriate reverence.

"In the first instance I thank you for the gift of my life, and in the second for seeing my health restored."

Anya instinctively sank down until water lapped at her chin but still she quickly responded to see another given rightful credit. "I could not work the deed alone. Indeed, to halt our foes 'twas Keir who wielded the same sling that brought you low."

Evain's dark head fell back and the velvet thunder of his laughter filled the air. "A sling. The last weapon I was prepared to defend myself against . . . but apparently also the weapon whose use our foes least expected. And it seems that to the many matters I must share with Keir, humble gratitude will be added."

Delighted by Evain's laughter, evidence of both an injury overcome and a lightening of spirits, Anya turned far enough to cast a brilliant smile over her shoulder.

"Nonetheless . . . ." Evain reciprocated with a slow, potent smile of his own. "I am grateful that while I was unable, you sought the aid of natural spirits on my behalf."

Sapphire eyes were full of meanings Anya hesitated to interpret for fear of mistaking them for the response fervently sought. So focused on thoughts of things unspoken was Anya that she failed to hear the plainly stated acknowledgment of her link in the chain of destiny.

Evain sensed Anya's hesitation to believe, but while his smile slipped into one-sided mockery, it was a mockery cushioned by gentleness. He knew how to completely drive her question into certainty.

Anya was stunned when another backward glance found Evain stripping off his own clothing with a speed belied by an innate grace. Though they'd loved in the dark shadows of a honeysuckle glade, this was the first time Anya had clear view of Evain nude, and breath caught painfully in her throat at the stunning sight. As he followed her into the spring, the water-reflected shades of sunset played across the hills and plains of his blatantly powerful body. Wishing in that moment for nothing so much as to feel its heat, as he moved within reach her hands curled against the urge while fires of remembered wanting smoldered.

The blue flame of Evain's gaze traced a burning path across her bareness before lifting to the exquisite face tense with desire and to the wide eyes which said more of admiration than mere words ever could. He felt the shy, green-mist examination moving over him like a phantom caress. It seared him with the need to feel its reality. Reaching into the water, he took her hands to lift and flatten them against his chest.

Anya's fingertips tingled with delight at the prospect of a journey through the wedge of crisp black curls. Free to fulfill wicked longings, they began moving, and the feel of his smooth skin raised an excitement so strong she bit at her lip. Unwilling to acknowledge the existence of anything beyond the sensation of a massive chest rising and falling heavily, her hands wandered in fascination over the erotic combination of hard muscle and abrasive hair. They moved slowly up to stroke the breadth of wide shoulders and then down, feeling every line and curve burn beneath her touch.

And all the while every particle of Evain's being centered on Anya's curious caresses. The cool water surrounding them did nothing to douse the passion blazing in his blood, rushing through his veins like wildfire through the forest, uncontrollable, unstoppable. Heavy lids half fell over the smoldering blue flames in his eyes. Exercising every shred of self-control, he remained rigid, determined to permit her this unrushed moment of exploration.

Anya loved the contact with the power of Evain's body, the male scent of him, and her small pointed tongue ventured forth to find a new pleasure in the taste of his flesh. Evain felt the contact like the lick of teasing flames. His breath turned harsh and uneven, and the sound of it quickened Anya's pulse. She could feel his potent hunger growing, spreading its raging need to her.

Beneath Anya's caressing hands, ever more daring in their sweet torment, Evain's restraints had been sorely tried. But his control was shattered by the brush of soft lips following the path of caressing fingers to settle over a flat masculine nipple. Deep groan rumbling from his depths, he buried his fingers into a cloud of moonbeam hair and for a long, devastating moment urged nearer this source of piercing pleasure.

Then, determined to return kind for kind, Evain's fingertips swept tantalizing pleasure from her throat through the deep valley between the perfection of generous breasts. Her head arched back and eyes closed on a strangled gasp as his hands started a return journey. Fascinated by her helpless response to his touch, Evain opened his fingers to slowly, slowly glide up, stroking welcome torment over sensitive skin that trembled.

Every feeling centered on the scorching touch, a small sob of protest escaped Anya when her sorcerer's fiery caress hesitated a breath below her throbbing breasts. Sensing Anya's legs threatening to give way, Evain swept her hips tight to his with one arm while the other hand remained curved around her rib cage. Her breath caught in an agony of waiting until slowly, aching moments later his palm moved up and in a warm, slightly abrasive caress cupped the delicious weight. He stopped again while an intense blue gaze fastened upon what his hand cradled.

"You are a delicacy I find myself unable to live without." The growled words were deep and darkly textured as he bent and pressed a whisper-light kiss to a pale rose crown. Withdrawing he watched with a faint, satisfied smile as Anya involuntarily arched toward his retreating lips—small payment for the agony of nights spent in hot, hopeless dreams. He returned to deliver a frustratingly brief kiss, a slight suction painfully sweet but able only to increase the cravings of them both.

Breath caught on starving need and an indistinct plea for the torment's return, Anya twined slender fingers into midnight black strands and tugged until he relented. Evain wrapped both arms fully around the hungry maid and urgently lifted her completely off her feet, bringing the luscious bounty of her flesh to the ravishment of his lips. Anya was lost in a haze of smoldering hunger and gladly surrendered to her sorcerer's enveloping heat, arms twining tighter about his neck, pulling him nearer still.

He allowed her to slowly slide down his powerful form until their bodies met, hard chest against soft breasts, hip to hip, thigh to thigh, and with a mouth warm and hard he drank the heady nectar of hers. The intimacy of the embrace dragged an aching moan from Anya's throat while under the welcome demand of his lips, she arched nearer. Readily yielding to her wordless demand, he deepened the kiss with a devastating slowness that sent wild shudders of sensation through her. His hands curved over her firm derriere and angled her to brush against the full length of his burning need.

Not certain what sweet quirk of fate had gifted her with this second experience of a pleasured love she'd thought would be ever forbidden but unwilling to question the good fortune, Anya purposefully sought the fire storm's hottest flames. Provoking the sorcerer's tempest, she clasped his hips nearer and surged against him in the feverish rhythm of passion's fury she'd learned in his arms. The flames leaped higher and higher as Evain moved her in a sweet, tender rotation. Lost in hungry need, her hands locked about his neck and nails dug into the smooth flesh of his shoulders as her body twisted against his, enticing, inciting.

Evain shuddered wildly. Admitting his own unmanageable need, he caught Anya up into his mighty arms, carried her from enchanted waters, and lowered her through the gentle lavender mists of dusk to a cushion of lush grasses. Toward the mage who held her heart and so easily summoned the storm of her desires, Anya lifted arms and glowing eyes filled with unshielded love. Permitting no moment of doubt for the right of his deed, Evain yielded to his elfling's magical temptations and his own unending love. He moved to settle above her, and Anya cried out with pleasure under his full weight, hot and strong. She wrapped silken legs about him as he lifted her hips to slowly join their bodies in the most intimate of embraces.

Like two flames dancing in the fire's midst they twined and surged together, stoking hungry flames to an ever more intense blaze. Anya clung to their source, striving to match the tempest's fury while her nerves stretched taut. Burning winds of desperate desire grew wilder and wilder until Anya thought she could bear no greater pleasure. At last, as the primal rhythm of all natural powers strived for its tumultuous pinnacle, Evain returned a precious gift given, whispering into Anya's ear, "I will love you forever."

Under the power of these longed-for words the unbearably sweet tension of Anya's feverish yearning burst into a passionate shower of fiery delights and delicious fulfillment.

Adrift in a haze of contentment, Evain's strong arms cradled a still trembling Anya close. With one hand he smoothed the tangled mass of her soft gold mane while a satisfied smile curled the lips pressing gentle kisses to the top of her head.

Snuggling into her sorcerer's embrace, Anya took joy in the feel of the hard chest beneath her cheek and the touch of tender lips on her hair. Willfully she lingered in the misty half sleep of honeyed satisfaction, refusing to blight the pure glow of a dream come true with a feared reality. But once acknowledged even so far as to refuse its company, the thought could not be squelched.

Anya went unnaturally still while in her mind loomed the fear that once cool sanity returned, Evain would rue the declaration of love made in the heat of passion. A kiss-swollen lip was firmly bit to stifle a moan of distress even as she blocked the bleak possibility with a certain fact. No matter what came after, the sound of the words uttered in his deeply textured voice while strong arms claimed her as his own was a memory to be cherished always.

Evain felt the uneasiness seeping into his elfling and found it worrisome—but only for a moment. Then, suspecting its source, he immediately sought to drive any doubt from her mind with words that caught her breath with happiness. And yet, Anya's happiness contained a faint, lingering echo of anxiety that Evain might later regret them.

"I have loved you always. While you were a toddling and then a child it was the uncomplicated, loving fondness of an older brother. Then came the day I returned to the keep and found you were no longer the serious child ever following me about. Nothing was ever simple again." Evain shifted Anya to rise up on one arm and gaze down into anxious green eyes. "With every visit my love for you deepened until I had to stay away from the maiden who was the heart of a terrifying emotion neither Druidic training nor sorcerer's spell could tame."

Though more precious to Anya than any other gift could ever be, Evain's declaration revealed seeds of truth she feared would eventually sour the sweetness of his love for her. Small teeth nibbled a full lower lip to rosy brightness while Evain spoke, but when he paused, she promptly confessed a growing guilt.

"I pray you will forgive me the selfishness in my stubborn attempts to seek a relationship able to threaten your destiny. It would be too high a price, one I'd never ask you to pay."

"Nay, I was the stubborn fool." Evain's soft laughter flowed over her like a comforting caress. "You knew what I couldn't believe, despite the signs. And by my disbelief I defied a basic Druidic precept: The sacredness of in-between, the magic of things that are neither one thing nor another. Like you—both Saxon and Cymry; Christian and Druid."

Deep blue eyes gone soft brushed love over the winsome face below that soon bloomed with shy pleasure.

"It was my wrong," Evain repeated in a voice deep with the anguish of what could have been, "and it nearly cost me the thing most precious in my life . . . you."

With the last word Evain's mouth dipped to meet lips willingly offered in a kiss of piercing sweetness that threatened to reignite passion's fires.

Evain pulled back, slightly shaking his ebony mane while with a smile as potent as the kiss he regretfully said, "We daren't yield to honeyed temptations again." He absently waved toward the soft darkness all around. "The night is full upon us and I suspect that in concern for our safety either my sister or Keir will soon set out to find us. To prevent that we must return to the cavern."

His own mention of the boy reminded Evain of a fact to be shared with the woman he need no longer keep at arm's length—as if he'd succeeded at that in the first instance.

"While you and Keir came out to gather wood, Elesa shared with me another vision."

Though the moon had yet to rise, golden hair captured starshine to glow as Anya nodded encouragement to the man who paused to speak although he'd said they must go.

"I had yet another unknown sister." These were facts so new to Evain that he paused to martial them into sensible order. "This one older."

"And Keir's mother." The realization struck Anya even as she spoke it. It fit with what the boy had told her about the grandfather who as a Druid sorcerer had been slain by those frightened of his powers. Indeed, she'd told Keir then that Evain's parents had died in the same manner.

A slight smile returned to Evain's lips as again he nodded. "Keir is my nephew."

He was not surprised that Anya had so quickly discerned the truth. Although he'd failed to sense her bond with nature, he'd always known how sharp were the wits residing behind her mask of solemn serenity.

That Evain apparently had no difficulty in accepting Keir as kin pleased Anya. But with thought of the scene during which Keir had told her of his Druid background came a realization that she had failed to tell him what had been learned in the barn at Ecley Abbey.

"As you are recovered, I have news near as important as Elesa's vision of Adam which must be shared." Though she ought to have told him when first he awoke, Anya comforted herself with the belief that 'twas better done now after his strength and clear wits were restored. "'Tis information over which Bishop Wilfrid gloated while telling me."

With blue eyes unwaveringly upon her, she recounted all that the bishop had said, from the threat against Throckenholt to his intent to use his captives as bait to lure others they loved to their doom.

By the time the sound of her last words faded into silence the air fair throbbed with Evain's determination to once again defeat the bishop plainly as vindictive as he was greedy. Evain donned his clothing with great haste only to discover Anya struggling unsuccessfully to match his speed in pulling on thankfully dry garb. Then, despite his impatience to set in motion the deeds meant to secure his goal, he gently brushed fumbling fingers aside to finish the task with an expertise whose source Anya chose not consider.

Evain sensed her thoughts and with one finger lifted her chin to place a quick, reassuring kiss upon soft lips before taking her hand to lead her from their private haven of sweet peace and fiery delight.

Chapter
17

"Aye, close to your home." Elesa's smile was wry.
"Another stone fortress of the ancients."

Sword already belted about his hips, Evain's eyes
narrowed on the bag repacked with a fresh supply of
foodstuffs and leaning against his satchel, both sitting
at the gloomy cavern's doorway awaiting an imminent
departure. His sister had no need to give the site a
name. He recognized it by the description and his lips
curled in disgust. How better to hide something than
where least expected—in plain sight? Hidden until
came the moment for a scheme's final scene, the one
forewarned by a bishop foolishly bragging of hostages
to be dangled as human bait luring prey to Roman
ruins long abandoned and ignored on their own
coastline.

Exercising her habit of solemn patience, Anya
waited to one side of the siblings facing each other

across the fire's low-burning flames. Her attitude of motionless quiet seemed to spread to the fox at her feet and to Keir standing a pace behind. She, too, had discerned the fact behind a Druid-trained seeress's less than definitive statement. And while closely watching the unfolding scene was glad she'd already arranged for Blossom to remain with Elesa. Though Anya was fond of the horse, the placid mare would be utterly useless on a journey requiring speed and was better left here in contentment.

Evain's attention lifted to their hostess. "Now share your magical means to see us reach our destination with promised haste."

Wanting to leave this area where the bishop held sway under shield of darkness, the better to elude would-be captors, Evain had sought an immediate departure upon return to the cavern the previous night. Elesa forestalled his plan by heatedly repeating earlier claims of an ability to see their journey completed with infinitely greater safety and speed—if they waited till the dawning. Now aware of their destination, he knew how long it would take them to walk there even were they to continue days and nights without rest, a deed which could see them dangerously weakened. In truth, the prospect of the length of time required was daunting and likely increased risks to the success of his strategy for blocking their enemy's intent. Their best hope lay in his sister's promises.

"Bring your supplies and come." Motioning her three guests to lift waiting baggage, Elesa roused Anya's curiosity by picking up a square package of carefully folded turquoise cloth bound with twine.

While the three visitors adjusted their burdens for the journey, their hostess held her package tight in one arm and with the other put the tallow dipped end of bound rushes into the fire. It smoldered and then burst into light. Elesa surprised the trio waiting at her haven's door to the forest above by turning to move toward the opposite wall.

Elesa could feel their curious eyes upon her back. Even her powerful brother was startled, a fact she found amusing. In the next instant she regretted that response, fearing the decade which had passed since she'd shattered her crystal and with it her connection to dark powers had not completely smothered the perverse nature that bond had spawned. Forcing her thoughts from a guilt likely to ever be hers, she pressed fingertips into one shadow amongst many on the rough and seemingly solid wall. At her command a large rock slowly rolled away.

Evain was annoyed with himself for his surprise over the trick of a boulder not unlike the one which guarded the entrance to his cave-home in the mountains of Talacharn.

When Elesa held her firebrand into the darkness beyond the opening, it revealed a steeply descending pathway whose one side dropped into a black void of unknown depth. She was first to step into the darkness.

Evain next sent Keir and then Anya, a wary but loyal fox at her heels. He waited to come last and guard the procession's rear against unknown perils. The thud of his staff striking stone as they moved cautiously downward was soon drowned out by the sound of rushing waters. A broad white smile flashed across his face. A river flowing beneath the earth, one unimpeded by the contours of the surface and able to flow in lines more direct. He began a quiet chant, summoning a claw held crystal to life. Soon its much brighter glow made Elesa's firebrand useless, save for the return journey she would make alone.

Neither Anya nor Keir yet possessed the secret training to know what to expect but not for a moment did they question the right in trusting those who did. And after the descending pathway took several sharp turns their doubts were lost in the awe of strange new sights. Formations like massive icicles of stone both dripped from the gloom above and rose from the darkness below.

The route wound around a sweeping corner to halt on a broad flat area verging on an underground river moving slowly at outer edges but rapidly in the center. The air was heavy with moisture. Against the base of one jagged spike soaring from the damp floor on one side lay a long, thin skiff.

As Evain settled the vessel into the shallows at water's edge, his sister offered a final piece of necessary information . . . and a last warning.

"On the banks where this river flows out to join the sea is the small hamlet of Ybryn where lives a fisherman known as Huw. Though taciturn and of ominous visage, he will sail you to your destination."

Elesa smiled grimly while adding, "I'd a vision last eve of a mighty storm brewing over Throckenholt Keep. I cannot tell if 'tis merely my past or your future, though I fear it more likely the latter."

As the seeress had not been told of the bishop's threats against his beloved's home and thus had no reason to feign such a portent, Evain agreed. However, sensing Anya's immediate tension though she went as motionless as if she'd become another of the odd stone formations sprouting from the tunnel's floor, he said nothing of it. Rather he questioned Elesa's first statement.

"How will this Huw be persuaded to carry us on the treacherous journey to where we must go?"

"When you emerge with my skiff, he'll know you come from me." Seeing this was not sufficient explanation to satisfy the wary sorcerer, Elesa added, "By deeds I foretold when first we met, Huw's family was spared from the deadly assault of stealthy night raiders."

Evain's half smile reappeared as Elesa further explained, "While the tide was out they hid in my sea-cave. The one through which you will arrive."

"How can we be certain to reach that point while the tide is out and the passage open to the sea?"

"'Tis why I insisted your departure must wait for the dawning." Elesa shook her head, gazing at him in mild disgust. That her brother bothered to ask made it clear he still hesitated to fully trust her.

Though never had he previously employed such routes nor was he familiar with this particular river, Evain had been taught of the secret pathways under the earth. And he had learned the rules that governed them well enough to know Elesa spoke true. It was not that he'd sincerely doubted her good faith but the same training responsible for his knowledge of underground passages had ingrained caution in him. It was why he'd felt compelled to present this minor test.

Anya felt the strain between the siblings and was relieved when Evain sent his sister a brilliant smile. Preparations for departure were quickly resumed. Anya was directed to settle in the prow while Keir was to sit in the middle and Evain to work the oar from the back. Nodding her understanding of these arrangements, Anya wasted no moment to bend and place the bag of foodstuffs between her position and Keir's. As she straightened, Elesa stepped forward.

"I noted that you've no change of clothes and thought you might appreciate this garment to remedy that lack." Elesa held out the twine-bound packet Anya had wondered about.

"Appreciate it I would . . . but are you certain you wish to part with a garment so fine?" Though as 'twas carefully folded Anya couldn't see what manner of dress it was, the cloth was rich and even in the eerie joined light of flame and crystal, the gleam of a gold edging was unmistakable.

"'Tis useless to me now." Elesa shrugged but the motion did nothing to lessen the stiffness of her wary wait for possible rejection. "I offer it in thanks both for saving my brother's life . . . and for the happiness my visions show you will bring him. Thus, your acceptance of my gift would give me joy."

Thrilled by the prophecy of future happiness with her beloved, Anya's sweet smile glowed as she clasped soft cloth close. She would value the rich gift but would treasure it more for the sincerity of the giver.

Elesa felt warmed by the smile, a warmth doubled by the approval in the steady gaze of a sorcerer upon her back. She turned toward the man standing behind with oar in one hand and in the other a staff topped by a luminescent orb.

"For giving us safe harbor, sharing your warnings, and providing this safe and hasty passage, I am grateful, *sister.*" Evain emphasized the bond. "But even more am I thankful to you for revealing a nephew unknown and directing me toward paths of knowledge even my great mentor did not know."

As he said the word *nephew,* Keir's ears pricked and he glanced toward Evain to meet the miraculously meaningful smile of the sorcerer who nodded toward him! He was bewildered but ecstatic at the possibility.

"Will we see you again?" Evain shifted his attention back to Elesa.

Anya was amazed by the rarity of a sorcerer asking such a question of someone lacking Druidic powers, but his sister recognized the action as a measure of respect she would treasure.

Elesa's somber expression broke into a beaming smile although she gave her head a slight shake before stating, "You may not see me, but I assuredly will see you in my visions."

Remembering his sister's forlorn statement that she was oft shown glimpses of what she'd lost, Evain felt stricken by regret on her behalf.

Seeing in his expression an emotion bordering on unsought pity, Elesa sternly cautioned, "Best you be off elsewise you'll miss the outgoing tide."

"And all our work will truly go for naught," Evain finished her warning.

With the three settled into their positions, belongings stowed and even a clearly apprehensive Noddi inside the skiff, pointed nose burrowed between Evain's satchel and Keir's bag of treasures, they pushed off from an underground shore. The sorcerer's staff, as well as his sword, lay lengthwise just inside the vessel. By the glowing crystal brushing his thigh, Evain maneuvered the skiff into the river's fast-moving central channel and the journey through an eerily beautiful tunnel was begun.

While they sailed up the mouth of a river with Huw manning the rudder as his oldest son started to bring down the boat's square sail, Anya could see the bay where they were to be put ashore. She was sore from so many hours—a whole day and night—in one water-borne vessel or another. After a sennight and more of walking, she'd never thought to be tired of sitting, but she was. And yet mundane discomforts were of small matter when laid beside perils looming over family, home, and, worst of all, her beloved, who beyond doubt would walk into the greatest danger before ominous threats were defeated.

Evain leaned against the side of the long, narrow boat to watch as the sun cleared the horizon and dawn's bright shades faded into pale blue. This new sunrise and the promise of safe landfall brought proof to the two fishermen of the truth in his claim of a power able to guide them safely around rocky shores in the dead of night. Throughout the dark hours he had both manned the rudder and chanted control over the wind filling their sail. Tasks which left him both physically and mentally weary.

As Elesa had promised, the fisherman she'd befriended had willingly accepted the request to sail a sorcerer and his two companions from village quay to the requested destination. Huw had, however, balked at the thought of beginning their journey shortly after the nooning hour. A deed which meant being asea during night hours, and one dangerous even with a full moon to lessen the gloom. Yet, faced with a Druid sorcerer and his mysteriously glowing staff, he'd reluctantly undertaken the task.

Sensing Evain's exhaustion, Anya turned to send a smile of sweet comfort over her shoulder to the man behind.

"Are you ready for our next adventure?" Evain asked his brave elfling who'd sat quiet and motionless through more than a few harrowing moments at sea.

Despite the certainty that a sorcerer could sense her emotions, Anya attempted to hide her apprehensions by calming them with the memory of Elesa's vision. The seeress's prediction of future happiness she would hold tight as a mental talisman against defeat and refuse to consider the possibility that the woman might've lied solely to provide comfort.

At the sound of Evain's voice, a sleeping Keir stirred and sat up. During their hours on the subterranean river the sorcerer had told the boy of his own parents and how it was that they were related. He'd also promised Keir his heart's desire—training to a sorcerer's skills.

"Are we there yet?" the youngster questioned.

"Very nearly so." Anya waved toward the shore to which they were rapidly drawing closer.

As the hull scraped against the shore's coarse sand and small rocks, Evain threw his sheathed sword, satchel, one bag of foodstuffs, and another with Keir's possessions safely into the dry grasses a distance up the bank. He hopped into shallow water, then lifted first Noddi down and next set the boy atop rocks sprayed by steadily rolling waves. After retrieving his precious stave, Evain stretched it out toward Keir.

"Hold it safe for me until I am ready to take it

back?" Evain asked this of his nephew in a first simple test of aptitude for the lessons to come.

Rightly deeming the safekeeping of a sorcerer's stave a sober responsibility, Keir's face went grave as he held the object near twice his size with great good care.

Evain cast the boy a quick smile before turning back to the boat. While his staff was diligently guarded, he reached up to welcome Anya into the cradle of waiting arms. Her he carried all the way into the shadows beyond forest edge.

Anya showed her pleasure in her sorcerer's acceptance of his nephew by the brilliance of the smile she gave him while cuddling closer into strong, possessive arms.

In return, suspecting this would be their last moment of privacy for some little while, Evain claimed a devastatingly passionate kiss of necessity too soon ended. Then reluctantly turning away, he went back to once more thank fishermen awed by a sorcerer's ability to navigate around treacherous impediments unseen in the dark yet assuredly plentiful along a rocky coastline.

"Will they be able to return to their home safely without you to aid them?" Keir asked as Evain approached him.

Accepting his staff from the boy, Evain answered. "By departing on their return journey immediately, they'll be able to reach their own harbor before sunset and in daylight they have no need of me."

As Huw and his son put back out to sea, the sorcerer and his companions moved into the woodland and began to climb the steep hill overlooking a fortress built on the shore around the first bend. The trail was arduous and rife with jagged outcroppings which forced them to deviate from a direct ascent and took longer than expected. An unfortunate reality made more serious by the certainty that a safe descent on the far side would require even more time.

Their difficult climb was accomplished in near silence, save for Evain's request that Anya tell him how she had won freedom from Ecley Abbey for herself and Keir. After she explained the trick played on the bishop with the spell of shielding, Evain gave his resourceful elfling a loving smile of approval. A hush broken only by bird song and sound of their footsteps then settled again over the band toiling to scale the tor. This while he spent the remainder of their upward journey devising a plan to perform the feat originally at the heart of the quest upon which he'd embarked when setting forth from Throckenholt.

When at last they stood at the hill's peak, from the shield of thick trees they could clearly see their goal. The Roman stronghold of Venda was known to Evain but to both Anya and Keir the ruins that had survived on a rocky finger of land jutting out from the coastline were both amazing and fearsome. Its position of dominance made it easily defensible and gave it an unobstructed view of all who approached. The latter fact explained why Evain had arranged for them to be put ashore before rounding the bend.

Toward the goal of winning freedom for the captives within, Evain closely examined not the fortress alone but searched for signs of life around it. There were few, only a small group of horses grazing inside a roofless stone room overgrown with vegetation. It was a good sign.

Initially Evain had rued the company of first Anya

and then Keir, but he now was thankful for both. He could easily perform the simple spell necessary to win their first goal. And yet, exhausted by his night's work and faced with the prospect of an infinitely more demanding challenge to come, he was wise enough not to do so. Rather he would entrust these two with the lesser mission and conserve his energies for the sake of successfully wielding them during the mighty confrontation by a seeress foretold.

"Keir—" Evain's call broke a hilltop silence into which few natural sounds intruded. "Will you do what I ask?"

Although he'd given the same promise before being permitted to accompany the sorcerer, Keir gazed up at Evain and instantly nodded.

"Cup your hands together and hold them steadily in front of you no matter what occurs."

While the boy obeyed, lifting cupped palms without pause, Evain dug into the pouch attached to his sword belt and pulled out a use-smoothed white quartz. After briefly rolling the stone between his palms and offering a short chant, it answered a sorcerer's call with a bright glow.

Keir silently gasped when Evain gently rolled the luminous crystal into his hands. Not for a moment did its brilliance flicker nor did the boy react with fear. Rather he gazed at it with wonder. Evain nodded, satisfied that his plan would succeed.

"We'll all descend the slope together but at the bottom, while daylight fades, the two of you must take the next step alone." Evain was pleased that neither questioned his statement. "Anya will chant her spell of shielding, enabling you both to enter the fortress unseen."

Anya was thrilled by words showing not merely that Evain honestly believed she possessed Druidic powers but also that she would be given a chance to fulfill her dream of proving her aid of value to him.

"Once inside, Keir, you must hold the glowing crystal near enough to her to keep you both hidden while she—who knows the proper amounts—pours a sufficient measure of sleeping draught into the guards' every source of ale. Once the rest of the wicked overtakes them, find their prisoners and free them, if you can. Should their cell be so firmly barred that you are unable to open it alone, you need only wave a firebrand from the tower you see there"—he motioned toward a ragged spire—"the one rising higher than any other, and I will come to help set them free."

Evain hadn't told Keir that 'twas his sister confined with Adam for fear something might happen to the child before she could be rescued, leaving the boy to twice grieve for the small maid's loss. However, Keir's unspoken and tentative hopes were already roused.

Solemnly listening to a sorcerer's plan, Anya saw Evain's purpose clearly enough to recognize his reasoning. She was unlikely to forget the warning that her home lay in the eye of an ominous storm. And well she knew Evain was the only hope for the people of Throckenholt, as he alone was capable of commanding the fearsome forces of nature to drive the armies of threatening foes into submission. To rouse, control, and then to quiet such unruly, violent forces his powers must be fully restored. Evain's would be by far the most difficult feat and she would do anything to see her love had no need to attempt it with his strength needlessly weakened.

Their descent through dense trees and around huge

boulders was as arduous as the climb had been. But, as planned, they arrived at the forest's edge while the sun slipped behind the western horizon. Under Evain's encouragement, Anya's sweet voice lifted in the chant of shielding and her crystal quickly responded.

For the first time in many years Evain stood back to watch while others wielded Druidic powers to undertake an objective alone. The event was most disconcerting for the fact that it involved his half-Saxon elfling going into night darkness and possible peril alone. He nearly went after the pair but an unwillingness to crush their pride in his trust of them held him back, and they moved rapidly forward until even the pinprick gleam of their crystal's light disappeared.

While a sorcerer anxiously waited, Keir reached for an outer door amazingly unguarded and easily opened. Staying close together, the two of them made their way toward the raucous sound of men obviously already ale-soaked. Anya recognized the signs from feasts attended at home and while visiting other keeps with her parents. Though it seemed much too early in the evening for such sotted behavior, she deemed it possible these fools were so near drunken stupors her potion would be unnecessary.

As Anya and Keir stepped into an area of the abandoned and crumbling fortress crudely patched into a makeshift hall, they found the source of the voices. Lolling about in rumpled, ale-stained clothing, it was obvious that these five guardsmen were either poorly trained or poorly supervised. Mayhap both. Whatever the case, they'd likely been drinking the whole day through. One's face already lay in a trencher which showed little sign of solid food having resided upon it in any recent time.

Quashing her distaste, Anya set about doing what she'd been sent to do. Carefully transferring her crystal into Keir's hands, she pulled out her vial of sleeping elixir. Weaving an odd path around reeling men, evading wildly swung arms and a body falling motionless to the floor, she led Keir in moving from mug to bottle to cask. To each she added a drop or more, depending upon the container's size.

Although Evain had faith in her ability to chant a spell strong enough to last until the sleeping potion took effect, Anya was not so certain it would continue that long and wanted to waste no time in locating the prisoners. While the loud, nearly indiscernible babble went on, she led Keir into a series of corridors, open to the stars overhead. Against each of a variety of doors she placed her ear in hopes of catching a revealing sound.

At last she heard a small girl's giggle. The metal rod running through two iron loops driven into stone on either side of the door was easy to remove. And the oak planks of considerably more recent construction than the fortress were quickly opened.

Only when a startled Adam looked up and with a distrustful look approached the open portal did Anya realize her spell prevented the golden-haired warrior as well as their foes from seeing either her or Keir. A fact which made it the more surprising when the little girl Adam had set carefully to one side as he rose jumped up. Plainly not blinded by the spell, the child squealed with glee and launched herself at Keir—knocking the crystal from his hold.

Keir was stricken by the dropped crystal but the guilt was swamped by the joy in having his little sister alive and returned to him again.

"Anya!" Adam growled, momentarily startled by the sudden appearance of this maid where a moment past had been nothing. In the next instant his gaze dropped to the stone rolling across an uneven floor and all was explained. Its purpose he knew well enough after ten years with his beloved Druid wife. The only surprise left was that Wulf's half-Saxon daughter could wield its powers.

Anya regretted her impatience in seeking out prisoners as the sound of their discovery drew the attention of leastways one of the captors. A burly man staggered into the corridor making a belligerent demand for quiet.

Before could be raised an alarm of questionable use, considering the only men who could be summoned were equally lost in befuddling seas of ale, Adam dropped the man with a quick blow to the chin.

While retrieving her now cold stone, Anya very softly cautioned Adam that they need only wait to slip away until the two still conscious dropped into sleep.

Adam grinned at the quiet young woman. He'd often wondered what lay hidden behind her serene mask and now he saw the fires of a determined spirit in glowing green eyes. It was she who crept forward to peer around the corner and surreptitiously watch until the last foe dropped into a deep, unnatural slumber.

As they slipped from the fortress, Anya felt secure enough to speak without fear of being overheard.

"Evain awaits our coming and will explain what must be done to defeat a great host gathering with the intent of shattering Northumbria into pieces of a size they can consume . . . starting with Throckenholt."

Adam's bronze brows arched in surprise. First, that not Evain but Anya had come with a boy unknown to him though plainly familiar to his little companion, Sian. Second, that this odd group had secured such vital information. However, his experience with Druids prevented an instant's doubt for the claim. It merely increased his wish to reach the sorcerer's side. Clearly, matters had worsened considerably during the months of his captivity.

Anya could see the long-held ealdorman was anxious to rejoin the fray and ensure that the toads who'd taken him would meet defeat. However, Evain had given her and Keir one more task. They must free the guardsmen's destriers and chase them into the wilds —unless Adam chose to claim one to aid his fulfillment of obligations owed his king. Anya knew Evain, accustomed to the wild terrain of the Cymry princedoms, found little use for the beasts. She understood his reasoning—only see what hindrance Blossom had most oft been in their journey. Thus, she wouldn't question him on the wisdom of taking horses for themselves, particularly not these war-horses whose power neither she nor Keir were likely able to control.

However, Adam did select a mighty stallion which he quickly saddled while Keir and Anya drove the others toward forest darkness. Once their small band reached the woodland's edge, toddler again cradled in the mounted Adam's arms, Evain stepped forward to meet them.

"What is this I hear about forces massing to conquer Northumbria?" Adam impatiently asked before the sorcerer could speak.

Rarely willing to bend to another's pace, Evain gazed into the solemn face of the child in his questioner's arms. It was framed by raven-dark hair and the eyes meeting his were a mirror of his own. An undeniable family bond. His mocking smile flashed in the moonlit night but it soon tilted with disgust for the answer to be given.

"Though King Aldfrith's designs were never in question, Bishop Wilfrid has again brewed a venomous potion. Combining the rulers of the Saxon kingdoms of Mercia and Wessex with the Cymry princedom of Gwyll, the brew is stirred with a potent vengeance for past foes such as you and spiced with hatred of all Druids. This he means to pour like scalding liquid over Throckenholt."

Adam's bronze brows met in a ferocious frown. "Not again!"

Evain nodded, black hair catching a white gleam from the night heaven's light. "I and my two companions mean to journey there immediately and see what spells we can conjure to forestall the bishop's intent."

Anya smiled, warmed with pleasure for this demonstration of her beloved's unspoken praise of the success won in the deed just done and his acceptance of her possible value in the dangerous scene to come.

"I hope," Evain added a request of Adam whose shire neighbored his king's personal lands and were on the path to the royal court, "that you will deliver to my sister *our* niece and then journey on to warn Aldfrith of the peril meant to see its poison flow out from Throckenholt and spread over all Northumbria."

Eyes narrowing on his wife's brother, Adam asked a single word question, "Niece?"

"Aye." Evain impatiently nodded. "I'll explain all . . . after our victory is won and the wretched bishop is once again scalded by his own brew."

Chapter
18

Although Keir peered up, looking for signs of the predicted storm, save for the first drifts of dusk's purple haze, the sky remained as clear as it had throughout their day's journey from the forest above Venda.

Keir had been born on Throckenholt lands yet had never visited its lords' keep and thus had no way of knowing how far or how near they were to that destination. But Anya did and the closer they came to her threatened home, the faster she walked. And at the last she rushed past Evain to sweep aside a final leafy impediment, anxious to view familiar tilled fields. Anya came to an abrupt halt with Noddi at her heels. After warriors were summoned to defend the kingdom, these fields had been laboriously plowed by people unsuited to the chore. The result of their toil had been laid to waste by the booted feet of massed armies. She glared at the forces encamped about palisade wall encircling village and keep. These unwelcome visitors had pitched their tents at the base of that protective barrier formed of sturdy tree trunks stripped of branches, set upright in lines, and tightly bound together with tip ends sharpened into points.

Evain came to stand behind Anya and, resting his staff in the crook of a tree trunk, placed his hands comfortingly on her shoulders while his sapphire eyes narrowed on the unpleasant sight. It had been his plan to send Lady Brynna, her sons, and all the village inhabitants to safety before this force could arrive and be greeted by a sorcerer's fury. Plainly he had erred in permitting himself to spend the previous night at rest in the forest, seeking complete restoration of powers sufficient to execute the formidable feat ahead.

As Evain's fingers unintentionally tightened on her shoulders, Anya suspected his regret and its source. This was her home and her family and never would she knowingly do anything to harm them. And yet she could not rue a past and unintentional action. She bit at her lip, refusing guilt for treasured hours wrapped in her sorcerer's arms. With Keir nearby, not hours spent in passion but rather in love.

"I'll never regret time spent with you." Sensing his elfling's emotions, Evain bent to whisper in an ear he lightly kissed. "Only that we've delayed too long to see my strategy employed afore these wretches arrived."

Anya nodded. She regretted that as well.

"As our foes are already here there is no longer any possibility of waiting for Adam to deliver Sian to my sister and bring your king with his fyrd to Throckenholt's defense." Evain had never intended to wait before dealing with the threat but spoke as much to himself as to his companions.

There was assuredly no need to restate the dark fact Anya had told him in recounting what Bishop Wilfrid had revealed to her as his captive. By the foolish man's own words they knew that the fiery destruction of Throckenholt Keep and its village was to be withheld only long enough for Brynna and her sons to be taken hostage. Moreover, with no credible protectors within, the burning of the keep and village was likely viewed as a deed easily done. And, Evain ruefully acknowledged, rightly so. He was far more aware than these foes camped at the barricade's foot that his foster mother's Druidic skills were honed to aid and heal, not to harm and destroy. Thus, her powers were utterly inadequate to meet this challenge alone.

Certain that the man who'd gone quiet was considering alternative plans to defeat the bishop and his allies, Anya made a tentative suggestion.

"Keir and I could repeat the feat of yestereve." When Evain failed to immediately discount her proposal, she expanded on the idea. "You could chant your small crystal to a shielding spell and Keir could carry it while I carry my own. And though the gates are assuredly barred from the inside, together he and I could bring them out through the hidden postern door."

Still at the tender maid's back, Evain bitterly smiled. Anya lacked both his experience and training in the methods of humankind's wars. He would not high-handedly dismiss her ideas. Rather, he sought to gently point out the flaw in her reasoning. "How is it that your mother, who is perfectly capable of the same feat, has not chosen to do so?"

Anya frowned, annoyed with herself for not stopping to consider such a simple fact at the outset. And yet an old habit which she'd thought left at Throckenholt's gates many days past reasserted itself. She questioned her sorcerer's statement before the words could be bitten back.

"Perhaps it would be too difficult to hold herself and the three boys safely inside the ring of light?" It was a foolish explanation and Anya blushed as she offered it.

Evain's soft laughter stirred pale gold locks escaped from tight braids. Had the neophyte sorceress already taken up a sorcerer's habit of odd mood shifts? No matter, the moment of amusement was welcome amidst great strain.

"Brynna's powers are such as she can easily summon a glow bright enough to cover both herself and the boys."

"Then why?" Anya briefly questioned despite an awareness of the answer as deep as Evain's. A pall of fear for her mother and brothers—and all in Throckenholt—descended like an overwhelming burden upon her slender shoulders.

While his strong hands pulled the dainty maid back against the strong comfort of his chest, Evain answered just as seriously. "I'm certain your mother knows what the bishop intends for Throckenholt once he has secured the captives he seeks."

Anya shuddered as to her mind came the immediate mental image of her home swept by a terrifying wall of flame like the conflagration which had consumed Keir's home. She reached out to the solemn boy who had moved to join companions quietly discussing the ominous view.

"Your lady mother," Evain softly finished the answer to Anya's simple query, "won't abandon her people to meet so ghastly an end." Since the day a young Evain had joined Brynna in a Druid's cave-home, now his, he'd realized this woman who became his foster mother had a particular affinity for life and all living things. "For any life lost at the expense of saving her own, she would never stop grieving nor would she ever forgive herself."

Anya knew it was so and yet more than her mother's life was at risk and she argued, "Mother might allow us to bring the boys to safety."

"Safety? Where? Not here unprotected from armed foes likely to find even well-concealed prey." Evain dryly added, "Can you envision either of your brothers easily bending to an order to remain quietly hidden?"

Anya grimaced, inwardly admitting that Cub and Edwyn, both rowdy by nature, were far more likely to make wildly impossible attempts to take on the entire opposing army by themselves. She chose not to acknowledge that this was precisely the feat being attempted by herself, Keir, and Evain. After all, they were Druids as her brothers were not.

"Nay." Evain shook his head. "What we must do is save the keep, the village, and your family. Not by individual pieces but in one whole."

Evain's face went impassive and his gaze intently studied unmoving shapes in the gloom. Though Anya could not see his face, she felt heartened. He was, of a certainty, worthy of the trust she put in him to find the answer. Only was she sorry that her suggestion had been of so little use.

"We cannot bring people *out* of Throckenholt

but . . ." As Evain slowly spoke, Anya angled her face to glance up and see his mocking smile appear.

Anxious to hear her sorcerer's plan, Anya turned full about in his arms while Keir took a step nearer.

"We can go *in* unseen through the postern door."

At the look of confusion on the faces of both his companions, Evain's deep laughter rumbled. He felt freed by this simple answer which his fears for those within had prevented him from seeing immediately— proof of the vital import of a sorcerer holding himself in complete serenity.

"Once inside, I mean to do precisely what I planned. Whether the keep be empty or filled to overflowing is of no matter. Though our foes cover the ground like a plague of swarming ants, they cannot possibly stand against the vast powers I will wield in Throckenholt's defense."

Anya felt currents of energy coursing through Evain. They calmed her every apprehension. She joined her beloved sorcerer in spreading their unspoken confidence to Keir.

Evain turned to take his staff in hand as he began a low chanting that summoned a brilliant glow to its claw-held crystal. By its shielding light three people and one fox boldly walked through the camp of their foes and circled the palisade to slip through its hidden rear door. Even after they were inside Throckenholt's walls, to prevent possible challenges or curious eyes from following their path, they continued in the crystal's concealment to cross fields behind the keep and enter that structure itself.

When the three entered the Lord of Throckenholt's great hall, Evain permitted the glow to fade, startling most of those within. Only Lady Brynna seemed unsurprised as from one of the two chairs ever drawn near the central hearth she gracefully rose to welcome the newcomers.

"Anya—" Brynna opened her arms for the daughter quick to fly into their loving embrace. "I will chant a song of gratitude for answered pleas."

"I've come through our successful quest all of a piece, Mama." Anya hastened to reassure a mother's fears, something to which she'd given too little thought. Confessions of dangers overcome and a captivity defeated could wait for a time of less tension.

· Even as the words left Anya's lips, Cub hugged her about the waist and Edwyn tugged at her hand.

"Who is he?" Edwyn's whisper was too loud for Keir not to hear and the latter blushed brightly.

"Keir is Evain's nephew and is to be trained in sorcery." Anya knew that though neither brother had a personal desire for such training, leastways Edwyn would be impressed by the prospect.

And Edwyn was. It was Cub who looked at the strange boy his own age with narrowed eyes and asked, "How can Evain have a nephew we don't know?" He followed up the eminently logical question with a firm statement. "Llys can't have had a child we never met."

"I'll explain how it came to be . . . later." As Evain was rarely impatient with their curious questions, when he leveled upon the doubter a forbidding gaze, both boys went still. "For now, won't you welcome Keir, and take him to the spring for a refreshing mug of cool water?"

Anya's brothers immediately turned to do as requested while Keir, despite the fact that they'd passed the well on their way to enter the keep, quietly went along with the blatant ploy to give his companions private moments with Lady Brynna.

Brynna recognized the maneuver as quickly as Keir and turned to her foster son with a wordless demand for news more specific than provided by Anya.

"'Tis true." Evain wasted no precious moment more and leaned his stave against Wulf's empty chair by the fire to take Brynna's hands. "The goal of our quest is won. By now Adam will not merely have reached my sister's side but moved on, carrying news of your plight to King Aldfrith and to Wulfayne."

Brynna nodded a dark head burnished by silver strands but spoke a forlorn acknowledgment. "I doubt they can arrive in time to save Throckenholt from the ravening hordes already braying at the door."

"I agree." Evain gently squeezed the hands in his hold. "'Tis impossible for them to appear so soon. But I have arrived and can do that deed in their stead."

Although granddaughter of a great sorcerer, and host to firm faith in Evain's incredible powers, Brynna worried. "Wait for the morrow." The possibility of altering a sorcerer's will was remote but still she tried. "They'll not attack at night, and by morn our warriors may be here."

Evain's sardonic smile appeared as he shook his head to negate the argument she had surely known would fail. And yet, he did break an unspoken but certain rule of wizardry. He explained his reasoning. "The Mercians below are despised for their dishonorable habit of striking defenseless prey with fire in the night."

"I have heard many such tales from people fleeing destruction on the borders to seek refuge here." With the admission, Brynna's tense shoulders slumped in defeat and she pulled her hands from her foster son's to turn away. "But Bishop Wilfrid announced from below that he would allow me peace until the morrow's dawn to consider the cost of not then surrendering myself and my sons to his custody."

"What cost does he threaten?" Anya softly asked, moving around to face her mother.

Brynna turned bleak gray eyes to her much-missed daughter and gave a mirthless laugh. "Fire to consume the whole of Throckenholt and everything within its walls." When the siege began, she'd been glad that Anya would not be a part of this ghastly end. Now, here she was. "I can easily sense their intent and am certain that 'tis precisely what they will do once they've secured their prize."

"Despite Wilfrid's fervent desire to take you for hostage and his claimed willingness to wait . . ." Evain saw danger beyond the bishop and could not be gulled by the promises of untrustworthy foes. "I've no trust in Saxon kings more apt to light fires in order to cause such an uproar of confusion they can enter unchallenged and seize you by force. Thus, I mean to put an end to their schemes without delay."

Brynna slowly turned back about to give the sorcerer a somber smile of acceptance for the dangerous deed she suspected he meant to perform.

Anya took a step forward and slipped a comforting arm about her mother's waist. "What Evain says he can do, he can do." With the confident words, eyes as dark and shiny as holly leaves lifted to meet her love's steady gaze and slight nod of appreciation for an unwavering support.

Brynna saw the glance exchanged and recognized

the depth of emotion behind it. Instantly she feared her daughter completely caught in the painful mire of an impossible love.

All too aware of Brynna's concern, Evain's attention shifted to her. "During the difficult journey just past, Anya repeatedly proved that she possesses a bond with nature's powers which, though untrained, is as strong as that wielded by her sorceress-mother." With this news he gave implied reassurance that no block lay between them . . . leastways not one formed of a sorcerer's Druidic duty.

Pulling a distance from her daughter's hold, Brynna gazed steadily into green eyes never able to deceive her. In a serene emerald gaze she found a glowing pleasure and proof of Anya's love for the man at the core of a sorcerer. Joined with Evain's statement, this was enough to win her approval. Wulf, however, might be another matter.

"Do you wish to be a part of this final scene?" Evain asked Anya as he lifted his staff.

That the sorcerer would permit her daughter's inclusion in so serious a matter was further confirmation, did Brynna need it, of both the depth of his commitment and his genuine belief in her daughter's powers.

Anya, too, recognized his offer for the incredible gift it was and quickly nodded. But even while accepting, she thought of another who had surely earned the same honor.

"What of Keir?"

In answer to his elfling's quiet reminder, Evain's crooked smile of self-mockery appeared, and he asked a thrall to beckon the boy. It was a summons which all three boys answered. But while Keir was invited to join his allies, Anya's brothers were asked to remain in the hall and watch over Noddi.

As Evain led the way from the keep, Anya almost skipped to keep up with her love's long strides, and Keir—as so oft on their quest—took up the honorable position of guarding the rear.

At the bottom of the narrow wooden ladder giving access to a walkway near the palisade's top edge, Evain paused and gave his companions a serious command. "Whatever happens, whether seeming physical danger or fearful spoken threat, betray your responses by neither movement nor sound."

Anya instantly nodded. As she'd practiced such quiet serenity from childhood, it was a part of her nature. Keir's agreement was as prompt.

Evain had one more command and it the most important. "When nature's fury rises, stay close to my side and safe in the eye of the storm."

Keir's eyes widened while Anya nodded once more and just as quickly. Promises given, her dainty form closely followed Evain's powerful figure up the ladder and the boy climbed behind. While they ascended, the sorcerer offered a brief chant that drew a gentle glow from his staff.

As Throckenholt's lady, Brynna deemed it needful to be near while the fate of the shire was decided. Leaving her baby son to a motherly thrall's care, she followed the young couple, though only to the ladder's foot. She arrived just as Evain set his plan into motion.

"Bishop Wilfrid." The ominous thunder of Evain's low call rolled across the encampment below, lost in deepening night shadows. "Long have you sought the sorcerer, Evain. And now I am here." Words roaring like the winds of a brewing storm drove other sounds into silence and spread the seeds of growing dread in the minds of even courageous warriors. "Come, meet me face-to-face."

In response to the man who named himself sorcerer and as proof held a staff from the top of which flowed a strange light, men scattered like fallen autumn leaves before the first gusts of winter. Some ducked into tents for weapons foolishly left behind while others leaped from shelters with gleaming swords at the ready. Soon every eye was held by the eerie sight of the black-clad man standing atop the wall. The summer evening was humid and perfectly still, and yet hair with the sheen of ravens' wings lifted on the same unnatural wind which swirled his cloak about him in a black whirlpool.

"Claud, fetch the bishop," Evain demanded, penetrating eyes drilling into the angular man easily spotted. "Fetch the man to whom you thought to deliver me as prisoner, and I will see that his wishes all have answer."

While a fuming Torvyn hustled away to do as his escaped captive bid, a babble of voices rose to fill the void following the sorcerer's command. Even amidst such strange events, Rolf took pleasure in seeing the arrogant thegn made to bend to the other man's demand.

As Bishop Wilfrid appeared, armed men gladly fell back to clear his path to the one demanding his presence.

"Evain, at last . . ." Wilfrid disliked being forced into the position of gazing up at a foe he meant to see humbled at his feet. "Surrender to us—you and all your Druid seed—and we will permit the *good* Christian folk of Throckenholt to survive."

Evain's laughter fell like a rain of blows over the intently watching company below. "I know your mind. Depart I, and you'll see the whole of Throckenholt put to fire."

The bishop's complexion deepened to an unhealthy purple shade while his hands went white with the struggle required to restrain them from curling into fists—a too revealing action. He was not used to being challenged and most assuredly not accustomed to having a foe so easily discern the falsehood behind a promise.

"Depart . . ." Evain turned the man's treacherous offer back upon him. "And I will permit you and your allies to withdraw in safety."

Long-smoldering venom burned through the cords restraining Wilfrid's anger and he snarled a heated threat. "We will burn you out!"

"No doubt you will *try*." Evain's mocking smile flashed. "But I will see your flames extinguished afore they do harm."

"Hah!" Wilfrid spun about, wildly commanding men to throw burning torches against the wooden palisade.

Evain instantly lifted his stave toward the new risen moon and as a low chant rumbled from his chest, clouds raced to hide that silvery orb. Crashing together, the impact broke them open as easily as fragile eggshells. Torrents of rain soon doused every torch and each of the campfires from which they'd drawn life.

"Strike down the heathens, Lord." Wilfrid thrust

his arms toward the stormy heavens, determined to regain control of this scene and intent on winning this most fervent goal. "Burn them with the fires of hell."

Thus far Anya had held to Evain's command, remaining quietly a step to one side and sheltering Keir in the gloom at Evain's back, but she was so offended by the bishop's surely blasphemous action that she stepped directly in front of her sorcerer. Amidst the stillness of a crowd gone quiet, waiting to learn who would be the winner in this grave conflict, her soft voice was easily heard.

"Wilfrid—I'll not name as bishop you who are less a Christian than any Druid—only God can judge the heart of a man. And for seeking His aid in unholy vengeance, it is you who God will hold in judgment."

Wilfrid was incensed that this girl, who once already had demonstrated the temerity to lecture a bishop on rightful piety, would dare to criticize him again. In another dramatic gesture he fell to his knees while lifting his hands to the sky. "Please, Lord, use this wicked creature as an example of Your righteous punishment. Strike her down with Your fury."

"Beware I don't see *you* struck down, *Bishop.*" Evain spoke the title in the same tone he would use to describe a particularly noxious poison. He'd no respect for Wilfrid, supposedly a man of peace and charity, but clearly disloyal even to his own faith.

The bishop's answer, a screamed dare accompanied by a vulgar epithet, as he rose to again stand defiant, only deepened Evain's disgust. Lifting his staff once more toward the tempest he had summoned, over and over Evain repeated a litany of unknown words. They gained in power and depth until they seemed to shake the ground beneath the massed armies' feet. And all the while, he directed the clouds into a swirling turmoil from whose raging center lightning flashed. A bolt streaked down toward the crystal atop Evain's extended staff and from that orb to the target he chose . . . the ground a scant distance from the furious bishop's toes.

Knocked off his feet by the reverberation of a powerful strike so near, as Wilfrid fell back his usual ruddy complexion was white as winter's first snowfall.

The bishop was not alone in his stunned response to this second demonstration of powers beyond the ken of men untaught in the secret knowledge of Druids. Under their panic, members of massed armies broke into pandemonium. Among the first to flee were two men who had earlier experienced enough to know the sorcerer was able to carry out any threat. Torvyn and Rolf led the way as men dashed from Throckenholt's fields as if each furrow were filled with white-hot coals.

Soon only three men were still within sight and they not by choice. The bishop's legs were unlikely to hold him steady anytime soon. His two allies, kings both, would not risk having it known that they'd been so terrified of a Druid that they fled from a bloodless conflict and deserted a cohort in need of aid. Thus they resentfully lingered to help Wilfrid from the scene but were unlikely to forget the debt owed for the deed. They assuredly would never forget who had again failed to bring down his foes or soon agree to any scheme the man proposed. Indeed, the only fruit borne of the bishop's plot to take this shire was the demoralizing of two armies. Those who had not personally been present would of a certainty hear every detail about the event and how a single man, vastly outnumbered, had defeated the massed armies of two kings.

Both kings wordlessly acknowledged that, whatever else was true and leastways for this year, the war was done. A defeat for which they would see the bishop bear the blame. And *never* again would King Ethelred agree to any manner of assault on Throckenholt.

While shamed foes slunk away in the night and an embarrassed Keir watched, Anya threw her arms about the man as able to command her hidden fiery spirit and loving heart as the unruly forces of nature. Evain returned the embrace with equal fervor for his sweet elfling whose quiet serenity contained a heated core and courage willing to dare much in defense of those she loved.

Their passionate exchange was interrupted by the loud cheers of Throckenholt's own. By a sorcerer's glowing crystal and demonstrated mastery over the tempest, people trapped inside a besieged village had been drawn to view the whole from behind.

As the sun dropped from the sky one day later, a vast army approached. With light hearts, Lady Brynna and her family—including her daughter and foster son—went out to lead a welcoming party of villagers to meet those arriving. The palisade's huge, iron-bound gates were opened wide.

Before Wulfayne had even swung from his destrier down to the hard-packed lane, he spoke to his wife. "I know you are not so foolish as to open our home in time of war without good cause—even though we've come in answer to the desperate call for aid delivered by a liberated Adam." Bronze brows arched in request for explanation.

"After freeing Adam," Evain immediately took up the task as he was at the center of the answer and able to more easily explain, "we feared you would be unable to arrive in time to stop the wretched bishop and his kingly allies . . . as we nearly were."

"Nearly?" Adam, too, dismounted to join the quest for answers. "Have they already come? And gone?"

Evain nodded and gave a slight shrug. "A bit of sorcery."

Two Saxon ealdormen exchanged a telling glance, eyes narrowed in mild disgust. Wed to sorceresses, they were familiar enough with Druid spells to know that nothing was as simple as those trained to secret ways would have it seem, left to their own choices. But now was not the time to pursue specific details, not with Northumbria's entire fyrd at their backs—the fyrd *and* their king. The latter fact was reinforced by the sound of Aldfrith's voice a brief distance behind.

"Many times I've heard the tales of how it is that I and my predecessors owe the safety of our kingdom to your Druids." King Aldfrith spoke to Wulf and Adam but his curious attention quickly shifted to the younger man, by his black hair clearly a Cymry native, and then on to the petite beauty bound close by a possessive arm.

"Is it to you whom I owe my gratitude for another such feat?" the king asked of Evain. "A deed I shall always regret not having seen for myself?"

Again Evain nodded although he gave this king a cryptic explanation. "I frightened off those who thought to take my foster mother and family hostage before putting fire to the village and its people."

"Alone?" Aldfrith's pale gray eyes were penetrating.

"Anya helped." With a gentle smile of amazing

potency Evain gazed into a piquant face before adding, "And in the quest my nephew, Keir, lent aid as well."

"Keir?" The king's voice was quiet but nonetheless demanded answer. The sorcerer's sister was wed to his ealdorman and he knew all their sons. Keir was not one.

Never comfortable with specific explanations even obliquely demanded and certainly not to Saxon rulers, Evain merely pointed to where Keir stood with Wulf's sons.

The king nodded toward the boys but immediately returned his attention to the sorcerer and his lady.

The pair subject to royal scrutiny examined the one who watched them. Anya thought Aldfrith, tall and slender, looked more the image of an ascetic bishop than ever had the squat, overfed, and impious Wilfrid.

Evain was uncertain what to make of this man, an unusual emotion for one whose senses were honed to judge such matters with ease. He had heard that this Saxon king, unlike the two defeated, was a man who prized peace. He seemed a quiet, thinking man—as well as a warrior. These were traits Evain could understand.

Seeing Evain's steady inspection of Wulf's king, Brynna chose to speak before the questioning could progress to the point where a sorcerer might refuse answers that a king would consider his right to hear.

"I regret, sire, that we have severely limited resources and cannot feed the whole of your army."

Aldfrith grinned and it warmed cold gray eyes to smoke. He recognized Lady Brynna's intent and easily yielded his desire to quickly learn the details of an obviously amazing feat. Doubtless this adventure, like those preceding it, would eventually become a tale to be told in halls throughout the kingdom and beyond. He could be patient and learn it later. For the moment he must answer the lady's concern.

"Never would I expect any single shire to provide such largess. Although our food did, in truth, come from the shires, we carry it with us and need not further impose upon your larders."

Brynna was relieved but quickly added, "We would deem it an honor if you and your thegns will join us for an evening meal to celebrate our lord's return."

Aldfrith graciously accepted and placed the lady's proffered hand atop his forearm to formally lead her back up the village's single narrow lane toward the keep. The rest of the lord's party followed while the men of Throckenholt returned to their own homes.

"Let us celebrate that and one thing more." Aldfrith suggested. "From the fact that Ethelred's army was earlier withdrawn from the points of conflict along the border but isn't here, it seems clear our friend, Evain, has managed to do what my military skills have failed to achieve."

The use of Evain's name proved the king had already won a measure of information about what had happened, likely from Adam.

"Thanks to his good offices, the war is done . . . leastways for a time." Aldfrith smiled benignly upon them. "Certainly long enough that I may release my warriors and send them home to their own lands. Then, if God be willing, they'll have sufficient time to reclaim ravaged fields and sew crops again with hope of a harvest to come." He paused long enough to charge one of his thegns to see the order carried to the fyrd making camp beyond the palisade wall.

As their small party passed through the keep's door and into the hall, Brynna glanced back and caught a glimpse of Wulf's expression as he glared at the sorcerer whose arm was wrapped around his daughter in anything but a brotherly fashion.

Moving to his side and sharply tapping his strong arm, she gave him a scowl of mock castigation. "You remind me of my grandfather."

"Glyndor?" Wulf was startled. Surely it was Evain who resembled the old sorcerer. "How could you think so daft a thing?"

Quite pleased with her success in winning that question from Wulf, Brynna explained. "I remember just such a heavy frown upon his face when first you asked to wed with me."

Anya's breath caught uncomfortably in her throat as she heard this unexpected shift in the subject of her mother's conversation—proof she, too, was adept at wielding a disconcerting mood-altering trickery.

"Wed?" Wulf's narrowed green gaze again swept over the couple before him—Anya full of hope and Evain looking ready to argue the matter for himself. In the next instant, the truth in his wife's statement washed over Wulf. He erupted in a growl of laughter that left a glitter of cheery amusement in his eyes.

Wulfayne had demanded his children be raised as Christians, not Druids. But apparently whether he willed it or no, inherited powers were beyond his control. By the rescue Adam had reported and hints of events here, it was clear his little Anya possessed them. As for the other . . .

"I fell in love with a sorceress and should not be surprised that my daughter loves a sorcerer." His eyes narrowed teasingly on the couple. "And if their courtship was anything like ours, the wedding had best be soon."

Anya blushed while Evain laughed. He was rarely startled by the reactions of others but assuredly was now and hugged his tender elfling tighter to his side.

"Foster son, son-in-law, part of our family from first to last." Wulf gazed warmly into Evain's pleased expression. "I ask only that you wed my daughter by Christian as well as Druid rites."

Evain instantly answered. "I welcome every known bond to ensure that Anya will remain mine forever."

King Aldfrith could hardly help but overhear this conversation, and when he stepped forward, his subjects welcomed him.

"I was puzzled by what I might do to repay the sorcerer and his lady-apprentice for their good deeds on behalf of my realm. They rescued Adam and put my enemies armies to flight while saving Throckenholt." The cool brush of his ice-gray gaze warmed as it moved from Evain to Anya. "Now I see there is an aid I can render them."

Everyone looked bewildered.

"Always in my retinue there travels a monk. Though all too oft he is called to perform the last rites upon fallen warriors, he is equally able to undertake the much more agreeable task of blessing a marriage."

During the next hour Anya felt as if she were again caught in the eye of a whirling storm but safely anchored by her beloved. The king's monk seemed truly happy to have been called for so pleasant a duty and undertook it with joy. The villagers where hastily invited to watch the simple blessing offered over their lord's daughter and the sorcerer who had saved them.

Wearing a chaplet formed of quickly gathered lilies and the beautiful gown Elesa had given her—soft cloth in a turquoise hue and trimmed with bands of gold thread—Anya met her dark and devastatingly handsome sorcerer at the top of the keep's steps. There, by Christian rites, Anya was bound to Evain. A treasured dream at long last come true.

Although Throckenholt's larders had grown alarmingly barren, between that of the lord and those of his people, a feast of sorts was provided to mark the important occasion. One whose merriment was increased by the great abundance of ale donated by their king. To the grassy area behind the keep where trestle tables were arranged, the people brought their pipes, timbrels, and even a harp to add cheerful music to the festivities. Originally planned by Lady Brynna and King Aldfrith as a simple meal of welcome and gratitude, it became one that would not soon be forgotten. Aye, it would linger in their memories— not for its lavish fare but for the joy of the pair in whose honor it was held and the pleasure it gave after days, weeks, and months of fearsome tension.

The banter included a laughing discussion of the high price Bishop Wilfrid would pay for his failed scheme—the loss of his patrons' goodwill with everything that entailed. It was deemed a cost dearer even than any physical wound for the arrogant, greedy man who would lose the ability to either live in rich comfort or wield the power he craved. Moreover, it was doubtful any Saxon king would longer support his attempts to woo Rome's aid in winning back the wealth and position he'd lost as a result of his first clash with those defending Throckenholt.

Evain sat at a joyous table with Anya close at his side and regretted only that his sister, Llys, was not present. But she would understand why the marriage had taken place now just as he understood why she had not come with Adam. She could hardly abandon either her children or the shire to accompany an army to war and had remained at Oaklea. Yet before the company fell too deep into revels, he and Anya had managed a quiet talk with Adam, Brynna, and Wulf to share the tale of Elesa and the part her visions had played in the winning of their battles—and the news of another lost sister and two children.

Between Adam and Evain it was decided that on Adam's return to Oaklea he would take Keir, permitting Evain and Anya to begin their marriage in privacy. Then, when winter neared, the boy would rejoin his companions of recent days in a sorcerer's hill-cave home where he would join Anya in serious study of Druidic knowledge. Sian would remain with Llys and Adam . . . leastways for now.

Anya danced with King Aldfirth. With her father, too. And even with Keir and her brothers. But it was with Evain that she rightly spent most of her time. Then as children began falling into slumber although the adults grew only merrier and the sound of increasingly loud laughter continued to join the spritely music, Evain retrieved his stave from where it rested against a tree trunk. He tucked Anya's small hand in the crook of his arm and together they slipped into shadows and away through the dark velvet night. Stepping unnoticed out the palisade wall's postern gate, the pair moved into one of nature's bowers, a private haven where Druids could be infinitely more comfortable.

"You are my beloved elfling. Mine always." Into a delicate face framed by moonshine hair, Evain's blue-flame eyes gazed with such warmth that Anya melted against him.

"And I, as I have since near the day of my birth, will love you forever." Under his potent smile, Anya's heart swelled and she lifted honey-sweet lips to him.

Evain accepted her gift, and to seal their oath fit his mouth to hers with exquisite care for a soul-binding kiss. And all the while around them on a warm breeze drifted a myriad of petals—nature's blessing on a sorcerer and his destined mate.

"Long ago," says Marylyle, "I learned the magic to be found between the covers of a book. I feel so fortunate now to be among those permitted to offer a few hours of enjoyment in the lives of busy readers. Often, it is hearing from you which keeps me going. If you've a moment to drop me a line, I'd love to hear from you (and I *will* answer, although with pressing deadlines, it sometimes takes me a while)."

Marylyle Rogers
P.O. Box 45352
Boise, ID 83711

POCKET BOOKS
PROUDLY ANNOUNCES

TWILIGHT SECRETS

MARYLYLE ROGERS

**Coming in Paperback
from Pocket Books
Fall 1994**

**The following is a preview of
Twilight Secrets . . .**

April 1101

Beams from a sun half done in its descent from zenith to journey's end below the western horizon shafted through the newly unfurled leaves of a dense forest gone quiet against the intrusion of humankind. Aware of possible dangers lurking near, Mark was alert to the fact that the only sound to be heard was the steady thud of his destrier's hooves over a narrow lane's soggy surface.

A rain shower quickly come and gone had left abundant moisture on the thick foliage of branches twined overhead. Thus, though the sky had cleared, droplets of water continued to fall upon Mark, but he lent small attention to either the odor of his cloak's damp wool or the chill it lent. Penetrating gray eyes constantly shifted from the muddy path ahead to delve into the green shadows on each side, leaving him prepared for what was too likely to come.

Of a sudden Mark's way was blocked by armed men who planted themselves three deep in the path a brief distance in front of him. The sharply honed edges of their bared blades glittered with stray gleams of sunlight.

"What have we here?" Mark's sardonic half smile appeared but his silver-ice eyes went so cold they threatened to freeze those daring to stand against him. "A welcoming party from Wroxton Castle? Or did you issue from Kelby Keep?"

"Our source can be of no import to any man fool enough to approach alone a destination surely known to be hostile." The man sneering these words was short, broad and completely bald. "Never will we permit that the Lady Elysia be wed to a bastard like you!"

Mark startled his onlookers by laughing freely, head tilted back until his hood fell away to reveal a thick mane of raven-black hair lacking the protection of the helmet he disdained. Leastways the waiting was done. In a single swift movement of speed and grace, he unsheathed and thrust his own broadsword toward the heavens. "Valbeau to me!"

Mark's stocky opponent dashed toward him, blade slashing. Before the man's weapon could crash against that of his mounted prey, the forest erupted with a mass of armed warriors who immediately surrounded the smaller band confronting their leader. But those thus trapped refused to easily cede the victory, and for a time the forest echoed with the sound of blade meeting blade in earnest conflict.

Unwilling to put his favorite destrier at risk in a useless battle with a foe afoot, Mark exercised an amazing agility and dismounted even while continuing to meet his opponent's relentless assault. Once on the same level, despite the ground's treacherous layer of mud, Mark met the attack with a ferocity that soon sent the bald man's weapon flying harmlessly into dense undergrowth. In desperation the man jerked a dagger from its sheath at his belt and lunged toward an unwelcome intruder. Mark twisted to the side and the man tumbled headlong into a briar patch.

The battle was forced to an end by both superior skill and the sheer force of greater numbers. As peace returned to the woodland, Mark towered above the earlier sneering foe who now lay flat on his back with the tip of a sword pressed against the base of a vulnerable throat.

"Hugh—" Without glancing away, Mark called out to the dark, taciturn friend ever first to arrive and fight at his side. "See that the lengths of rope we took pains to carry with us are used to safely truss our quarry."

Habitually stingy with words, Hugh curtly nodded a head as dark as the one belonging to the man who'd asked the deed he immediately set about fulfilling.

As an erstwhile foe was pulled to his feet and wrists were tied together at his back, Mark studied the sorry sight and quietly mused.

"Seems the priestly messenger has delivered the

king's decision." Dark head tilting to one side, Mark couldn't resist returning the man's ridicule for his parentage—no matter that 'twas true—with a jeer of his own. "I trust even your sort refrained from the sin of harming a man in holy orders?"

The one addressed glared but would not respond. Mark had expected no answer. Yet that lack deepened his cynical amusement—an amusement tinged with regret. Both this man's refusal to speak further and the actions he and his fellows had taken to forestall the king's threatened intent were only to be expected. However, such demonstrations of friction could only make more difficult Mark's path toward assuming his new position as these people's lord.

Mark would far rather have arrived unannounced, but Henry had insisted upon dispatching a priest to Wroxton Castle with a royal decree certain to be resented. The wily new king had argued that it was best to enter any conflict with one's enemies unmasked. Thus Henry had sent his messenger ahead for the purpose of smoking out the snakes in a thicket of traitors. Mark could not dispute his friend and sovereign's logic but would rather have worked toward the same end with a lighter touch . . . particularly where he was expected to wed with one of their number.

"I won't do it!" Pulling away from the brush wielded by her childhood nursemaid and now companion, Elysia twisted about to lift a brown gaze gone near black to the comfortably plump female at her back. "I shall simply refuse."

Ida patiently watched while the younger woman once again rose from the three-legged stool where she'd perched to have tangles smoothed from dusky locks prior to their braiding. She refrained from pointing out the folly in heated claims to the maid of a certainty already aware of the futility at their core. The message sent by Prince Henry—Ida hadn't yet come around to thinking of the conqueror's youngest son as her king—had put the whole of Wroxton in a tizzy, but her lambie worst of all.

Elysia fair stomped from one side of her bedchamber to the other, loose curls tumbling in a dark cloud to her hips. "I am to wed with Gervaise—a deed that would soon have been complete had King Rufus not been ruthlessly slain by those who now think to force another upon me."

"Ah, lambie—" There was no point in disputing Elysia's words when the man's death rendered the question moot. Yet Ida knew 'twas unlikely the avaricious king would ever have allowed the rents drawn from her lambie's heritage to flow into another man's pocket . . . unless that groom were in such a position as to compensate for the loss with either wealth or military aid. Gervaise was not such a one. Indeed, Ida had never trusted the neighboring landholder. And though marriages between those well born were commonly arranged for the sake of procuring property and titles, her Elysia believed Gervaise's motives far more personal. Ida harbored doubts and feared her lambie doomed to disillusionment.

"Calm yourself." Ida stepped forward and in comfort wrapped a thick arm about the young woman who'd had little rest in the hours since the priest had arrived bearing an unwelcome royal decree. In truth, Elysia had slept not at all until dawn peeked over the horizon. As a result, the maid's fiery spirit simmered too near the surface. It was also the reason Elysia had only just completed what should have been morning ablutions and why wild curls had yet to be tamed into braids.

"You *have* sent my missive to Gervaise?" 'Twas near the hundredth time Elysia had asked this question.

"Aye." Ida quietly repeated the reassurance yet again. "'Twas dispatched a full day and more past."

"Then why has he not come to me?" Doe-brown eyes were soft with anxiety.

"Mayhap your beloved is taking steps to see the mischief undone." The success of such an action Ida knew to be impossible, but she saw no reason to further burden her tender lambie with unpleasant facts.

"Elysia?" A quiet voice tentatively spoke from the doorway. "Have I committed some wrong that you are so angry?"

Forcing an upward curve to frowning lips, Elysia pulled from Ida's comforting hold and moved toward the timid girl hesitating in the shadows beside a barely open portal.

"Of course not, Eve." Elysia put an encouraging arm around the maid's shoulders much as Ida had so recently done for her. "I am upset by deeds that threaten to alter my life's path. But these are deeds in which you have no part and for which you can no more bear the blame than you ought for any wrongs done me or others in Wroxton."

With the latter statement, Elysia cast a meaningful glance over her shoulder to the friend behind. Ida had unaccountably joined other castle inhabitants in rejecting the company of this innocent woman-child bearing both the visible and unseen scars of a sin not her own.

Head ever lowered to ensure that loose flowing hair the shade of dirty thatch would cover her disfigured cheek, Eve nodded appreciation of her protector's reassurances even while quietly giving news she'd come to impart. "Lord Gervaise awaits your coming in the great hall."

Elysia flashed a smile bright enough to warm the chamber's spring chill. Then, heedless to the impropriety of appearing with hair neither bound nor covered, she hastened from the chamber. With as much haste as safety permitted she hurried down a narrow, steeply winding stairway whose gloom was lessened only by burning rushes dipped in tallow and placed in rings widely spaced and driven into stone walls.

Pausing beneath the arch where stairwell opened to a sizable hall, Elysia fondly studied the tall, wiry man standing with his back to her. Gervaise's russet head was bent over the central hearth while he peered into flames leaping beneath a huge caldron of stew and several spitted birds. She smiled. Never would he admit it, but his sight was not as keen as once it had been. A failing that bothered her not one whit. 'Twas to be expected of a man who carried the age of two score and a wee bit more—an age that brought with it a restraint and wisdom she admired.

Though Gervaise was a contemporary of her parents and more than twice her age, Elysia had idolized him since childhood. She'd been thrilled when, after her father's death, he had proposed an alliance between them, though the offer had been delivered with a list of dry facts upon which he based his belief that joining her inheritance to his lands, despite Kelby's lesser size and importance, would be advantageous for them both. She'd chosen to believe his lack of any passionate declaration was born of his respect for her tender years, and her longing for fervent words and deeds merely proof of her impetuous immaturity.

Once given the excitement of dreams come true in Gervaise's proposal, she'd been left with but a single block to her happiness. But it had proven an immovable rock: King William Rufus's greedy determination to ensure that Wroxton's sizable rents and taxes would continue flowing into his own coffers by keeping its heiress unwed and in his ward. When Rufus died and his brother Henry seized the crown, she'd hoped the change would ease their position, but Gervaise had warned her that their new monarch's cooperation would be even more difficult to win. Her shoulders slumped. Gervaise had spoken true. With King Henry matters had gotten infinitely worse!

"Gervaise," Elysia quietly called. "Tell me you've had word that the events of this past day were naught but some horrible mistake. Better still, tell me that a scribe's error in naming the groom has been corrected and that 'tis our wedding rites that soon will be performed."

The russet-haired man turned to face the willowy creature hastening toward him, arms outstretched. Once within reach, Gervaise took Elysia's hands into his, halting the headlong rush and restraining her to stand demurely a brief distance from him.

Elysia could feel her cheeks burn with bright color. Once more, as too oft in recent months, Gervaise had wordlessly staved off her impetuous action. 'Struth she would have thrown herself into his arms had he not wisely prevented her from making a private matter public by enacting such a scene before the small army of curious house serfs laboring to set up trestle tables for the meal to come.

"Nay, Elysia. 'Tis all too real." Gervaise's lips thinned in a tight smile as he shook his head. "But I have dispatched a messenger to plead the cause of our betro—"

"Well, I *won't* marry him." Elysia tamed her voice to a mere hiss. "Not this stranger, this bastard . . ."

With a pained grimace, Gervaise squeezed Elysia's fingertips to end this too-well-watched discussion of personal matters, but it was another man's voice that stole her own and banked the coals of her temper.

"If the king wills it . . ." Mark stood in the open

portal, having left the force he'd led into the castle's inner bailey with their prisoners at the foot of steps leading up to the castle's drawbridge and double doors. "If I will it, then, milady, wed me you *shall.*"

Startled by the unfamiliar voice, Elysia spun around to find a stranger silhouetted against twilight's purple haze. As the unwelcome visitor stepped further into the hall, she took one look at hair as dark as night and black-lashed silver eyes and inwardly named the man far too handsome to be trusted.

Mark felt the lingering brush of a suspicious brown gaze and was amused. He had feared the hesitation of others to provide a description of his bride borne of a wish not to be forced into an honest report of the woman's severely limited attractions. But his suspicions were proven utterly unjustified. She was elegantly slender and her large, dark eyes were beautiful. Moreover, her thick mass of curls—unbound as few well-born women would permit—caught and reflected ever-shifting gleams of firelight while framing a lovely face. This quashing of erroneous apprehensions brightened Mark's mood and his lips slowly curled upward in an action whose rare honest warmth she could nowise appreciate.

However, that potent smile did succeed in washing over Elysia with a physical impact able to halt the breath in her throat. Under its power she was instantly convinced that this devastatingly attractive man would expect every woman to fall weak to his charms. But not she! She was already bespoken, and best he learn it was so!

"I am betrothed to another."

Mark's black brows scowled. "Betrothed?" No mention had been made of any such bond. The next moment, his forehead smoothed and a mocking half smile tilted his lips. That he hadn't been warned was surely proof no such arrangement had been formalized and lent reason to doubt the veracity of the maid's desperate claim.

"Aye." Gervaise spoke, uncomfortably aware that a hall recently filled with the dull roar of activity had gone so silent it seemed even the walls had sprouted ears. "Eighteen months past, a betrothal was performed between Elysia and I, Gervaise of Kelby Keep."

For the first time, Mark turned his penetrating gaze full upon the lanky man at the heiress's side. He was older than Mark had expected, as proven by the threads of gray liberally sprinkled through red hair. Henry had warned him to be wary of this man whose loyalties near certainly lay with Robert of Normandy. But Mark hadn't expected to face him as suitor to his bride.

"Have you documents bearing King Rufus's seal proving her guardian's assent to the match?" Mark's question held the sharpness of a flashing blade. "Without his agreement, the bond you claim is meaningless and one I need not honor."

"Would you make that decision for *your* king?" Gervaise parried the thrust.

Mark shook his head while wryly responding.

"Having no reason to fear King Henry's decision, I am willing to lay the matter before him."

"Then you must leave now." Elysia wanted the dangerous man gone and with all possible haste. "You have no right to tarry here."

"Have I not?" Mark reached into his tunic and pulled out a leather packet from which he withdrew a crackling parchment. The clearly visible royal seal drove the other two into silence. *"Our king has placed the heiress of Wroxton in my ward."*

"You've been named Elysia's guardian?" Gervaise's hazel eyes narrowed while his face went so pale it made his hair seem to flame the brighter.

Mark could almost see the wheels of his opponent's mind at work. "King Henry would not drive me into a commitment I found unpleasant. And yet he took action to ensure that Wroxton rest in my care no matter my choice of bride. The decision of whether to wed with Elysia or hold her as my ward is mine to make. Thus, no matter my choice, remain here I and my army will."

That this man was to wield power over her future lit golden fires in the depths of Elysia's dark eyes. Facing him with clenched fists firmly planted on slender hips, she made a heated declaration. "I will *not* wed you!"

While silver eyes gleamed with delight, Mark's potent smile returned. Few women had ever refused his attentions and many had sought the honor this one would spurn. By her action Elysia caught his interest and promised to hold it as few woman had for any length of time in recent years. This unexpected beauty's temper might well add spice to the tasteless gruel of a struggle to uncover and thwart traitorous plots.

Look for

Twilight Secrets

Wherever Paperback Books Are Sold
Fall 1994

From Bestselling,
Award-winning Author

Marylyle Rogers

A return to the British
Middle Ages.

Twilight Secrets

POCKET
BOOKS

Available from
Pocket Books
Winter 1994